A TEMPTING PROPOSITION . . .

"*I* think it's a good idea," she whispered, and she nipped his earlobe.

He didn't move. She had no idea what that meant. Damn it, she'd never done this before. Josh was supposed to have fallen over himself as soon as she'd suggested the possibility of a hookup. He should have been *giddy* with excitement. That was how this was supposed to work, wasn't it?

This was . . . Ashley had no idea. She'd think about it when she sobered up. For the time being, she kissed her way down Josh's neck. His skin was warm and surprisingly soft, and she felt a churn of desire in her gut when she felt his pulse beating strong and fast beneath her lips. Ashley genuinely wanted this man. She hooked her fingers into the waistband of his jeans, and that was when he caught her hand in his.

"Not a good idea," he said, and he stepped back, holding his arms out to keep her from following.

"Why not?" she demanded.

"You've had too much to drink."

She stared at him. "What? You're the bar police now? You watch people's drinks and then decide who gets to go home with whom?"

"No. Just who gets to go home with *me*."

Just a
Summer Fling

CATE CAMERON

BERKLEY SENSATION, NEW YORK

**BERKLEY
SENSATION**

THE BERKLEY PUBLISHING GROUP
Published by the Penguin Group
Penguin Group (USA) LLC
375 Hudson Street, New York, New York 10014

USA • Canada • UK • Ireland • Australia • New Zealand • India • South Africa • China

penguin.com

A Penguin Random House Company

JUST A SUMMER FLING

A Berkley Sensation Book / published by arrangement with the author

For information, address: The Berkley Publishing Group,
a division of Penguin Group (USA) LLC,
375 Hudson Street, New York, New York 10014.

ISBN: 978-0-425-28205-2

PUBLISHING HISTORY
Berkley Sensation mass-market edition / August 2015

PRINTED IN THE UNITED STATES OF AMERICA

10 9 8 7 6 5 4 3 2 1

Cover art by Jim Griffin.
Cover design by George Long.
Interior text design by Kelly Lipovich.

Penguin
Random
House

I'm deeply grateful for all the support I received while writing this book. Special thanks to Sharon Cox—you're a very effective cheerleader!

And, of course, thanks to my agent, Andrea Somberg, and my editor, Julie Mianecki. Who knew the publishing process could be fun?!

❧ One ❧

ASHLEY CARLSEN WAS drunk. She'd been drinking at the lake house all afternoon, and then they'd piled into the car and been driven to town where they'd found *more* delicious alcohol, and now? Drunk. It wasn't unheard of for Ashley to have a few drinks too many when she was at home with her friends. But she'd never been so reckless as to lose control of herself out in a public place. She had an image to cultivate and maintain. Now that she'd dared to cut loose, though? She thought maybe she liked it.

"I love this band!" she told Jasmine McArthur just as their song ended.

"I think you've loved everything about this bar so far," her friend replied with a laugh. "The name, the neon sign, the wooden door, the sports posters, the mismatched tables, the servers' aprons . . ."

"It's a good bar!" Woody's wasn't fancy, but that was fine by Ashley. She squinted up at the stage and saw the musicians packing up. "Wait a second! Are they leaving?"

"Just taking a break, I think. There's a jukebox if you want to put a song on."

A jukebox. Like they were in the fifties or something. It was too damned perfect and Ashley absolutely *did* want to put a song on. Jasmine pointed to the far wall, past the bar, and Ashley craned her neck to see. Her gaze got caught on a broad set of shoulders before she found the jukebox. The man was facing away from her, but even from behind he was worth paying attention to. When he half turned, giving her a look at his silhouette, she forgot the jukebox entirely.

"Oh," Ashley said. It came out more like a moan than it should have. "Nice."

Jasmine draped herself over Ashley, leaning across to see what had caught her eye. "Oh," she said with a bit less enthusiasm than Ashley had displayed.

"He's lovely," Ashley said. But that wasn't the right word. "He's . . . God, what *is* he?"

"A bit of a whore," Jasmine answered. "He's a local handyman. He takes care of our place, and quite a few others. But that's not *all* he takes care of, if you know what I mean. He's a handy man when husbands aren't in town, as I understand it."

Ashley didn't have any reason to feel so disappointed. This was just one more man unable to keep his dick in his pants. She'd come to this small Vermont town to escape one man-slut and no sooner had she stepped into a public space than she'd encountered another. It was tedious maybe, but certainly not a reason for her to feel let down. "Oh," she said quietly, and took a sip of her wine.

"I'm not saying he's off-limits, Ashley. . . . He's . . . well, I'm having trouble thinking of any man who's more *on* limits than Josh Sullivan."

"Josh *Sullivan*? Like . . . *Lake* Sullivan? That kind of Sullivan?"

"According to him, his great-grandfather was one of the

first settlers to the area." Jasmine sounded bored. "Who knows if that's true. But, yeah, he says the lake's named after the old guy." She shrugged. "Honestly, though, who cares about his family?" Her face grew more animated and her smile was almost crafty as she said, "He could be just what you're looking for after that mess with Derek in the city! I know you say it was just your *pride* that was hurt, but even if that's all it was, it still has to sting. Getting a little action from a rugged country boy? That could be the perfect antidote to a bad case of cheating-boyfriend syndrome."

Ashley had only been staying with Jasmine for two days, and she'd already figured out that the woman liked drama. If there was none naturally occurring, she'd go out of her way to create some. Ashley tried to laugh it off. "Oh, I don't think Derek made me sick enough to need any medicine."

"So maybe it's not about Derek, then." There was something new in Jasmine's voice, something Ashley wished she was sober enough to puzzle through. But she and Jasmine didn't know each other all that well, and Ashley couldn't get a read on what Jasmine meant when she said, "You're looking for something new, aren't you?"

Was she? Professionally, yes. But that couldn't be what Jasmine was talking about. "Something new?"

"You just got dumped. You've flown across the country to escape a messy breakup. You should live a little. Take your tight little ass over there and let Josh Sullivan know he's yours for the night."

That was *not* Ashley's style. Not even close. Her best friend, Charlotte, was the take-charge type; Ashley usually just sat back and watched. She had a pretty good come-hither stare, but it only worked if the man would look in her direction long enough to get stared at. And that was about as forward as she'd ever gotten.

"It's the twenty-first century," Jasmine said firmly. "You *say* you want to be in control of your life and your career.

But you're still sitting around waiting for some man to notice you and decide whether you're worth his time! *You* decide, Ashley!"

"It's just not really—"

"You're scared!"

This was ridiculous. They were both grown women but Jasmine was acting like a little kid. And not a very nice one. "I'm not scared," Ashley said as calmly as she could. "I'm just . . . There's a difference between admiring someone's appearance and wanting to have sex with him."

"Why? Because you've got a boyfriend to be faithful to? Oh, nope, you don't. Because you're saving yourself for . . . Oh, no, there's no way Derek Braxton dated you for two years and didn't get any sex out of the deal. Unless *that's* why he had to go and sleep with his little tramp? Because he wasn't satisfied at home?"

Ashley stared at Jasmine. She knew her mouth was hanging open, but she couldn't pull herself together enough to close it.

Jasmine watched her with an arched eyebrow, then smiled almost sweetly. "No," she said. "That's not what happened. Derek cheated because he's an asshole, not because you're a prude. Right?"

"I'm not a prude," Ashley managed to say. At least she got her mouth closed at the end of the sentence.

"*I* know that." Jasmine was almost motherly now. "But does anyone else? I see how they treat you at home, like some kind of frilly little ornament. Because they still see you that way. They don't think you've got the guts to be a strong woman, the kind who sees something she likes and then *takes it*."

Ashley had no idea how she'd gotten into this conversation. She felt like anything she said would be stepping into one of Jasmine's traps. And she couldn't afford to offend Jasmine; she was part of one of Hollywood's biggest power couples, and she wasn't afraid of throwing her weight around. The invitation to the McArthur summerhouse had been a professional dream, but it would end up a nightmare if Ashley pissed Jasmine off.

"It's just . . . it's not really my style," she said.

"You want to play with the big boys? You've got to *act* like the big boys. And the big boys don't see something they like and then decide it's *not their style* to go get it. They fucking take it."

Ashley wished she'd had a little less to drink. "Okay, I think maybe we're talking about something a bit beyond picking up people in a bar."

"It's all the same. You've either got the fire or you don't."

"I have plenty of fire!"

"So prove it," Jasmine said with a cocky grin. "I'll bet you . . . lunch at The Warwick when we get back home. You chicken out, you owe me lunch. You go over there and take that rugged lumberjack home, and you win twice over. Sex, plus I owe you lunch."

"This is ridiculous," Ashley protested.

Jasmine smirked.

"I'm serious! This is not . . ." Not what? Not her style, she'd said, and that was true. But what the hell good was she getting from being true to her style? Her acting career was stagnant, her last relationship had just publicly imploded, and she'd practically run away from home. Maybe Jasmine was right and it was time to change her style. "I could go *talk* to him," she said.

"You have to actually leave with him," Jasmine warned. "This isn't a points-for-effort situation. You take him to bed or you lose."

Ashley looked again at the broad shoulders by the bar. Josh had turned away and she couldn't see his face, but she remembered enough of it to know that she'd really like to see more. And getting an up-close view might be nice, too.

Bet or no bet, she'd rather talk to that man than to Jasmine McArthur. All she had to do was find the guts to approach him. She looked at her empty wineglass, then reached for Jasmine's vodka tonic and lifted it to her lips. She had it drained in two gulps.

"Okay," she said. "I'm doing it."

Jasmine clapped her hands. "Fun!"

There was no point in thinking too much more about it. So Ashley stood up, straightened her clothes, and then headed for the bar. She tried to look confident, as if this was something she did every day.

Josh Sullivan was standing at the bar, his back turned to the crowd. He seemed to be dividing his attention between a baseball game on the television behind the bar and a few casual comments to the guy sitting next to him. And, damn it, the guy next to him was the tall, blond lead singer from the band that had just left the stage. Shoulders as wide as Josh's, so the two of them had to sort of angle themselves in just to have room next to each other at the bar. *Two* handsome men were even more intimidating than one had been.

How exactly was Ashley supposed to do this? If he'd been at a table she could have snuck around to the far side and caught his eye, but as it was she was stuck behind him, being ignored, and she felt like an idiot. Was she supposed to tap him on the shoulder to get him to turn around? That wasn't too cool.

People talked to strangers in bars all the time. There had to be a system. How did men approach *her* in bars? No, that wasn't a good line of questioning. She generally found the men who approached her in bars to be annoying, or even sleazy. Not the impression she was trying to create here. But it was probably better than the *other* impression she must be creating, hovering there behind the guy's back like a dog hoping for a treat from the dinner table.

She turned and looked back at Jasmine, who was laughing her ass off, of course. Ashley threw her hands up in a "What now?" gesture, and Jasmine just responded with a little shooing motion. Ashley waved emphatically behind her to show that there was no access point, and her flailing hand met soft fabric covering a hard, warm stomach.

She jerked around to stare at Josh Sullivan, who had apparently stood up to give his bar stool to a friend. Excellent.

"Sorry," she blurted.

She realized she was apologetically patting his stomach, then realized that her motivation was only partly apology. Damn, the man was *solid*, and very nice to touch. "I'm a little drunk," she said. The words were out loud, but she'd only meant them for herself.

"If you're going to be drunk, you picked the right place for it," Josh said. His voice was low and warm, loud enough to be heard over the din of the bar without sounding like he was yelling. He smiled gently at her and she knew she was staring but she didn't seem to be able to stop. The alcohol was part of the problem, but there was absolutely more to it than that.

She wanted to stare at him all night. But for some reason he was turning around, edging to the side, going back to his damn conversation about the stupid baseball game. He was blowing her off!

He was . . . this lothario, this man who was *handy* for so many women . . . and he was done with her? He hadn't seen anything to catch his interest?

She glanced back toward Jasmine. Jasmine just grinned and made the shooing gesture, urging Ashley to keep trying.

She wasn't going to slink back over to the table with her tail between her legs, so Ashley stepped around Josh's broad back and smiled at him. "Can I buy you a drink? As an apology for that little groping thing I did?"

He looked at her, assessing, then said, "Sure. I've been drinking beer, but I was just about to make a switch. You want to try something new?"

"I absolutely do!" She tried to make it sound as if she were feeling adventurous about more than her choice of beverage, but probably just came off as dementedly enthusiastic about alcohol. Damn, she was going to regret this when she sobered up. But now that she'd set it all in motion, she wasn't quite sure how to stop.

Josh turned to the bartender, caught his eye, and then tapped his watch and held up two fingers. What the hell kind of mountain-man sign language was this? But the bartender seemed to understand. While he was working, Josh edged back a little, making room for Ashley near the bar and forming a sort of half circle with the blond guy. "This is my cousin, Theo Linden," Josh said, and Ashley stuck her hand out to shake. A bit more traditional than her ab-patting move with Josh.

"Nice to meet you," she said. "I really like the band! Do you guys have any albums out?"

The guy's smile was sweetly self-deprecating. "We're just a bar band. Just covers, no original stuff. But if you need any roofing done, I'm your guy."

"I do *not* need any roofing done. But I appreciate the offer." Damn. If Ashley hadn't already seen Josh Sullivan, this guy might have been her crush for the evening. But she'd seen Josh first, and she was satisfied with her choice.

"Cal Montgomery," Josh said, and Cal turned and smiled. Another fine-looking man, tall and lean and strangely refined, despite the setting. Did Ashley have the world's worst case of beer goggles or was this town absolutely full of gorgeous men?

The bartender arrived then with two pint glasses, both filled with ice and a clear liquid, garnished with slices of lime. Intriguing.

"Cheers," Josh said as he handed her an icy glass. She took it in two hands and raised it to her lips at the same time he did.

An enthusiastic swig from him, a cautious sip from her. Then she snorted. "Water?"

He grinned. "I have to drive home. And you've been hanging out with Jasmine, right? So you could probably use a break, too." He stopped with a frown, as if he'd just realized something. "Or not. I can order you something else, if you want."

"No. The water's good. You're right, we've been drinking since noon." She decided to accept it as a small victory that he had at least noticed what table she'd come from and who she'd been with. "You call her Jasmine? You work for her, right?"

"You think she should be Mrs. McArthur?" Josh smiled, but it wasn't quite as sincere as some of his other efforts. "I have one pair of clients that I call 'Mister' and 'Missus.' They're in their eighties, and I think they appreciate the respect. The rest? First names."

"That'd be nice," Ashley said. "My housekeeper always wants to call me 'Miss Carlsen.' I mean, she washes my underwear! I feel like we could cut past the formal titles, you know? But she doesn't want to."

He nodded. "Probably not a bad idea." His voice was so quiet in the noisy bar that she was reading his lips more than hearing him. "It's good to remind yourself of things sometimes."

She was pretty sure she wouldn't have understood that even if she *hadn't* spent the day drinking in the sun. She glanced over at Jasmine, who raised a glass in a silent toast to what Ashley had accomplished so far and then made another "go on" motion with her free hand.

Damn it. But Ashley couldn't afford to blow off Jasmine McArthur. And maybe Jasmine hadn't been totally wrong about the best strategy for getting over a breakup. If one horse bucks you off, maybe you don't get back on the same one, but you should get back on *someone*. She had no idea what the appropriate next step was, but she hoped that a man like Josh Sullivan would appreciate the direct approach. Theo had faded out somewhere, maybe back off to the band, so there was a bit more room for Ashley to maneuver as she leaned in toward Josh. "It's loud in here," she said. "You want to go somewhere quieter?"

Josh froze for a moment, then sipped his drink. He obviously knew she was suggesting more than just conversation. Finally he said, "Better not. I'm not safe to drive yet."

"We could take a cab."

"You're staying at the McArthurs'? But you don't want to take me back there. So to my place. But I live out in the country. There's only one cab in town and Tony's not going to waste most of a Saturday night driving way out there and all the way back."

One cab. It was ridiculous. But not unsolvable. "He'll do it if we pay him enough."

She could tell it had been the wrong thing to say, but she really didn't know why. Then Josh said, "Not everyone's for sale, you know." He sounded almost hostile.

She tried to laugh it off. "I don't want to buy him. Just rent him."

Josh's smile was tight. "Still. No. Not a good idea."

"The cab's not a good idea? Or us going somewhere else isn't a good idea?"

"Neither one's a good idea." He said it with finality, and there was something about his tone that pissed her off. She'd been hearing too much of that lately. Men telling her that what she wanted *wasn't a good idea*, as if they were doing her a favor. As if they knew better than she did what she wanted and what was best for her. She'd had enough. Jasmine was right; it was time for a change, and this was as good a place as any for that change to begin.

She set her glass on the bar, then leaned forward and

brought her mouth to Josh's ear. "*I* think it's a good idea," she whispered, and she nipped his earlobe.

He didn't move. She had no idea what that meant. Damn it, she'd never done this before. Josh was supposed to have fallen over himself as soon as she'd suggested the possibility of a hookup. He should have been giddy with excitement. That was how this was supposed to work, wasn't it? She had no idea, but she knew he still wasn't moving.

She needed to do more. She had no idea how this had become so important to her. This was . . . Ashley had no idea. She'd think about it when she sobered up. For the time being, she kissed her way down Josh's neck. His skin was warm and surprisingly soft, and she felt a churn of desire in her gut when she felt his pulse beating strong and fast beneath her lips. This wasn't about Jasmine McArthur anymore. Ashley genuinely wanted this man. She hooked her fingers into the waistband of his jeans, and that was when he caught her hand in his.

"Not a good idea," he said, and he stepped back, holding his arms out to keep her from following.

"Why not?" she demanded.

"You've had too much to drink."

She stared at him. "What? You're the bar police now? You watch people's drinks and then decide who gets to go home with whom?"

"No. Just who gets to go home with me."

"Like you're some sort of prize?" she said, trying to dredge up some face-saving scorn.

"You seem to think I am," he said quietly. "But, no, I wouldn't put it that way." His voice was harder as he said, "I wouldn't think of myself as an inanimate object that has to go home with whoever wins it."

She stared at him. What the hell was going on? How had everything gone so wrong? And more importantly, how much of it was her fault?

Pretty much all of it, probably. She was out of control. She'd had too much to drink, she was frustrated by her career, her boyfriend had just cheated on her very publicly, and now she was making a fool of herself in a backwoods Vermont bar.

"I'm sorry," she said. She took a step backward. "I'm . . . I don't know. Sorry."

His face was impassive as he looked at her, then over at Jasmine, then back at her. "It's okay," he finally said. "We all do stupid things sometimes. It's not a big deal."

And that was that. She'd messed up, been forgiven, and now it was over. She reluctantly turned away, heading back over to Jasmine's table.

She didn't make it all the way.

"Hey! Ashley! Ashley . . . something! From that show . . . the one with . . . with the family . . ." The man who had accosted her was obviously drunk and leaning toward her in a way that suggested he was about to sprawl all over her, but she was more upset about his ignorance of classic American television.

"*Mayfair Drive*," she prompted. "One of the longest-running drama series in television history? Following the trials and triumphs of the Anderson family, including their youngest daughter, plucky Amanda Anderson, played by . . . ?"

"Ashley something!" the guy said triumphantly. "Yeah, I knew it was you. Hey . . ." He leaned even closer and breathed on her, and she knew what was coming. "I saw you in something else. Last year. That movie. That thing with . . . with the chick from that high school show." His eyes were wide with excitement as he stage-whispered, "I saw your tits."

"First time you'd seen any?"

He scowled. "What? No! I've seen plenty!"

"Oh. So . . . I'm not quite sure why you're so excited about that."

"Might be the first time he saw any and didn't get slapped

in the face right after," a new voice said, and Ashley half turned to see Josh looming into the conversation. Damn, he was tall. And wide in the shoulders. And his big, strong hand was hovering protectively just over *her* shoulder while his amber eyes were locked challengingly on the guy who'd stopped her. "That what it was, Driscoll?"

"Fuck you, Sullivan," Driscoll said, but the words were clearly just to save face. Ashley wished she was sober enough to catch the subtleties of the way he took in Josh's hand placement, his size, his confidence. She could use those reactions in a future role, if she ever needed to play someone who was backing down from a superior opponent.

Josh didn't respond to the words. He just stood there, staring, and Driscoll faded away without another look in Ashley's direction. She couldn't decide whether to be grateful for Josh's protection or annoyed at his interference. "Thank you," she said. "I could have handled that—it's part of my job, really. But thanks."

"You shouldn't *have* to handle it," he said. "I guess you know what your job is better than I do, but putting up with assholes shouldn't be part of anyone's job." Then he caught himself and shrugged. "At least, I don't think it should be."

"I . . . yeah, I agree, actually."

"Well, sorry. You know, on behalf of Lake Sullivan, or whatever. We're mostly not like that."

"I know," she said quickly. "I mean, I haven't been here very long, but almost everyone's been really nice." She supposed it was rude to push any further just because he'd been a gentleman, but she was having a really hard time making herself go back to her seat. "Everything's so beautiful up here. The lake and the forest. And the *rocks*. They're so rugged and wild."

He nodded cautiously. "I don't know if rocks can be tame, really. Or wild. They're just rocks."

"Yeah, okay. Good point." Ashley knew she wasn't making

much sense, but she didn't seem to be offending him, either. "Jasmine said there's wildlife, right? I mean, *wild* life. She said we have to be careful not to leave food out or we'll get bears. That's crazy. Like, at home, I'd worry about getting ants! Up here, I might get bears!"

"And ants." He was smiling. They were okay. It shouldn't have been so important to her, but it was.

She smiled back at him, trying to get her pulse rate back where it belonged, and trying to forget the feeling of his skin under her lips. "It's like a kids' alphabet book. A list of hazards in Vermont. 'A' is for ants, 'B' is for bears, 'C' is for . . . ?"

"'Cobras.'"

She stared at him, startled. "No. Not cobras."

"Yeah. Sorry, but it's true. There are three species of cobra that live in the Vermont wilderness."

She was pretty sure she would have heard about this little fact, but he seemed sincere. "What are they? The three species."

"Rock cobra, river cobra, stone cobra."

"Rock cobras are different from stone cobras?"

He kept his face still for a moment longer than he should have been able to, then let it fall into a grin. "I panicked. I couldn't think of a third cobra name."

"Lake cobra. Swamp cobra. Forest cobra. Or you could have gotten away from the habitats entirely. Grey cobra, hooded cobra, spitting cobra . . ."

"Damn. Next time I play 'let's make up snake names,' I want you on my team."

"But not in your bed." Damn it. Why had she said that? Just when things were going nicely, she had to ruin it.

But he didn't seem too offended by her bluntness. "Not when you're drunk. Not the first time, at least."

So. It was that simple. He had a rule, and it didn't really seem like a bad one. She was pretty sure that she'd approve of it when she sobered up. For the time being, though, she was still tasting his skin on her tongue and still wanting to peel away that raggedy T-shirt and find out just what lay beneath it. But he'd said no. Repeatedly. It was over. But that didn't mean she had to go back and admit defeat to Jasmine. It didn't mean she had to tear herself away from Josh Sullivan.

"Just so we're clear," she said, "there *are* cobras up here, or there aren't?"

"There aren't," he said reluctantly. "Not technically. Maybe 'C' could be 'coyotes.'"

"Okay," she agreed, and they went on with their game.

❧ Two ❧

JOSH WONDERED IF he would have had the self-control to say no if Jasmine McArthur hadn't been sitting over at her table watching them with such wicked interest. If it had just been him and Ashley. She'd been tipsy, maybe, but not really drunk. And, damn it, she was a beautiful woman. Long auburn hair, dancing green eyes, and a hell of a body. It was too bad that she was an actress, but everyone had faults.

And now, in the bar, she wasn't acting like a spoiled movie star. They were working through their alphabet of Vermont hazards. "M" had been easy, both of them saying "mosquitoes" at the same time and then moving on. "N," though?

"'Norwegians?'" Josh suggested. "There are a lot of them up here. But they're ex-Norwegians. They came generations ago. And I don't know if they're a hazard, exactly. Not all of them."

"I think Norwegians are a noble people. Not a hazard. And I already let you have 'Dutch' for 'D.' This list is serious business, Josh! It can't just be an excuse for you to slam different countries of origin."

Josh nodded. "Yeah, okay. That's fair. So . . . 'N.' Maybe 'neighbors'? Mine are okay, but only because they're distant. Most people up here like their space."

"I guess that's why you'd live here." She nodded as if pleased to have an answer to the question of why anyone would settle in such a godforsaken land. But then she smiled and he wondered if he was being a little oversensitive. She liked the lake, after all. "Okay, 'neighbors.' What's 'O'?"

But that was when Jasmine arrived. Josh smelled her familiar perfume before she'd even tucked her hand into the back of his jeans, that familiar claim of ownership that he hated so much. He reached behind him to pull her hand out, but he tried to do it subtly. Ashley couldn't see what was going on back there and he'd just as soon she not know about it.

"So, you two are getting along?" Jasmine asked. Her smile was sharp. "I was just going to call for the car. For myself. Josh, can I trust you to make sure Ashley gets home safely? Eventually?"

She'd taken her hand out from inside his jeans but now she had it resting on the curve of his ass, her fingers digging in a little where they wrapped underneath. How many people in the bar were seeing that? Seeing her treat him like a possession that she could paw at will, or give away to her friends if the whim struck her?

He stepped away from her entirely. She and her husband had a lot of friends, and most of those friends were Josh's clients. He really couldn't afford to alienate her, but he wasn't going to stand there and let her molest him, either. "I'm just about to head out myself," he said, working to keep his voice light and calm. "Ashley, maybe you want to go with Jasmine?"

She nodded slowly. "Yeah. Okay."

"Oh," Jasmine said. Her disappointment was a little too blatant to be real. The emotions Jasmine displayed for public consumption rarely had any relationship to her actual feelings; Josh had learned that the hard way. "But you two seemed to be getting along so well. Do you just need a little more time? I don't *have* to leave now. . . ."

"No," Josh said firmly. He didn't want to get dragged into whatever the hell this was. "Like I said, I'm about to go." He set his empty glass down on the bar and nodded. "Ashley, it was nice to meet you. Enjoy your stay in hazardous Vermont. Be safe."

She grinned at him. Damn, he liked her smile. And he liked how often she used it.

"I'll try. I'm a little worried that I haven't identified all of the risks yet. If I'm approached by something from 'A' to 'N', I feel like I'll be prepared. But if something from 'O' on attacks . . ."

Jasmine laughed. "You two have a little game! How adorable!"

Josh was not a fan of being called "adorable," and from the expression on Ashley's face he could tell she felt the same. So he smiled just at Ashley as he said, "We are pretty fucking cute."

"Might as well accept it," she replied, and her shoulder shrug was a lot more relaxed than it would have been a moment earlier. Somehow, in that quick second, they'd become a team. The two of them united against Jasmine.

And Jasmine could tell. "Fine, then," she said, her joking tone gone. "Ashley, if you're coming with me, let's go. Josh, I really would like the path through the trees re-mulched as soon as possible. I asked you to do that several days ago. And there are some boards on the dock that are rotting. We need them replaced before someone puts a foot through them."

Yeah. Good reminder of his place in their social structure. He told himself to be grateful for it. "I can try to get to the dock tomorrow—you've got some extra boards in your boathouse, so it won't take long to replace a few weak ones. I'll probably get to the mulch early next week. Everyone came up this week and found a lot of stuff they want done, so I'm working through the list as quickly as I can."

"Most of the names on that list are there because *we* referred you to them. Why don't you do the boards *and* the mulch tomorrow?"

Another good reminder. So he made himself smile. "I appreciate the referrals. But the mulch is a bigger job, and nobody's going to get hurt if a path isn't mulched. So it's lower priority."

"It would be a shame if we had to find someone else to recommend to people."

Okay, there had to be an end to it. "If you can find someone else who does work of my quality at my price, I guess they deserve your support." He stepped backward, disengaging from the conversation, then said, "Good night," and turned for the parking lot.

He was halfway to the door when he felt a warm hand catch his, and he turned to see Ashley looking tentative but determined. "Good night," she said quickly, and she brought her free hand to the back of his neck and pulled his head down. She stood on her tiptoes and pressed a quick kiss to the corner of his mouth. "Thank you."

It made no sense to let her go. He wanted to drag her out of there. No, not drag her—pick her up and carry her. But she'd been drinking, and Jasmine was . . . Jasmine was Jasmine. Always playing her games by rules only she knew. Josh wasn't interested in being her pawn anymore, and he felt a bit protective about Ashley, too. He had no idea what Jasmine was up to, but Ashley shouldn't get dragged into whatever it was.

"It was nice to meet you," he said, and he gently eased out of her grip.

She blinked and let him go. "I'm here for another week," she said. "Until next Friday. Do you think maybe—"

"This is the busy season for me," he said quickly. "Paths to mulch, you know? Very important stuff. No time for much else."

Another blink. "Okay," she said.

She sounded sad, but he bet he could kiss her into a better mood without much trouble. Except he wasn't supposed to be thinking that way. He knew better. "Good night, Ashley." He turned before she could say anything else that tempted him to do something different. He was dimly aware of people watching him, trying to figure out why the hell he was walking away from the woman behind him. It was a small town and half the bar knew who he was. They knew he'd made different decisions in similar situations in the past.

Ironic, he supposed, that he gave up on summer women right before he met one who seemed like she might be something a bit more. But he shook his head as he headed out the door and toward his pickup. Ashley was in town until Friday. Had he lost his mind, thinking there was going to be something more that developed over that time? Summer women were transient. For a while, that had been their biggest charm. But he was too old for that crap now, and he was tired of being the one getting left behind when they went back to their glamorous city lives.

"You heading out early?" he heard, and turned to see Theo standing just outside the bar door. It was the smoking area, but Josh had never seen Theo actually light up—he probably figured just being around smokers was enough of a nod to the rock 'n' roll lifestyle. "Had enough already?"

"I guess so, yeah. I'm getting too old for it maybe."

"Ninety percent of the guys in the bar would have cut off a body part to have either of those women fighting over them," Theo said philosophically.

"You want an introduction? Ashley seems nice enough, but Jasmine? Mess with Jasmine at your own risk."

"What would you do if I said yes?" Theo leaned a little closer, trying to get a better look at Josh's face in the dim light. "Not Jasmine. . . . I've already been chewed up and spat out by women like that, thanks very much. But if I asked for an introduction to Ashley . . ."

"I'd say you didn't need it. You've already met. She likes your band, remember?"

"She likes my band, but as soon as you gave her the time of day, I might as well not have existed. That's Ashley Carlsen, you know. The *movie star*. That's who you just walked away from."

"Yeah," Josh said slowly. "I think I noticed that."

Theo shook his head in amusement and mock disgust, and they stood silently for a moment before Theo headed back in to his band and Josh started for home.

He was climbing behind the wheel of his pickup as a black sedan pulled up to the bar door. It looked completely out of place in the surroundings, but he knew why it was there. He'd spent enough time in the backseat of the damn thing. Sure enough, Jasmine came staggering out of the bar, her arm looped through Ashley's. They were both dressed for city clubbing, totally over-the-top for a Vermont bar, but Josh hadn't noticed that inside. He'd just seen Ashley, a pretty girl with a sweet smile.

Now, as Jasmine's shrieking laughter stabbed his eardrums even from across the lot, he could see how ridiculous it all was. Ashley was part of another world. A glamorous land where housekeepers washed her underwear, drivers took her home from bars, and handymen spread mulch on her friends' pathways. He'd visited that world, but he'd never belonged. And he didn't want to be a visitor anymore.

He had enough to worry about. He wasn't a kid anymore,

and he didn't have the energy for getting involved with something he knew was going to end badly. So he watched the car pull away and he drove home by himself.

JOSH usually got caught up on his paperwork on Sundays and then took the rest of the day off, but he wanted Jasmine McArthur off his back. And, maybe, just maybe, he wanted one more look at Ashley Carlsen. He knew it was stupid, but once she'd dropped the whole seduction routine, he'd really liked her.

Yet in his typical contrary manner, he carefully arranged to visit the McArthur place at the time he was least likely to run into anybody. Especially anybody who'd been out late the night before, drinking and carousing.

The sun was barely over the horizon as he parked off to the side of the driveway, well away from the expensive cars of the people who belonged there, and hoisted his toolbox and the replacement boards out of the truck bed. The McArthur cottage was, like many others on Lake Sullivan, on top of a low cliff overlooking the lake; he found his way to the long wooden staircase that connected the house to the waterside and made his way down.

That was when he saw her. She stood on the end of the McArthurs' dock, still and graceful as a heron, silhouetted against the rising sun. She was wearing a simple one-piece bathing suit, watching a family of loons swim past.

Josh felt like a peeping tom, invading Ashley's moment of peace and solitude. Just as he was about to turn away and find somewhere else to start his day's work, she raised her arms and gracefully dove into the water, like a mermaid returning home after too much time among the humans.

She stayed under a long time, long enough that he started worrying about submerged rocks her head might have connected with. His feet were on the gangplank when she reappeared thirty feet away from the end of the dock. She'd turned around underwater, so she was looking back toward the shore, and he still had the sense that she was returning to her own world. He could see it in his mind, the way she'd dive again and disappear with a quick flash of her tail fin.

But she didn't. She just raised an arm to wave at him, then ducked back underwater. By the time he got to the end of the dock he could see her skimming along just under the surface of the water, a long, pale line against the dark green of the lake.

She smiled as she lifted her face out of the water and looked up at him. "You're here early. Is there a mulch emergency?"

"Just trying to get the dock fixed before it's covered with people."

"Should I stay in the water, out of your way?"

"No, it's fine. One person won't be a problem."

She didn't climb out right away, though. She floated on her back, her eyes closed, as he tried not to look in her direction. He was there for a job.

He had the old boards unscrewed and stacked by the time she climbed up the ladder and wrapped a towel around herself.

"You're up early, too," he said. If he'd thought about it he'd have kept his mouth shut, but he'd been distracted by trying not to watch the towel as it edged down over her breasts. "Especially since you were drinking yesterday."

"Swimming's the best hangover cure I know," she said with a smile. "Nice cool water, and I swear the pressure of it against my skull helps squish my brains back where they're supposed to be."

"That seems medically unlikely."

She shrugged. "I don't ask questions, I just feel grateful that it works." She settled onto the diving board and leaned back, her eyes closed again, her face turned toward the sun.

He worked quietly for a couple minutes, then glanced over to find her watching him. "You know what you're doing, huh?"

He frowned. "It's not too tricky. Take out the old boards, put in the new ones. They're already cut to the right length, even."

"I wouldn't know how to do it."

"You already do." He held his cordless drill out toward her. "I'm using this as a screwdriver. I just place the board, slap in a couple screws, and it's done. You want to try?"

She didn't answer right away, then said, "Yeah, I kinda do. Is that okay?"

"Sure, if you want. There's not much to mess up."

She practically skipped across the dock, and stood so close to him he could smell the clean lake water in her hair.

"This trigger controls the drill. Push it gently for slow, or speed it up by pushing the trigger all the way in."

She took the drill, played with the trigger a little, and then they crouched down and he held a board in place while she drove in a few screws. "That easy?" she asked, a pleased grin on her face.

"That easy."

"Can I do one all by myself?"

"Be my guest."

So he took her place on the diving board and she found a board and fit it into place. She didn't look totally natural. She dropped one screw and it fell between two slats, landing in the lake below with a soft splash, and she looked up at him with an almost comic expression of guilt.

"It's not a big deal," he reassured her. "They don't cost much, and one wood screw won't hurt the lake."

She nodded and went back to work, and when the board was attached she turned to him with a triumphant grin. "Look! I did that!"

"Nice work. Looks secure."

"Holy smokes." She was still beaming. "I can't believe how proud I am!"

"Neither can I," he admitted with a laugh. "You want to keep going, or should I take over?"

She looked tempted, then shook her head and held the drill out to him. "You'd better take over. I want to go out on top, before I mess something up."

They traded places again and Josh quickly finished the remaining boards. He was done. It was time to go. But for some reason he was reluctant to leave.

"Hey!" Ashley whispered excitedly. "Look! I saw those guys before. Are those loons?"

Josh looked out at the lake. He kept his voice low as he said, "Yeah. A nice little family, huh?"

"I saw them yesterday, too!"

"You come back next year, you'll probably see the same ones. At least the parents. They fly south for the winter, but they come back to the same lake every year."

"Yesterday it looked like . . ." Ashley frowned. "I was going to look it up on the Internet, but I got distracted. But it looked like the babies were riding on the mom's back. Do they do that?"

"Yeah. I'm not sure why. . . . They do it more when the water's cold, so maybe it's to help them stay warm? But I guess it would be good protection against predators, too."

"Predators? Who eats baby loons?"

"Turtles. Big fish. Hawks, probably."

Ashley looked toward the lake as if she were worrying about an attack.

"I've been on this lake for thirty-one years and I've never actually seen it happen," Josh said. He didn't want to ruin the poor woman's vacation with imagined loon carnage.

Ashley relaxed a little. "Did we count any of those on our list of Vermont hazards last night? We haven't gotten to 'T' yet. Maybe that should be 'turtles.'"

"Or 'S' for 'snappers.' There's some nice little turtles up here who wouldn't hurt anybody, not even a baby loon. It's the snappers you want to watch out for."

"I think 'S' should probably be reserved for 'snakes.' Anywhere snakes live, they should be the number one 'S'-related hazard."

"Fair enough," Josh agreed. He didn't mind snakes himself, but he wasn't in the mood to argue.

They watched the loons in companionable silence for a few more minutes, and then the dock vibrated a little as someone stepped onto the gangplank. They both turned.

"Well, you're up early!" Jasmine said with exaggerated cheer. She had a glass of orange juice in her hand, and Josh knew from past experience that it would have at least champagne but more likely vodka in it. Ashley might swim to control her hangovers, but Jasmine preferred a hair of the dog approach. Just one more thing Josh wished he had no reason to know.

Ashley and Josh had been speaking quietly enough that the loons had come quite close, but with Jasmine's arrival they were heading away. Josh figured it was time for him to follow their example. "I got the boards replaced," he said, nodding at the wood beneath their feet. "And I'll be by on Wednesday, probably, for the mulch."

"Wednesday." Jasmine pronounced the word as if it had an unpleasant taste. "You're here today. Why not today?"

"Church," Josh said. He hadn't been inside a church since the last wedding he'd attended. And Jasmine would know his Sunday routine as well as he knew her hangover cures. But he didn't think she'd want to explain how she'd come by that knowledge, not with a witness. So he smiled blandly at her then nodded in Ashley's direction. "Snakes and turtles," he said. "But I think we missed a couple letters in the middle somewhere."

"Next time," she said.

He knew better, but he smiled anyway, then gathered the discarded boards and tucked them under one arm while he carried his toolbox with the other and headed off the dock. He tried not to react at all when Jasmine followed him.

When they reached the top of the stairs she said, "So you two are still being adorable, are you? With your little game?"

"We just can't help it, I guess. We were born that way, you know?"

"Well, I hope Ashley doesn't think that *our* game is still in play."

"Whose game?"

"Ashley's and mine." Jasmine looked at him and her face transformed into the first genuine smile he'd seen from her in ages. "Oh, Josh! She didn't tell you?"

Anything that made Jasmine that happy was going to make someone else sad, and Josh had a pretty good idea who the "someone else" would be in this situation. "So hopefully I can do the mulch on Wednesday. Might not be until Thursday, though."

But Jasmine wasn't so easily distracted. "I'm surprised she didn't mention it to you, with all the giggling you two have been doing together."

Josh was pretty sure he hadn't been giggling, but he was at the truck now, tossing the wood into the back and not bothering to secure his toolbox as carefully as he usually did. He wasn't going to engage with whatever Jasmine was up to, certainly not to debate whether he'd been laughing. Then he turned and saw Jasmine leaning against the driver's door. She wasn't going to let him leave until she said whatever it was. He braced himself and she smiled wickedly.

"I bet her she couldn't fuck you." Jasmine waited for a reaction, but Josh was pretty sure he managed not to give her one. Jasmine's shrug was over-casual. "She's having a bit of a tiff with her boyfriend at home, and I thought she could use a little distraction. For all your failings, Josh, you've always been a good distraction that way. So I thought you might be good for her, but she wasn't interested. I mean . . ." She ran her eyes down Josh's ragged clothes. "Not really her type, obviously. But with the bet? The girl's a competitor, I'll give her that. That's what made her come over to you in the bar."

It was just one more sleazy interaction with Jasmine. Just one more opportunity for her to poke at him, looking for holes in his armor. This wasn't anything new. There was no reason for Josh's stomach to be churning.

"I need to get going," he said, but she didn't move from her spot by his door. He could have picked her up and set her aside without any trouble, but she was a client and he was on her property. He supposed he could have gone around to the passenger side and worked his way across the cab, but it would have been awkward, especially with her laughing at him the whole time. So he just stood there and waited.

"She's a movie star, Josh. Did you honestly think she'd be interested in you without a little outside encouragement?" Jasmine smiled sweetly.

And he managed to return the expression. "No, not really. I mean, you and me? Yeah, okay, that made basic sense. But someone like Ashley? Totally out of my league. We were just talking about loons, Jasmine. Nothing for you to be jealous about."

He saw her eyes narrow and knew he'd gone too far. But he just couldn't make himself care. She had more money than God and she had a lot of influence with the Lake Sullivan summer people. She wasn't a good person to have as an enemy. But she was an even worse person to have as a friend.

"Excuse me," he said, and she stepped aside, letting him climb into the truck. He watched her in the rearview mirror as he pulled away. She wasn't moving, just standing there, staring after him. Planning her revenge, he was sure.

Damn it. He'd worked so hard to keep his cool around her, and he'd managed it for so long. And then he'd blown it with one stupid conversation.

He didn't want to think about what had made him so angry. Didn't want to think about Ashley and her stupid grin when she'd attached the board to the dock. So she'd been playing around. So she hadn't really wanted him. Big deal. He'd known she was trouble, and he'd stayed away. He'd done the right thing. He was fine. Just fine.

He wondered how long it was going to take before he started believing the lines he was telling himself.

❧ *Three* ❧

"SO, WHAT'S THE mulch *for*?" Ashley tried to sound light and relaxed, as if she hadn't been compulsively watching the driveway for days, waiting for Josh's pickup to appear. But when he'd finally shown up, he hadn't smiled at her like he had on the dock. There was none of the warmth, none of the casual joking. He'd just nodded in her direction and then gotten to work.

And now, even after she'd strolled over and greeted him with enthusiasm, he still wouldn't look at her. He was shoveling wood chips from the back of the truck into a wheelbarrow, and apparently that was a job that required his full attention. "The mulch goes on the paths," he said without expression.

She made her laugh a little louder than it normally would be so she could be sure he heard it. "Yeah, I got that! But *why* does it go on the paths?"

He stopped shoveling at least for a moment, but he still didn't look at her. "I have no idea," he admitted. There was a tiny bit of expression in his voice and she was thinking about counting it as a victory, but then he swung down out of the truck bed, graceful and light despite his size as he landed on the rocky ground, and he said, "You should go find Jasmine. It was her plan, so she'd hopefully know why she wanted it."

"Okay. I'll ask her when I see her." There was that topic of conversation closed off. "Do you need any help with anything?"

"I charge by the hour for jobs like this," he said, taking the handles of the wheelbarrow and heading along the path into the woods. "If you helped, you'd actually be taking money out of my pocket."

She hadn't thought about it in those terms. "Well, do you want me to get in the way, then?" She was pretty sure he would have been charmed by her smile if he'd bothered to look in her direction. "I could drag this out for so long you could buy a new truck!"

"There's nothing wrong with my old truck." And with that he was out of earshot and the conversation was over.

She could have gone after him. This was the McArthurs' property and she was their guest. If she decided she wanted to hang out in the forest, she'd be absolutely within her rights to sit right on top of the damn path Josh was trying to mulch. But a tiny sprout of self-respect poked up through the muddy soil of her infatuation and wrapped around her ankle to keep her from chasing after the man.

She should go back to the cottage. She was an early riser, at least compared to the rest of the guests, but she could hang out in the kitchen with the housekeeper, or take a mug of coffee down to the dock, or . . . anything, really. Instead, she pretended to be fascinated by a weird brown growth on a nearby tree trunk. She reached out to touch it. Surprisingly hard. What the hell was it? She crouched down to see it from underneath and wondered if she could break it off the tree to see how it was attached. But she didn't want to damage it. Or the tree. It really was quite interesting.

This was her strength as an actress, she knew. When she first started with a role, she was just pretending. Just playing make-believe, like a kid. And then, like a kid, she'd slip away from reality a little, away from her own life and into something else. GiGi, her great-grandmother, had been a stage actress, famous in her time, and she'd been the one who encouraged Ashley to act. She'd shown Ashley how to find one thing, one prop or gesture or idea, and how to focus on that and let everything else fill itself in. "Magic Time," she'd called it. "Okay, Ashley, is that how a bear would walk? So you walk like that. Walk like that, and let Magic Time happen. Soon, you'll be the bear." Ashley had been cast in *Mayfair Drive* three days before GiGi had faded away in her sleep, and Ashley had always been so happy that the old lady had been around long enough to receive the phone call from Ashley to share her success.

Now, in the backwoods of Vermont, Magic Time had come unbidden, as it sometimes did. Ashley had acted like someone who cared about growths on trees, and all of a sudden, she *did* care. She heard the soft rolling of the wheelbarrow behind her and couldn't help asking, "What *is* this thing? It looks like a huge mushroom, but it's hard. . . ."

"Conk," Josh said. He paused, as if fighting with himself, then apparently lost the battle and added, "That's what we call them, at least. I think they're a kind of fungus. They eat away at the tree, making it rot inside."

"So they're bad?" Ashley stroked the smooth, warm skin of the conk.

"Circle of life," Josh said. "They're not good or bad; they just are."

"But they're bad for the tree?"

"Yeah," Josh said. He looked at her then, his amber eyes cool. "They're parasites, I'd say. They find a weakness and work their way inside, and then they get strong while the tree weakens. It takes a long time, but it happens. Eventually it'll kill the tree."

The words were innocuous enough, but there was something about his gaze that made her feel like she was being accused of something. Was he . . . was he calling her a parasite? Comparing her to the conk? She frowned at him in confusion and with the beginnings of irritation, but he was already turned back to his task. "How come you're acting like a virgin who got felt up at the dance?" she demanded. So much for her attempts to be charming. "I messed up a bit at the bar but we got past that, then we were friends at the dock, and now you're pissy again?"

"I'm at work," he said. "I'd like to concentrate on that, if you don't mind."

"You're shoveling wood chips. That takes your full mental energies?"

"Maybe you heard Jasmine threatening to fire me and blackball me with her friends? I'd like to make sure she doesn't have any reason to do that."

"I'm sure she wouldn't."

"You're sure of that, are you?"

Well, no, she supposed she wasn't. But, still. "The job doesn't really seem that demanding."

She knew as soon as she'd said the words that they were wrong, and sure enough, he straightened and stood for a moment, controlling his temper. He kept his face turned away from her as he said, "I'm just a simple country boy, not all sophisticated like you big-city folk. A job like this is about all I can handle."

Shit. "I didn't mean your job *in general* doesn't seem demanding," she tried. "Just this one part of it. And, I mean, it's not like *my* job is all that complicated, if you're just looking at it from the outside. I play make-believe for a living, right?"

"And for a hobby, too, from the looks of things."

Neither of them spoke after that. She wasn't quite sure what he was accusing her of, but she was definitely tired of the attitude. She wanted to fight back, demand clarification and an end to the snide remarks. But instead she stepped away from the tree with the conk and headed for the house. She was on vacation. She didn't need this crap.

JOSH refused to feel bad about it. At least, he tried to refuse, and when that didn't work, he refused to *admit* he felt bad about it. That was something.

He wished the mulch job *was* a little more demanding, so he could let it distract him from his thoughts, but Ashley had been right. Shoveling wood chips really didn't take a lot of brainpower.

He kept his back to the cottage as much as he could and his eyes down when he couldn't, but he hadn't figured out a way to turn off his ears. So he heard the sounds of the cottage coming alive, guests and hosts meeting for breakfast on the deck, talking and laughing. There was no problem with him doing work while the McArthurs entertained. They were *always* entertaining, after all, and he was a common laborer, invisible to the wealthy unless they decided they wanted to see him. There'd been a time when they *had* wanted to, but after a year or so of politely refusing all of their invitations, they'd gotten the message and allowed him to sink back into safe anonymity. But he could hear *Ashley*, her voice sweet and clear, and he wished . . .

He had no idea what he wished for. He just wished things were different. But they weren't. So he concentrated on his work, and when he finished he loaded the wheelbarrow into the now-empty bed of his truck and headed for the driver's-side door.

"Josh!" A man's voice from the deck.

Josh looked over and raised a hand. He tried to ignore the stab of guilt he always felt when dealing with Jasmine's husband. "Hey, David. That's one load done, but I'll need to do another." He moved closer as he spoke, trying to seem relaxed. "I'm supposed to be down the road for a meeting at ten, but I can come back here early afternoon, if you want. Or else tomorrow."

"This afternoon would be best. Jasmine wants this job done."

"Okay."

"She asked me to speak to you, Josh." David came a few steps closer, but he was still on the deck. Any of the guests who wanted to hear him would be able to. "She's not too impressed with the service we've been getting lately."

Josh kept his face blank, trying not to think about the exact nature of the *service* Jasmine wanted him to provide. "I'm sorry to hear that. But I think I've been getting everything done pretty fast. If someone else has an emergency, like a leak or something, I need to fix that first. But otherwise, I'm on schedule."

David shrugged. "She's also concerned that you're not behaving professionally. I know you used to be part of . . . well, you used to be friendly with Jasmine's crowd up here. Right? She's concerned that maybe you've gotten a little confused about your place in all this."

Josh kept his mouth shut. Cal Montgomery was on the deck, one of the few locals rich enough to fit in with the summer crowd. He was standing next to Ashley, both of them listening without looking in his direction. Josh tried not to guess what either of them was thinking about it all. He waited to see if David had more to say, then stepped backward. "I'll bring the rest of the mulch this afternoon."

"And you'll give us priority service in the future," David said. "How many of your clients came because we gave them to you? So you'll give us priority, and you'll watch the way you speak to my wife." He smiled, but his gaze didn't leave Josh's face. The man was some sort of big shot in Hollywood business, and he was clearly used to giving orders.

Josh wanted to just walk away. He remembered Jasmine's complaints, back when they'd been spending time together. David's numerous affairs, which were apparently common knowledge all over town. David's controlling behavior, Jasmine's fears that he was going to trade her in for a newer model . . . Looking back, Josh knew she'd used her vulnerabilities as a tool to seduce him, but he didn't think they'd been completely manufactured. No, nothing with Jasmine was ever that simple. And now, staring up at David, Josh was supposed to pretend he didn't know any of that and was just a recalcitrant handyman.

It would be so easy to just walk away. But damn it, he wasn't fired yet, and he needed this job. Not just this one, but all the others that came with it. So he stared at David, and David stared back, and Josh had no idea which one of them was going to blink first.

Then Ashley was there, looping her arm gently through David's and smiling as if he was her hero. "Are you still interested in kayaking this morning?" she asked sweetly. "I was just going to go out, so if you're ready."

It looked like David was going to brush her off, but then Cal stepped forward and said, "You're probably tired, David. Don't worry, I'd be happy to show Ashley around the lake."

David frowned, clearly not wanting to seem like he wasn't strong enough for a little kayaking. "No," he finally growled. "I can take her." He turned without another word, and Josh was dismissed.

He tried not to watch Ashley guide David away. Tried not to notice the way her head tilted toward him, her hair falling to brush his arm. Damn it, he knew how that hair would feel bunched in his fist, the soft thickness of it, the way he could use it to tilt her head just right. And the way she'd smile up at him as he did it, her green eyes dancing with . . .

With what? That was the problem. With desire? Or with amusement, laughing at his weak will and inability to stay away from her? It was all just a game to her, he reminded himself. Just a game to all of them. But he wasn't playing.

"Be careful with him," Cal said quietly.

Josh almost laughed, although nothing was funny. "I'll be as careful as he lets me be." Then he turned and headed for the truck.

As he drove out of the driveway he used the Bluetooth phone to dial a familiar number. "Kevin? You want to work this afternoon?"

Kevin was Josh's cousin, six years younger, full of good nature and absolutely without ambition. He worked when he felt like it or when he needed some cash. Or, sometimes, when Josh needed a favor. "I could," he said now. "What's the job?"

"Just spreading some mulch at the McArthurs'. They're getting bitchy about how long I'm taking."

"I could use your truck?"

"What's wrong with yours?"

"It won't start."

Josh sighed. Kevin wasn't exactly proactive about things. And he was annoying. But he was distracting Josh from other problems, at least. "Okay, but what's wrong with it? *Why* won't it start?"

"Cursed, I think."

"Probably not."

"Maybe."

"You're seriously just going to . . . what, leave it in the driveway? Not even try to figure out what's wrong?"

"I don't have a witch doctor handy."

"Good thing it's not really cursed, then."

"We don't know that for sure."

"Okay. Fine. You can use my truck. I'll pick you up around noon and you can drop me at the Fergusons'."

"And, just to be clear," Kevin said, "this is because you're busy, right? It's got nothing to do with Jasmine McArthur shoving her hand down your pants the other night at the bar."

Of course Kevin had heard about that. Jasmine hadn't been subtle, and gossip spread fast in a small town. But Josh could honestly say, "No. It's not because of that."

"And it's got nothing to do with you making out with Ashley Carlsen at the bar, and her staying with Jasmine McArthur? Scott Mason lost twenty bucks on that, you know. He bet you were going to take them both home for a three-way."

"Scott Mason's an idiot. But I hear he's looking for work. You want me to call him for this afternoon, leave you a bit more time to find your witch doctor?"

"Well, I'd probably have to pay the witch doctor, so I'd better do some work." Kevin paused long enough that Josh thought the conversation was mercifully over. But then Kevin said, "Hey, you know who won that twenty bucks from Scott?"

"I don't know or care."

"It was me. He called me, told me about it, and I bet him you wouldn't do it. I bet him you'd pussy out."

Yeah, the complexities of Josh's life decisions simplified to "manning up" or "pussying out." Kevin was not a fan of subtleties. "I'll come by around noon. If you're not ready, I'm calling Scott."

"Fine, Captain Grumpy. I'll be ready."

Josh hung up the phone. His cousin was taking bets on his sex life. Was it that different from the games Jasmine and Ashley were playing?

Yeah, it was. Because Ashley had been in on the game and Josh hadn't been. Josh wanted something real, something that wasn't for public amusement. He wasn't playing, not anymore. But no one else seemed to care about that distinction.

He turned the radio on and found a Springsteen song, then rolled his windows down and blasted the volume. He needed to stop being such a drama queen about it all. He'd made mistakes and he had to live with them. Life would go on, with or without work from Jasmine and her rich friends. He just needed to stop thinking about sparkling green eyes looking at him like he was something special, something real. The woman was an actress; it was an act.

He just needed to remember that.

≳ *Four* ≲

"I THINK I'M going to stay up here a bit longer," Ashley said into the phone. Her manager, Adam Wagner, was on the other end of the line, and she braced herself for his reaction.

"How much longer? Another week?"

"Longer than that. I found a place I can rent for the rest of the summer. Until mid-September, actually. I think I'm going to do it."

"What? Why?" Adam sounded almost hurt, but he'd been managing her since she was a child and she was mostly immune to his theatrics. "Why would you do that? Is it about that nonsense with Derek? Because, no! You can't hide away! You need to be out there, dating, partying, having lunch with handsome men in all the right places for the paparazzi to see you. You are *over* Derek Braxton, Ashley!"

"I *am* over him," she said firmly. She'd been over him even before his oh-so-public affair with a costar. "But I think I'm over the rest of it, too. The partying and lunching and paparazzi. At least for a while. You know how long I've been in the business, Adam. I love acting, I truly do. But I'm not getting the jobs I want, so there's no need to come running back down for work. You can look for something for me starting in October, if you want. Find me a big paycheck or a promising indie or something. But not until October. I'm taking a vacation."

"A three-month vacation?"

"Call it a sabbatical if it makes you feel better. I'm recharging. When I come back down I'll be full of energy and ready to start auditioning for serious jobs. So you could spend some time setting that up. You know what I'm looking for. Real acting. Challenging roles. Directors and costars I can learn from. Find me something like that."

"We've had this conversation before—" Adam started.

Ashley cut him off. "Yeah, we have. And I've listened to your advice, and I've decided that I don't want to follow it. I *know* there's more quick-and-easy money in the B-movie stuff. I *know* it's easier to get those parts, and really hard to cross over to the top-quality projects." How could she explain the yearning she had, the *need* to explore and push the boundaries? She'd tried before but she'd never been able to make Adam understand, and she had no new words to offer him this time. So she took a simpler approach. "I don't need more money; I need a career I can be proud of."

"Oh, *you* don't need more money. That's nice for *you*."

Adam was paid a percentage of Ashley's income, and they'd both known that was a factor in his reluctance to let her take a chance with her career, but this was the first time he'd ever acknowledged it out loud. Ashley wasn't sure if she was relieved or apprehensive, but she managed to say, "I don't need the money. I understand if you do. I've never asked you to make me your only client, and if you feel you need to diversify, I understand." She'd be thrilled, really, but she didn't think it was wise to be quite that honest. "But for me? I'm looking for a different type of role. Please do what you can to make that happen."

Damn. She didn't think she'd ever been that forceful with Adam. He'd been her manager for so long and the habits of deference she'd learned as a kid were hard to break. But since she was on a roll, she added, "And I'll be up here until mid-September. You can call me if something huge happens, but otherwise please stick to e-mail. I'm trying to get away from it all, not bring it all with me."

"I don't think this is wise, Ashley."

"I'm not too worried about being wise. But thanks for your concern. I'll talk to you later." And she hung up. She stared at the phone, waiting for it to ring, and she knew she'd used up all her resistance for the moment. If he called back and kept after her, she'd give in. So she switched off the phone. Then she stared at it. She didn't think she'd ever willfully turned the thing off before.

It felt good to be free.

And it felt even better to stuff the last of her clothes into her smallest suitcase and head for the door. She was going to be free of Jasmine, too. Ever since that night in the bar, Jasmine had been different. Crabby, crusty, looking for flaws and weaknesses. She spent a lot more time laughing *at* Ashley than she did laughing with her. And David had flown back to the city midweek, so there was no need to stick around to develop that connection.

No, Ashley was leaving all that behind and starting something new. It was a bit strange that she seemed to want to start it up here in backwoods Vermont, but there was something about the place that called to her. As soon as she acknowledged that, of course, she was forced to spend a little time kicking the image of Josh Sullivan out of her head. Yeah, okay, there was something about him that called to her, too, but Vermont was a lot less likely to be a snotty jerk to her for no reason, so she was going to focus on the place rather than the man.

She hauled her luggage downstairs herself, even though

Jasmine had said she'd send someone up for it. The new rental car was waiting in the driveway, Ashley was packed and ready to go, and there was no way she was sitting around waiting for Jasmine to arrange cartage. No, Ashley was leaving on her own terms.

"Oh, I could have had someone do that," Jasmine scolded gently as she saw Ashley descend the stairs. Most of the last round of guests was gone, but there was a newly arrived middle-aged couple from New York sitting in the den, watching Ashley struggle. The man stood to come and help her, but Jasmine waved a hand in his direction, telling him to sit down. "I have staff for this sort of thing! If she wants to do it herself, let her!" Ashley didn't look in her direction but she could hear the eye roll in her tone. "But try not to scratch my walls, sweetie."

The walls were solid wood and Ashley's luggage was soft-sided. There was nothing at risk but Jasmine's sense of control, and Ashley didn't mind if that got a bit banged up.

"Thanks so much for having me," she said when she got to the bottom of the stairs and set down her largest bag. "It really is a magical place!"

"I must say I'm a little surprised by your enthusiasm," Jasmine said with a tight smile. "Most of my guests go home after their visit; they don't generally move in a few doors down."

Ashley tried to make her smile a bit more genuine, but it took all her acting skills to do it. "Well, I guess I fell in love."

Jasmine raised an eyebrow. "With *Vermont*? Sweetie, this place is . . . it's a fun little make-believe place. Somewhere to pretend we're pioneers or bush people or something. It's not—" She stopped and her smile got a little more pointed and her eyes danced wickedly. "Unless you didn't mean the place. But, no, surely you didn't mean the *man*!"

"What? No, of course not! The place. The lake and the forest." Ashley felt almost panicked. Obviously it was stupid to think about falling in love with Josh Sullivan. But it was disconcerting to have Jasmine think of him as any part of the reason Ashley was staying in the area.

"Oh, that's a relief," Jasmine said. "I was worried there for a moment. I've got to tell you, sweetie, he was *not* too impressed when I told him about our little bet. So it's just as well you aren't pining over him!"

"When you . . . what? When you *told him*? Why would you do that? *When* did you do it?" Ashley made herself stop talking. The panic in her voice was too clear, and Jasmine was feeding on it like a bear gorging itself on honey.

"Oh, sweetie, was that meant to be a secret?" Jasmine's voice was dripping with saccharine apology. "I'm so sorry! I didn't think it would matter, and it was just so funny! I didn't think you'd mind."

"When did you tell him? Why? When?"

Jasmine shrugged. "That day he repaired the dock, I suppose. Anyway, it doesn't really matter, does it? He's just . . . he's like Vermont, sweetie. He's a fun little game, but he's not real life. Is he?"

Ashley was pretty sure she was going to clock Jasmine the next time the word "sweetie" came out of the woman's mouth. She could just imagine the way it would feel, her fist connecting with Jasmine's fragile little jaw, rocking her damned head to the side. . . . "Of course it doesn't matter," Ashley said with a smile to match Jasmine's. "I was just curious. And now I'm curious about my new place, so I'm going to head on over. Thanks so much for having me, and let's get in touch as soon as we're both in L.A.; I owe you a lunch, after all."

"Of course you do," Jasmine agreed. "I'll be sure to collect." Then she herded Ashley out the door, somehow making it seem as if she was being thrown out rather than leaving by choice at the prearranged time. Ashley just bit her lip and climbed into the car. She pointed it toward the road and made herself drive at a sedate speed rather than speeding away as if being chased by the hounds of hell.

When she hit the main road, she was tempted to just drive. Maybe she could find a good song and roll down the windows and just go. But she also wanted to see her new accommodations, and that urge won out over the other.

Her shoulders relaxed a little more with every turn the rental car took, and as she guided it into the long, tree-lined driveway that would lead her to the lake, she felt completely renewed.

She'd made the right choice. She pulled up in front of the sprawling log home she'd rented and let herself sit and stare for a moment. The dark green of the forest stretched as far as she could see in any direction. She knew her neighbors were actually fairly close on both sides, but she couldn't see them, so she could pretend they didn't exist. There was nothing but her and the forest and the lake. *This* was what she'd been craving at the McArthurs'. This sense of tranquil solitude. She'd enjoyed her mornings at the other cottage, waking before everyone else and going down to the dock, or walking through the forest, but then she'd been expected to return to the cottage and be social. Blech. No more of that.

She parked the car and stepped out of it, stretching her arms wide and breathing in the forest scent. She had a crazy urge to own this land, not just rent it. She wanted it to be her sanctuary, her retreat. She wanted a sense of permanence in this one area of her life.

She was startled out of her musings by the sight of a man walking down the winding driveway toward her. A familiar man. She reminded herself that she hadn't known who the property's caretaker was until *after* she'd decided to rent it.

"Josh," she said as calmly as she could. "Hi. The rental agent said you'd be around, but were you waiting in the forest or something? I thought I'd have to call you."

"I was working two doors down. Saw your car." Laconic, as he tended to be before he warmed up. As if he only gave people as many words as he thought they deserved, and he'd decided she wasn't worth many. She hated to think of him hearing about the stupid bet; it would be easier to be angry with him than to feel guilty.

But that wasn't what she was supposed to be thinking about. "You have the keys?" she asked.

He held them up, then reached out to pass them to her. He dropped them when her hand was about six inches below his, as if she had the plague and he wanted to avoid any chance of contagion.

It was a nice touch, and she resolved to remember it. She could use it in some future role where she was required to show absolute disdain for someone, but hopefully the memory could also inoculate her against any further errors of judgment around this man.

"Thanks," she said. "And . . ." Did she want to bring it up? Not really, but she didn't want to leave it unmentioned, either. "Jasmine said she talked to you. Told you about that little game we were playing in the bar. I hope—"

"The bunkie needs some work," he said, as if she hadn't been speaking. "The roof got damaged in the storm last week. I put a tarp on it, but it's not repaired yet. Curran knows about it, and he wasn't too worried, but now that you're renting the place he wants me to make sure it's back in order."

The bunkie was the tiny guesthouse, just a bedroom and a bathroom, part of the quaintness of the spot. And Sam Curran was the retired NHL star who owned the cottage. This was all just business. Josh didn't want to talk about anything personal. Ashley tried to adjust. "Okay . . . do I need to do something for that?"

"You shouldn't need to do much, but the bunkie's out of service for at least a week or two. If you need it sooner, let me know and I can try to get to it faster or find someone else to do the work."

"No, I won't need it. I'm not planning to do any entertaining at all."

He cocked a disbelieving eyebrow. "You're going to stay up here all by yourself for the rest of the summer?"

"That's the plan." It was none of his business, really, but she wanted to say the words, wanted to announce her intentions and luxuriate in her decadence. "I'm on vacation."

He didn't seem to appreciate the significance of that. "People usually go on vacation with other people, you know."

"Not me. Not this time." She saw his skeptical look. "I'm not totally isolated up here. I have friends I can visit with." At least if she counted Jasmine as her friend. And if she didn't, which felt a lot more likely, she'd find new ones. There were lots of cottages on the lake, and lots of people in the town. She wasn't planning to be a total recluse. "I'm just taking a break from the whole industry thing."

"Okay," he said, but the word was clearly a dismissal, not an agreement.

Ashley had to stop herself from continuing the argument. She knew what she needed and what she was going to do to get it. "So whenever you want to do the bunkie repairs, that's fine."

"There's some other maintenance stuff, too. Some of the screens need to be replaced, and the railing on the back deck needs to get stained. Do you want me to call you when I have a schedule, or should I just go through Curran?"

Ashley kept her cell number private. Very private. So the temptation she was feeling to share it with Josh Sullivan was just another weird quirk she needed to control. "Go through Sam, I guess. He'll want to know what's going on, I'm sure."

Josh nodded as if that was the answer he'd expected. "Yeah, okay. I'll leave you to your vacation, then."

And with that, he turned and sauntered along the gravel driveway, back toward the main road. Ashley only let herself watch him for a few moments; she was proud that she turned away before he was completely out of view. She was an international star, damn it! She wasn't going to act all moony over a small-town handyman who wasn't even that good-looking by the standards she was used to. She thought about that for a moment. No, damn it, even by Hollywood standards Josh Sullivan was hot. Less groomed, more authentically rugged than the actors she knew, and all the hotter for it.

She grabbed the closest couple of bags from the car and headed for the cabin. She was on vacation. This thing with Josh Sullivan was . . . She had no idea what it was, but he clearly wanted it to be over, and she supposed she couldn't blame him. She was looking for peace, not confusion. So she should stay the hell away from Josh Sullivan.

❧ Five ❧

"YOU NEED HELP repairing that bunkie roof?" Kevin asked eagerly. He was helping Josh clean up some trees that had fallen in the same storm that had damaged the bunkie. Josh had thought about sending Kevin over to Ashley's with the keys instead of going himself. He didn't like to think about why he'd decided to make the drop in person. And Kevin apparently hadn't been surprised by Josh's decision.

"Or there's other work over there, too, right? You need help with any of that?" Kevin continued. He wasn't that much younger than Josh but sometimes it seemed like he was from a whole different generation. One that wasn't quite as tired of it all.

"Later on, maybe. It's not on top of the list."

"What if she's gone by then? We could be blowing our chance!"

"Our chance to *what*?" Josh asked. "What do you think is going to happen? She's going to look up from her fashion magazine or whatever and see you slaving away on the bunkie and fall in love with your manly working-class sweatiness? She's going to invite you down for a beer on the dock and you'll spend the rest of your lives together?"

"Whoa." Kevin stared at Josh as if he questioned his sanity. "Fall in love? No, man, that's not what I was thinking of at all. Fall in *bed*, yeah. That's what I'm shooting for."

Josh sighed, his energy draining away. "Not a good idea. You know that."

Kevin snorted. "Yeah, okay. Easy for you to say. Convenient that your big realization came after you'd already bagged half the summer women on the lake."

"It came *because* I'd already slept with them. Messing around like that is not a recipe for long-term success."

"It ever occur to you that maybe you just weren't doing it right?" Kevin grinned. He probably knew he was pushing his luck, but he didn't know that Josh's time with Ashley earlier had made him even more irritable than usual. So the younger man grabbed his crotch in what was obviously supposed to be a macho way and said, "After a shot of this, they'll be crawling back for more!"

"You can't even keep a *local* girlfriend happy," Josh growled. Then he saw Kevin's expression and wished he'd kept his mouth shut. Was the guy still stinging over the Kelli thing? They'd broken up months ago, but Kevin suddenly looked like a little kid trying not to cry. Damn it, this was what happened when Josh let himself get sucked into these stupid conversations. "Get that load of firewood up to the house. We should be able to get the Danielson place done today, and maybe start the Kirpals'."

Kevin did as he was told, his obedience a clear indicator of his unnaturally subdued mood. Josh fitted the blade guards onto the chainsaws and set them by the driveway, ready to load them into the bed of the truck when Kevin returned. Then Josh started raking sawdust and small branches out of the way, all the while trying to keep himself from think-ing about Ashley.

He picked up a chunk of bark too heavy for the rake and whipped it into the woods as if it were the cause of all his frustration. It wasn't all about Ashley. Not really. But damn it, she was a bigger part of it than she should be.

He found another piece of bark and threw it, too. Then another. The conversation in the bar? It had been a setup. A game. She was an actress, and for twenty minutes she'd acted like a real person, someone fun and friendly and appealing. That was all. And the conversation on the dock had been another illusion. He'd thought she might be a mermaid, for Christ's sake—obviously his brain hadn't been working too well.

"Bad day?" The woman's voice was strong but had a quaver of age to it; or maybe that was just amusement, con-sidering the source.

Josh turned to see Mr. and Mrs. Ryerson standing on their driveway, clearly back from one of their many walks. They were holding hands, as they always seemed to do when they were within reach of each other. Which was most of the time.

"We got things cleaned up here," Josh said by way of reply. "Kevin's just dropping the wood off at the house. I can come back sometime in the fall to split it, if that works for you."

"Sounds good," Mr. Ryerson agreed. "There's always something comforting about having firewood seasoning for next year. We might be a bit old to be planting trees and expecting to see them grow, but at least we can plan a few years ahead."

"You guys stop walking a marathon every day and I'll start worrying about your mortality." Josh bent to greet the Ryerson's spaniel, then looked up and said, "Until then, you'd better keep up with your firewood."

"Exactly," Mrs. Ryerson agreed with a firm nod. "And don't listen to him—we're still planting trees, too. Maybe we'll be around to enjoy them full grown, maybe we won't, but they'll still be good trees, with or without us."

They headed off down the driveway then and Josh finished tidying up with a slightly better attitude. Ashley Carlsen was a frustration, but she was a passing problem. Like all summer people, she'd soon go home, and unlike some she wouldn't come back year after year. By the time Kevin returned, Josh had himself back under control and was his relaxed, sardonic self again. No big worries, no strong emotions, and certainly no insane crushes on random movie stars.

He didn't even kick Kevin out of the driver's seat like he normally would, a wordless apology for hitting a sore topic earlier. Kevin might never realize he'd been apologized to, but that wasn't really the point. Josh had done what he could. Yeah, he was fine. Everything was back to normal.

And it would stay that way as long as he could keep away from Ashley Carlsen.

"EVERYBODY wants to use the wheel," Laurie Palmer said with an amused smile as she wiped the worst of the clay from her strong hands. "You're thinking of *Ghost*, right?"

Ashley grinned. "Maybe a little."

"The wheel's fun. You should definitely use it, eventually. But you need to get a feel for the clay first while it's sitting still, and *then* try it out at a couple hundred RPM."

Ashley nodded. She'd come to the pottery studio on a whim; she'd been walking down Main Street, celebrating her first day as a sort-of local and getting a feel for the town, when she'd seen the window display. She'd thought maybe she'd pick something up to send to her mother, if she could get it packaged securely enough to ship. But the potter had been at work when Ashley arrived, and had just nodded her invitation for Ashley to look around before going back to her wheel. Ashley had found herself more intrigued by the work in progress than she was by the finished pieces. Laurie had started talking, explaining what she was doing, and Ashley had pulled up a stool and watched. Laurie was about Ashley's age and size but she seemed more substantial somehow, as if she'd drawn the solidity out of her clay and imbued herself with it. Ashley had asked about classes as a general possibility, but Laurie had tossed her a smock and told her to give it a try right then.

"There's something really satisfying about it," Laurie said now, handing a fist-sized chunk of clay to Ashley. "Technically it's inorganic, but it *feels* like it's alive, you know? You warm it up, work it for a bit, and it changes, becomes more pliable. So even before you put your creativity into it, you're already adding a part of yourself to the project. And then when you start shaping it . . ."

"I totally know what you mean!" Ashley was probably a bit more excited than a conversation about clay warranted, but she didn't care. She felt like she'd found a kindred spirit. "I'm an actor, and I feel like when I read a new script—a really *good* script—I feel like there's a symbiosis. The script and I work together. Technically I guess a script isn't organic, either, but it feels like it's growing and changing as I work with it."

"Cool," Laurie said. She sounded like she meant it. "Maybe we should trade lessons—I can teach you pottery, you could teach me acting."

Ashley laughed. "I wouldn't know where to begin. But isn't there a community theater or something up here? There must be something."

"The high school puts on a play each year. That's about it. Damian Forrestal used to run a bit of a community thing, but he quit a couple years ago after his wife died and I don't think anyone's really picked it up since then." Laurie shrugged. "Okay, then, no trade. You can just pay me for the lessons. First one's free, though. Play around with that chunk.

See how it feels now, and then just squish it and knead it and work with it for a few minutes and see how it feels then. Try to make a little pinch pot with it." She made a gesture with her hands, showing how her thumbs would make the inside of the pot while her fingers smoothed the outside. "And then crumble it up and try again. Add some water, but not too much. Then add a little more and see what happens."

Ashley complied and they worked in friendly silence for a while, until Ashley finally held up her goo-covered hands. She'd added water until the clay had turned into a near-liquid slurry, and she had no idea how to do anything constructive with what was left. Laurie saw the mess and grinned. "Okay, good. A bit of water is useful, but don't get carried away. Everything in moderation."

"I'm not too good at moderation."

"Mistakes are how you learn. Sometimes you've got to just go for it." Laurie nodded toward the deep metal sink at one side of her shop. "And then you just clean up and move on."

"Nice philosophy," Ashley said. She was pretty sure she meant it. Maybe she needed to adopt it a little more fully in her own life. She couldn't worry about making mistakes; she'd just make them, and then clean up. It was the only way to learn.

She arranged to come back to the shop in a couple days for her first real lesson, and then stepped back out onto Main Street. The day had warmed up while she'd been inside the studio and now it was hot enough for Ashley to start thinking about getting back to the cottage and having a swim.

That was when she saw him. He was across the street with the guy who'd finished spreading the mulch at Jasmine's place, and they were leaving the little café with paper bags in their hands. Josh looked across the street and saw her, and she had her hand half raised, her lips starting to curve into a smile, before she even thought about it. It was just instinct. She liked him, damn it.

But she liked him a good bit less when he jerked his head

in a tiny quarter-nod of acknowledgment and then turned away as if he'd done the bare minimum and had no interest in doing any more.

It was the bet. He didn't like her because of the bet, and that was just so stupid! She wasn't sure she'd even *made* the bet, and if she had it was just to get Jasmine off her back. He'd understand that, surely, if she could just get him to sit down and listen to her explanation. She'd tell him the whole story and they'd laugh, and they'd figure out the rest of their alphabet of Vermont hazards and then move on to talk about other things. They'd be friends again, and then something more.

She hadn't even realized where she was going until she had her hand on the door of the little café. A bit worrisome to realize she didn't clearly remember crossing the street, but obviously she'd made it safely. She pulled the door open and stepped inside the too-warm, wood-paneled interior. Well, now that she was there she could buy something for lunch, at least, and take it back to eat on the dock. Then she saw the sign on the wall behind the counter and everything in her mind stopped for a second, then spun back into gear. The sign was a message, surely. A suggestion from the universe. She just needed to get Josh to sit down and talk to her. And maybe, with a little help, she could make that happen.

IT was amazing how long she managed to keep herself from realizing it was a bad idea. A really, really bad idea. And even after she realized it she still seemed unable to stop herself. She could have called it off with one phone call, but she didn't. A couple days between conception and execution apparently wasn't enough for her to come to her senses.

"Yeah, right there," she agreed as the server from the catering company looked over with a question in his eyes. "That's a good spot for watching the sunset. And then there's white linen for on top, right?"

"And flowers," the server confirmed. "A low arrangement, so you can look over it and still do as much gazing-into-each-others-eyes as you want."

Oh, it was a terrible idea. But Ashley really wanted to gaze into Josh's eyes. She wanted to explain herself. Most importantly, she wanted to know if what she'd felt was real, and if it was, she wanted to figure out a way to get a constant supply of it.

"Josh Sullivan is here," the chef said as she poked her head out the cottage door. She worked at the café in town and had taken all the information when Ashley had asked about the catering poster behind the counter. Now, at the cabin, Ashley had assigned the chef to be her spy, since there was a window in the kitchen with a view of the driveway. But she didn't sound too pleased with the report she was making. "Is he . . . Is this all for *Josh*?"

The server and the chef exchanged looks, making Ashley even more nervous than she'd already been. "I didn't know you knew him."

"He's my cousin," the chef said. "He went to school with Paul." She nodded toward the server.

"I thought his cousin was a man." Ashley's brain wasn't working properly. "There was a man who spread mulch for him, and they said he was Josh's cousin."

"It's a big family," the chef said. "That would have been Kevin. He and his sisters are on the other side of things. I'm from Josh's dad's side. There's not as many of us."

There was a knock on the door then, and Ashley didn't have time to figure out any more of Josh's family relations. She ran her hands over her cream linen dress—it was designer but looked simple, and she knew it hugged her curves just right—and then headed for the front door. She'd committed. She'd made the call, and now she needed to follow through.

She ignored the instinct to run upstairs and hide in her bedroom until everyone just went away.

"Josh!" she said as she opened the door. Her voice was too loud, too excited. She sounded like she was on coke. "It's good to see you." And by trying to be more sedate, she'd ended up with a voice that made it seem like she was about to pass out. Damn it, she was better than this! "Come on in," she managed in a fairly moderate tone.

"You've got a leaky pipe?" He stepped inside and she noticed the large metal toolbox in his hand.

"Actually . . ." Oh God. He already thought she'd lied to him about the bet, and now she was going to have to tell him she'd lied about the pipe as well. How the hell had she thought this was going to work? In her ridiculous plan, she was supposed to just laugh now, admit her trickiness, and he'd laugh along with her and join her for dinner. Was she insane? That would never work.

But maybe she could bluff through it. "Yeah. A leaky pipe. In the . . . the downstairs bathroom." But she didn't want him looking at the toilet. That was too gross. "The sink. There was a puddle of water under it, and I cleaned it up. But then it came back." She was walking as she talked, leading the way to the bathroom with the nonexistent leak. "So I cleaned it up again."

They reached the bathroom and both looked in at the bone-dry floor. Ashley tried to giggle. "Oh. Wow. It's . . . Did it fix itself?"

"That doesn't usually happen," Josh said. He set his toolbox on the floor and bent to peer under the pedestal sink. He reached up and ran his hand over it all, the pipes and the wall and the floor, and then he looked up at her. "How long since you cleaned it up?"

What was a good amount of time? She had no idea. "Uh . . . an hour?"

"And how long was it the last time, between cleaning it up and the puddle coming back?"

"An hour?" It had worked the first time, so she was going to keep using it.

"So it should be wet again by now." Josh turned both of the taps on, then crouched down again and felt around.

Ashley wondered if she could distract him somehow and then splash a little water onto the floor. There had to be something.

"There's no sign of it coming through the wall," he said. "How much water was there? It might have just been condensation, if you were running cold water in the sink."

"I *was* running cold water!" She seized on the idea like a life preserver. "And it was really humid earlier. And I guess there wasn't really that much water on the floor. Maybe I panicked a little." Damn, she was going to get away with this!

Except that, as usual, she wanted more. "I feel like an idiot," she said. "I dragged you out here for nothing. But, look. I was expecting someone for dinner, and he's cancelled on me. If you wanted to join me—"

"I'll bill Cullen for the trip," Josh said. "Just travel time, unless there's something else you need me to look at while I'm here."

The sunset. She needed him to look at the sunset. And her eyes. Hell, she'd settle for him staring at her boobs. "Just a snack?" she suggested. "Something for the road?"

"I've eaten. So, if there's nothing else you need . . ." Then he stopped and looked behind her.

Ashley turned to see the chef—Josh's damn cousin—standing by the kitchen door, smiling neutrally. "Appetizers in here or on the deck?" she asked.

Josh stared at her, then back at Ashley. Everything was fine, Ashley assured herself. She'd *said* she was expecting someone for dinner. Her story still held. But then Josh turned and squinted at the sink. Then he turned back to Ashley, and she knew that he knew.

"Sam Curran's a good guy," Josh said quietly. Ashley couldn't tell exactly what emotion was simmering beneath Josh's still surface, but she was pretty sure whatever it was would boil over if she wasn't careful. "He trusts me. I assume he trusts you. I wouldn't want to bill him for something that was . . . something that didn't have anything to do with his house."

She stared at him. "Bill *me*!" she blurted out. "I'll pay for your time. I'm sorry. I just . . . I thought . . . there *was* water!" But he just looked at her, and she had to drop her eyes. "No," she admitted. "Sorry. There wasn't water."

She heard the chef easing back into the kitchen, retreating from the tension. But Josh didn't retreat. He stepped forward, closer to Ashley, close enough that she could smell him, soap and wood and other things she didn't recognize but wanted to understand. She could practically feel the heat of his body and she felt herself swaying toward it.

"Stop it," he said quietly.

She looked up at him and felt like a little girl being scolded by her teacher. Her hot teacher.

"There's lots of people up here who'd like to spend time with you. Lots of men who'd like to take you to bed, if that's what you're looking for. Find one of them."

"I found you," she said. It seemed stupid, but it was true. She'd found him, and she didn't want to lose him.

"I'm not interested." He bent down and picked up his toolbox. "I'm not playing this game."

She had her mouth open to argue, but then she shut it. Had she really been going to claim she wasn't playing a game, when she'd lured him over to the house on false pretenses? When she'd maybe made a bet about sleeping with him? "I'm not . . . I'm not doing it on purpose," she managed.

He snorted. "Fine. It's all an accident. Just have your accidents with someone else, okay? I'm out."

And then he left. His broad shoulders, his tight ass, the shaggy hair that would give her a great grip for controlling where his mouth went . . . She watched it all walk away. And there was nothing she could do to stop it from happening.

❧ Six ❧

"YOU BACK AT it, Joshy?" Abigail was Josh's cousin, and they usually got along. But she had a wicked tongue and as much of a love/hate relationship with summer people as he did. "Hanging out with the rich and famous?"

Josh had known it was coming. He'd thought about buying his lunch somewhere else, but he knew he'd have to deal with her sooner or later, and Abi's café had the best sandwiches in town. So he'd come in before the lunch rush and braced himself. Now he said, "I was there to repair a leak."

"Was it a leak in her *heart*?" Abi asked with exaggerated concern. She snorted. "Mom and Dad say you should go for it. They can't keep her DVDs on the shelves at the store ever since she came to town. They want to know how long she's staying so they know if they should order more."

All summer, Ashley had said, but Josh didn't think his aunt and uncle should be making business decisions based on that report. "Don't be so stingy with the turkey," he said instead, frowning at the sandwich Abi was making him.

"It's a careful balance, Joshy. For the flavors to blend properly, ingredients need to be kept in proportion." But she slipped another couple of chunks of turkey onto the bread. "You should have stuck around for dinner the other night. I made that cold soup you like, and some really tasty ravioli. Actually, if she'd told me the food was for you, I wouldn't have had to make many changes to the menu. It was pretty much all stuff you like anyway."

"So you didn't know?" He'd been wondering about that a little. "You weren't part of the setup?"

"No. Honestly, the way she was fussing, I thought somebody really important was coming over. When I saw you pull up, I figured there was a mistake."

"There was," he said. Then he added, "A bit more bacon wouldn't kill you, would it?"

Abi looked at him thoughtfully as she added a few more crisped strips. "You know, she was actually pretty nice. And she was nervous about it all. It was cute. And after you left she just sat there on the deck by herself, staring out at the lake. . . . Paul and I ended up eating the dinner. Which was delicious. You missed out on good food, at least, and probably on good company."

Josh squinted at her. "Are you serious? You practically threw a party when I stopped hanging out with the summer people. You said I'd dragged the family name through the mud for long enough. Now you're saying I should be going back to that?"

"Not to all summer people. Not to that McArthur dragon lady. But Ashley seemed different."

Josh thought of the bet and shook his head. "She's no different. She's just a better actress. Besides, I thought you were trying to fix me up with Martina Walker?"

"You were too slow on that one. She gave up on you and she's dating that new guy, the dentist. What's his name, again?"

Josh had no idea what the dentist's name was and didn't really care. It wasn't like he'd been interested in Martina in the first place. She was a nice enough girl, but there was no spark, nothing. . . . Damn it. He was back to thinking about Ashley Carlsen. But it was true. There hadn't been a connection with Martina like there was with Ashley.

But that was too damn bad. "Toss in a couple butter tarts, okay?" Better to think about food than women. "And maybe one of those big cookies."

"Careful, Joshy," Abi said as she wrapped up his food. "Ashley's used to all those Hollywood hard bodies. If you get pudgy, she won't want you anymore."

At least they both agreed that she was only after him for his body. "Make it two cookies," he said.

The bell on the door rang as Josh was paying for his lunch, and he glanced over to see Scott Mason walk in with his arm around a vaguely familiar woman. He and Josh had been in the same class all through school and gotten along fine until somewhere about sixth grade when they'd both liked Wendy Trainor and she'd decided to like Josh instead of Scott. Scott had held a grudge ever since, even though he and Wendy had ended up dating all through high school. Now Scott saw Josh and leered. "I lost twenty bucks on you the other night, Sullivan! What the fuck happened with you and Ashley Carlsen?"

"Nothing happened. That's why you lost the bet, right?" Josh left the change with Abi and started for the door, but Scott stepped sideways. Not quite blocking the path, but making it so Josh would have to dodge around him. Josh didn't like to dodge.

"What were you thinking, man? A hot little piece like that? And she wasn't going to put up a fight, obviously. And that McArthur woman was watching the whole thing like she wanted in on the action. You could have had a hell of a night! Man, I know summer women are slutty, but—"

"Watch your mouth," Josh said.

Scott didn't seem to catch the warning in Josh's tone.

"What? She met you for the first time that night, right? And she was all over you. She wanted to go home with you, right? Sherry was next to you at the bar and she heard that much. If that's not being slutty—"

"She was playing around," Josh said firmly. "Having fun. That's all."

Scott looked like he was thinking about arguing the point. Then he took a moment to look at Josh's face. "Okay," he grumbled with a shrug. "Fine. She's a saint. Whatever. You still cost me twenty bucks."

Josh didn't think he'd get into that. Instead, he turned to say good-bye to Abi and saw her watching him contemplatively. He had no idea what she was thinking, and figured it was best to leave it that way. "Thanks for the sandwich," he said, and he headed out of the café. He wondered if the "O" on the list of Vermont hazards should be "overprotective." And his first instinct should *not* have involved sharing that idea with Ashley Carlsen.

ASHLEY wasn't stalking the man. But her pottery lesson had been prescheduled and she'd needed something to take her mind off her stupidity. Laurie had set her up with a chunk of marble on top of a rustic wooden table in the middle of the shop and was showing her how to use slabs of clay to make interesting shapes; then Ashley had glanced out the window and seen Josh striding out of the café across the street, an angry frown on his handsome face.

Laurie noticed her distraction and glanced across the street. "Josh Sullivan," she said as if the words were a complete and meaningful sentence. Then she looked back at Ashley. "I heard a little story about you and him at Woody's. . . ."

"Just me," Ashley said quickly. "He put up with me, but just because he's a good guy. None of that was his idea."

Laurie looked a little skeptical. "Make sure the seam's tight, then dip your finger in the water and use it to smooth out the edges," she directed. As Ashley worked Laurie peered back out the window. "I don't know him that well. I used to be friends with Anika, one of his cousins. Have you noticed yet that he's related to practically everybody? That's because his mom's a Linden, and they have big families and none of them ever move away. I used to go over to her place—they still have a bit of lakefront, which is pretty damn rare for any locals up here—and we'd hang out on the dock and I'd ogle all the handsome boys in her family. But then Anika broke the family tradition and actually did move away, so I kind of lost touch. Josh was definitely nice to look at, though. But he's . . ." She made a face. "He's got a bit of a reputation, you know. For . . . well, for stuff like that night at Woody's. Going home with strangers. Especially rich strangers."

"He's made it pretty clear he wants nothing to do with me," Ashley said firmly. She liked Laurie and was pretty sure the woman was trying to warn her rather than trying to be a busybody, but there was no need for a warning. Josh Sullivan had been a brief visitor to Ashley's life and he'd run away as quickly as he could at the first opportunity. He wouldn't be coming back.

She looked back down at the vase she'd constructed. It was clumsy and rough compared to the smooth grace of the one Laurie had made, but Ashley still liked it. And she liked having something under her control, something that responded to her efforts. "Should I squish this one and start over?" she asked.

Laurie shrugged. "Your call. We can fire it and glaze it if you want, and you can still make another. Clay doesn't cost all that much, really, so if you want to keep it, you should."

Ashley looked down at the rough shape. "I'm keeping it," she said firmly. "I want to glaze it a nice deep blue and put it in my living room at home and if people don't like it, that's too damn bad."

Laurie raised an eyebrow. "Okay. Pottery as expression of defiance. Very nice. Let's put that bad boy over there for now and you can make something *else* to tell the world to go to hell."

"Not the whole world," Ashley said sweetly. She took the lump of clay from inside the plastic bag on the floor and tossed it hard on the marble slab. No, not the whole world. But Josh Sullivan the Unforgiving? She gathered the clay up and slammed it down again. She was done with Josh Sullivan. He wasn't the only one who could walk away from a bad situation.

She managed to keep the resentment burning through the rest of her lesson and for about half of the drive home, but then it faded into a vague sense of disappointment. It was stupid. She barely knew the man. She'd made her play and she'd been shot down. That was all there was to it.

She thought about heading back to L.A. She hadn't decided to stay in Vermont because she was chasing after a man, but it was a bit difficult to forget about him when she knew she might see him again, when everyone in town knew him or was related to him, when he shared a name with the damn lake she was staying on. . . .

Her phone rang and she looked down at the call display. Charlotte Samson for the third time that day, and for the third time Ashley ignored the call. Which was a pretty clear sign that she should stay in Vermont a little longer, she figured. Charlotte was a good friend, one of the few Ashley had in the industry, and if Ashley wasn't ready to talk to her, then she wasn't ready to talk to anybody. In a few weeks, Ashley would be able to gossip a little and start speculating about what roles she should be looking at. But she needed more time.

But apparently she wasn't going to get it. She'd assumed

Charlotte had been calling from California, but when Ashley pulled into the cottage driveway, there was a convertible parked by the house. And Charlotte was leaning on the hood, her smile wide and excited. Ashley might not have been ready to go back to Hollywood, but apparently Hollywood had decided to track her down.

❧ Seven ❧

"THERE'S TWO OF them now!" Kevin grinned excitedly as he shoveled scrambled eggs into his mouth. He'd heard about the new arrival from Tom Armstrong at the gas station, who'd almost passed out the day before when a woman in a rental convertible had pulled up to ask for directions and he'd realized he'd seen her on the big screen. "And there's two of us. And that place needs work. And if it's a little hot out and we have to take our shirts off . . . oh well."

"You really think either one of them is going to be impressed with your shirtless chest?" Josh shook his head and concentrated on spreading strawberry jam evenly over his buttered toast. His aunt Carol made good jam, and he didn't want to waste any of it. He also didn't want to pay attention to Kevin's nonsense.

"You're missing the beauty of this situation," Kevin said confidently. "Down in Hollywood or wherever, no, they're not going to notice us. But we're not *in* Hollywood, Joshy! And you and me—well, me, mostly, but you a little—we're the best thing this town has going! Two single ladies, looking for a little fun. Two single gents, ready to show them the sights. . . ."

"What sights are you thinking about, exactly? You going to take them to Montgomery's furniture factory?"

"So if there's nothing worth their time, maybe we'll just stay in," Kevin said with a leer that would have been a lot more effective if his mouth hadn't still been full of scrambled egg.

Josh was done with the conversation. "Find another wingman."

"I can't just drive up and introduce myself, asshole. I need a reason to be there. A reason like bunkie-roof repair." Kevin tilted his head, his expression suddenly crafty. "Or you could send me there with someone else. Matt Carter's always looking for work. . . ."

"Matt Carter's always looking for work because he never gets hired again after he's worked for people one time. You're not going to wreck my reputation doing shitty work on that roof, Kevin, not just because you want to—" He broke off as Aunt Carol wandered into the kitchen, where they were eating. Kevin's mom probably didn't need to hear the details of Kevin's intended debauchery. Then again, maybe she should. Maybe that would teach Kevin not to start conversations like this while he was sitting at his mother's kitchen table.

"You boys getting enough to eat?" Carol asked sweetly.

They were both adult men by any objective standards, but they knew they'd always be boys to their mothers. And Kevin wasn't really helping to dispel that image, considering that he'd moved back into his old room after breaking up with Kelli and wasn't showing any signs of moving out. In fact, he wasn't showing any signs of moving on, either. Nothing except for this sudden interest in movie stars. An interest that Josh was currently discouraging for his own selfish reasons. Damn it. Was he his cousin's keeper?

"We ate all the eggs," Kevin admitted sheepishly. "I'll pick up more on the way home, okay?"

"Since the girls moved out you two are the only ones who eat them," Carol said unconcernedly. "You know how I feel about embryonic chickens."

"You think they're disgusting," Kevin said. "And *you* know how *I* feel about nature's perfect food."

"You think they're delicious." Carol patted her son's shoulder as she leaned over and put a slice of homemade bread into the toaster.

The whole scene was a bit too sweet to feel real, but Josh had experienced this mother-son act enough times to know that the affection was genuine and heartfelt. His mother was Carol's sister, but she either hadn't inherited the same nurturing gene or she'd decided that her only child was somehow not an appropriate recipient. She'd made sure Josh was fed and had clean clothes, but if he'd wanted any more parenting he'd made his way over to Aunt Carol's. Now his mom had remarried and moved to the city, and Aunt Carol was still babying Josh every chance she got. Even if Kevin had been a bad worker, Josh would have still given him jobs because he was Carol's kid. And Josh knew Aunt Carol was worried about Kevin. Damn it!

"You better brush your teeth and check yourself in the mirror before we leave," Josh said to his cousin. "You aren't going to impress any movie stars with egg all over your face."

Kevin sent him a startled look, then broke into a wide grin. "Yeah? We're going over there?" He looked up at his mother. "Hey, Mom, guess who's going to bag a movie star today."

Josh winced, but Carol just raised an eyebrow. "Is it Josh?" she asked, and smiled sweetly in his direction. "Congratulations, Josh. Although I think you know how I feel about using language like 'bagged' to describe what should be a respectful and mutually enjoyable activity."

Normally, Josh would have agreed with her completely. This time, though? "'Bagged' might be the right word, actually. But kind of the reverse from what Kevin was thinking of.

"You know those big-city hunters who are always coming up and shooting our game, acting like they're wily outdoorsmen?" Josh shook his head and spoke to Kevin instead of Carol. Maybe he wouldn't get in the guy's way, but he'd at least make sure everyone understood what he was getting in to. "These women are just trying to bag a trophy buck."

But Kevin only spread his arms out to the sides and smiled cockily. "I am an easy damn target, and I am ready to be in their sights."

Josh sighed and pushed away from the table. "Okay," he said quietly. "Go get cleaned up, and let's get this over with."

Kevin almost knocked his chair over as he stood and dashed for the bathroom. Carol caught his chair and looked after him with an amused but worried expression. "Is this real?" she asked softly. "I mean, these women—these movie stars—they're not going to be interested in someone . . ."

She paused as she searched for the tactful words. Josh's smile was only a little bitter. "Someone like Kevin or me? No. They won't be interested. Not in anything real. But playing around a little?" He shrugged. "I don't know. I guess it depends how bored they are." When Ashley had moved in she'd been planning on some sort of retreat, cutting herself off from all her Hollywood friends. It hadn't taken her too long to get tired of that idea and invite someone up to entertain her, so she'd probably be looking for a new distraction any second now. "Depends what other options they come up with. Depends how long they're here for, and who they're trying to impress or piss off." It depended on a lot of things. But none of it was going to be about finding a real connection between two people. Josh knew that much.

Carol huffed out a breath that showed she wasn't completely

happy with the situation. "And you? Kevin's 'ready to be used.' Is that your plan as well?"

Sometimes Carol asked questions that she didn't really want to have answered. Josh was never quite sure what to do in those situations. "Not my plan," he said. "It's never my plan."

"But sometimes it happens all the same, doesn't it?" She smiled at him, then patted him on the cheek. "You're such a romantic, Josh. I have no idea how you turned out like that, but you sure did."

He made a scoffing face because that's what he was supposed to do when a woman said something like that. She just laughed at him, a sweet, delicate sound.

Then Kevin was back, grinning like a little kid about to go on a ride at the fair, and Josh wasn't sure whether he wanted to protect his cousin or hit him in the face. He settled for a grumpy scowl and a head-jerk toward the door. "We're burning daylight," he growled. "And I'm calling Sam Curran on the way. If he says this is a bad day for the work, we're doing something else. Understood?"

Kevin didn't stop smiling. It was good to see, really. Maybe a quick roll in the hay was just what the guy needed. Or maybe the movie stars wouldn't even glance in his direction, and the whole thing would be over before it even started. That would be excellent. Josh's brain was getting ahead of him, as usual, worrying about things that hadn't happened and that probably never would happen.

It would all be fine, he told himself as he backed the truck out of the driveway. Sure, he was breaking his rule about staying away from Ashley. But he could be physically present without being there in spirit. He'd done it before with other women, and he could do it with Ashley if he had to. He'd just keep his guard up. And he'd try to ignore the tiny stir of excitement in his stomach at the thought of seeing her again.

* * *

"IT'S brilliant," Ashley said as she dropped the bundle of paper into Charlotte's lap. "And with Lauren Hall directing? It's going to be . . ." Her words trailed off. She wouldn't let herself get excited about this script. She was supposed to be on vacation, for one thing. But more importantly, she knew the limits she was working within. She knew how she was seen in Hollywood, and she wasn't going to let herself get too excited about a role that would never be hers. She and Charlotte had heard about the project, dreamed about being part of it, but it seemed too bold, somehow, for them to actually try for parts.

But Charlotte wasn't being nearly as careful. "We can do it!" she proclaimed. "You and me. It'd be . . . Oh, Ash, it'd be *perfect*. People have said we look alike. Playing sisters would just make sense. And this is real acting, not just standing there and looking gorgeous."

"It's not a question of what I want. If I could get this job, I'd take it, no questions asked. I'd do it for free. But this is a serious film. It's got multiple Oscars written all over it. They're not going to cast a former child star who's made a career out of slasher flicks, rom coms, and being the romantic interest in action movies."

"Don't be such a baby," Charlotte retorted. "There's lots of child stars who get real careers. It's been almost ten years since *Mayfair Drive* went off the air, and you've been working steady the whole time. You have a real career, one that would make most actors completely jealous."

"I have a great career," Ashley said, trying to sound like she meant it. She certainly couldn't complain about the money, but she was starting to worry about the longevity. Hollywood wasn't kind to women over thirty, not if all they'd been cast for was their looks. "I've been very lucky.

But they're not going to look at me for this role. You have a
better chance, really, because you're newer. They don't know
you as well." It was hard to say, but it was true. And Ashley
needed to be a good friend about it. "I'll help you prep, and
you'll be great, and you can thank me when you win your
Oscar."

Charlotte didn't look convinced, but after a moment's
thought she said, "Okay. You'll help me—" She broke off
as she watched a pickup truck make its way down the driveway. "You expecting visitors?"

Ashley recognized the truck and cursed herself for wanting to run inside and throw a little mascara on. She needed
to get over the stupid crush. "It's the caretaker," she said,
trying to sound nonchalant. "See that blue tarp on the bunkie
roof? Not part of the original design."

"Oh," Charlotte said, her interest clearly fading. Then,
"Oh!" with a bit of a moan at the end as the men climbed
out of the truck. "Very nice. Double the fun."

Josh and his cousin. Josh scowling as usual, Kevin looking open and friendly, like Josh had, back before everything
had gotten messed up.

It was Josh who approached them, coming up the path
and standing on the ground just in front of their seats on the
wide front porch. "We were thinking of working on that roof
today," he said quietly. "Would that be a problem for you?"

"No problem," Charlotte said quickly, and a little lascivi-
ously. She grinned at Ashley. "Right?"

Josh frowned at her, and Ashley knew why. He didn't
like being an ornament. But that was too damn bad. It was
one thing for Josh to judge Ashley's behavior and find it
wanting. Quite another for him to presume to judge Ashley's
friend.

People on vacation, messing around with the locals—it
was a time-honored tradition. Fun for everyone involved.
Everyone except Josh "Puritan" Sullivan, apparently. For

the first time in too long, Ashley didn't feel embarrassed being around Josh; she felt annoyed. Yeah, she'd made a fool of herself, repeatedly, but that didn't mean he had to be such a princess about it all. It wasn't like she'd forced herself on him or something. "Fine," she said with a cool smile, one she didn't really try to warm up. "It shouldn't affect our day at all if you work on the roof. Will you need anything from us?"

Josh raised an eyebrow at the absurdity of the suggestion. Arrogant bastard. "We'll be fine," he said. Then, almost reluctantly, he stepped a little sideways and drew their attention to the other man. "This is Kevin. If I'm not around and you need something, you can talk to him."

Now it was Ashley's turn to raise an eyebrow. "I can't imagine that we'll need to do that."

"Actually," Charlotte said quickly, "we were talking about carrying that metal table down to the dock." She smiled at the men. "It's an awkward shape, hard for two people to get a grip on it, but too heavy for one person to carry it alone. At least, too heavy for one of us. . . ."

"I could have a look," Kevin volunteered quickly.

And that was all it took. Charlotte abandoned Ashley with a merry eyebrow waggle, and Kevin followed behind her like a happy puppy, leaving Ashley alone with Josh. It was exactly what she'd wanted only a few days earlier, but she'd given up on trying to apologize to him; he didn't want to hear it, and she was tired of trying to make it happen.

So she just sank back into her chair. It had felt good to stand up to the man, and she didn't think she wanted to back down just because Charlotte had decided to consort with the enemy. "Can you get started on the roof without him?" she asked pointedly.

"Of course. I wouldn't want to ruin your solitude. Oh, wait . . . you changed your mind about that, I guess."

She felt guilty for half a second, almost long enough to

start explaining how Charlotte had just shown up, without an invitation. Then she remembered that it was none of this clown's business. "So. The roof." He was dismissed.

And he didn't like it, she realized. He didn't like being the one who was judged and found wanting. Well, that was too damn bad. She refused to even look at him, just picked up the script she and Charlotte had been talking about and started reading. She was dimly aware of him turning away from her and walking toward the bunkie, but she kept her attention locked on the script.

It was a modernized Western and she'd started rereading somewhere near the start, a scene where the two sisters had realized that their husbands had almost certainly been killed in a cave-in at the mine. They were clinging to one another, one sister crying while the other was trying to be strong. There was hardly any dialogue, but with a director like Lauren Hall, the scene would be powerful. Ashley could see it in her mind, the way it would look on the big screen, and in her imagination she was playing the crying sister, the one who would get stronger later in the movie, and it was Charlotte trying to comfort her. In her mind, it felt powerful, and right. They could do it.

Of course, they wouldn't be allowed to. Ashley wouldn't be given the chance to prove that she was capable of being anything but glamorous and empty. But just because she wouldn't be given the part, it didn't mean she shouldn't try for it. She loved acting because it gave her a chance to live so many different lives, to be so many different people. And with the good roles, the ones that really meant something, she could pull something out of the character and keep it as part of herself moving forward. She looked down at the script in her hands. What would either one of the sisters have done, confronted with a man like Josh Sullivan?

Well, they wouldn't have made idiots of themselves in

the first place. But if they had, they sure as hell wouldn't apologize for it. They wouldn't back down or go crawling to him with an apology. Yeah, even if Ashley didn't have a chance of getting the role, that didn't mean she couldn't lift a little bit from the characters and keep it for herself.

She looked up from the script, over to where Josh Sullivan was setting a ladder against the side of the bunkie. She knew who she was, and who she'd been. She knew the mistakes she'd made, and she knew that sometimes she'd been flaky. But she knew who she *could* be, too. And she needed to stop letting people try to keep her from turning into that person, just because they expected her to be someone else.

JOSH tried to keep his mind on the job. By the time Kevin returned from his errand at the lake, Josh had cleared the damaged shingles and squared off the hole in the plywood. As soon as Josh saw the younger man's expression he knew he was in trouble, but he tried to ignore his intuition. He also tried to ignore the extra movie star, who was standing beside Kevin and peering with apparent interest at the tools in the bed of the truck. "I'll call down measurements," Josh said. "You write 'em down and cut the plywood."

Kevin looked startled, as if he'd forgotten that he was supposed to be working that day. "Yeah, okay," he said quickly, with a furtive glance in his companion's direction. Then he added, "Josh, have you met Charlotte before? Charlotte, this is my cousin Josh."

Josh nodded wordlessly in her direction, then said, "Thirty-two inches."

Kevin took a moment to understand, then scrambled to find a pencil and record Josh's measurement. "They need to learn to ride," he announced as he searched through the toolbox.

Josh wasn't going to acknowledge what he'd just heard. "Seventeen and three-quarters," he replied. "That's the first piece. Then a smaller one . . . nineteen and a half by . . . sixteen even."

"Shit," Kevin muttered. Then he straightened, with a pencil finally in his hand. "Could I get those again?"

"Thirty-two by seventeen and three-quarters," Charlotte said calmly. "And nineteen and a half by sixteen even." She smiled beatifically up at Josh. "So, Kevin said you keep horses. I said I wouldn't want to impose, but he said there isn't really a boarding stable in the area. No one who offers lessons on rented horses."

"It's the country," Josh said. He knew he was coming across as churlish but he absolutely didn't care. "If people want a horse, they keep it at home."

"So that makes it kind of hard for us to find somewhere to ride and someone to teach us," Charlotte said, as if she were glad they were in such perfect agreement. "We've both ridden before, but English. We need a few Western lessons for a couple of parts we're interested in."

"Wait. Both of you?" Somehow Josh had missed that before. He swiveled to look at Kevin. "You're a terrible rider. You can't teach them to ride."

"I'm not terrible," Kevin said with a don't-embarrass-me-glare for Josh and a nervous grin for Charlotte. "But, yeah, I wasn't thinking I'd be the one doing the teaching. . . ."

"Sorry," Josh said to Charlotte. He wasn't interested in talking to his idiot cousin. "It's a busy time of year. And I don't teach riding. I just keep a few horses for messing around on."

"You taught Emma," Kevin interjected quickly. "And her little friend, what was her name?"

"They were kids. And Emma's family. And I did that in the winter. It's not the same thing at all." But Kevin was staring at Josh, his face carefully angled so Charlotte couldn't see his pleading expression.

And it made Josh even more reluctant to be part of this stupid idea. Because Kevin's expression didn't say she's-hot-and-I-want-in-her-pants. It said I-really-like-her-and-I-want-to-spend-more-time-with-her. And Josh knew that he was looking at an expression just like his would have been when he'd first started hanging out with the summer people. Josh had managed to get out before his heart got more than a little bruised, but Kevin? Kevin was an idiot, and he charged into these things with no caution whatsoever. Kevin was going to get fucked up.

And still, somehow, Josh found himself giving in. Not because he was a romantic. Aunt Carol was just plain wrong about that. No, he wasn't a softy, wasn't hoping things turned out better for Kevin than they had for him, and he sure as hell wasn't secretly intrigued by having an excuse to spend more time with the other beautiful movie star visiting their fair community. No, it was none of that. He was just tired of protecting Kevin and wanted the kid to grow up a little. Yeah, that was all.

"Fine. You groom and saddle, you do some chores around the place, and you bring me a case of beer. And you understand that I'll be drinking the beer as we go. And we do this, like, once. Maybe twice. Just the really basic stuff."

"Absolutely," Kevin said in the voice of someone who'd just been offered the chance of a lifetime. "That works, right, Charlotte?"

Josh wasn't sure he liked the way Charlotte was looking at him. There was something about her expression, something that suggested she was seeing more than he really wanted her to. But all she said was, "Sure. That sounds great. And we can bring the beer, if you want."

"No," Josh said quickly. "If you bring it, I'd have to offer you one, and then maybe you'd take it, and then you'd be drinking around my horses, and letting rookies ride them is bad enough. I don't want to make them deal with rookies who've been drinking."

"Complicated," Charlotte said, and Josh definitely got the impression she was talking about more than his ban on drinking and riding. "But, okay. Your barn, your rules."

Well, he liked the sound of that, at least. So he gave her a nod, then turned back in Kevin's direction. "You measuring down there?"

"Oh," he said. His smile was more of a grimace. "Could you just give me those numbers one more—"

"Thirty-two by seventeen and three-quarters, and nineteen and a half by sixteen even." Charlotte smiled, then said to Josh, "Kevin said maybe we could have a lesson tonight, after it's cooled down a little but before it gets dark. Maybe around seven?"

Damn. This was really happening. Josh wondered what state the house was in, and then resolved to just keep them outside. He'd clean the front bathroom. That was it. Make sure the hallway that led to it was in good shape. No more. "Yeah," he said reluctantly. "Okay. Kevin told you how to get there?"

"He didn't. He wasn't quite *that* presumptuous! Maybe you could come up to the house when you're done working? We could give you a down payment on the drinks, and you could give us directions?"

But there was no way he was going to sit around on the deck of one of these fancy cottages and drink with the movie stars. Those days were gone, and he was glad of it. Besides, she'd already demonstrated that she had a good memory. "Take the highway north out of town, turn left at the abandoned church, then right at the top of the hill, and I'm the third driveway on the right."

She blinked as if taking a moment to store the information in her memory banks, then nodded. "Okay. No down payment.

We'll see you around seven." She turned and headed for the house, and they both watched her go.

"There is no way you can handle a woman like that," Josh said to his cousin. It wasn't a warning, just a calm statement of fact.

Kevin shook his head. "I'll do it or die trying." Then he looked down at the sheet of plywood he'd hauled out of the back of the pickup. "Could I just get those measurements one more time?"

⇒ *Eight* ⇐

"SO, WHAT'S THE story?" Charlotte asked as she and Ashley headed out on the highway. They both had jeans on, but Charlotte was wearing a fitted, low-cut blouse while Ashley had opted for a long-sleeve work shirt in an unflattering army green that she'd found at the town's small department store that afternoon. It was a shirt that clearly said I-have-no-interest-in-you-sexually-or-otherwise, and it was the best purchase Ashley had made in months.

"The story? What story?" She knew it wouldn't work, but she decided to play dumb anyway. It seemed appropriate to mount some level of defense. "I just decided that I wanted the part. Well, no, I always knew I wanted the part. I just decided that I owed it to myself to *try* for the part. I'm not going to do the bastards' dirty work for them. If they want to reject me, they can at least go to the trouble of doing it themselves instead of brainwashing me into doing it for them." That's what the sisters in the script would have done.

"Okay, that is all excellent, and I love it that you're going to try. But I think you know that's not what I'm talking about," Charlotte said.

"You played a psychiatrist for two episodes of a TV series. You are not actually a therapist."

"Ah, but isn't it interesting that your mind automatically went to 'therapy' just because I asked you a simple question. Yes, very interesting, I think. Don't you?"

Ashley refused to look over and see Charlotte's triumphant grin. Instead, she focused on navigating down the town's main street as if she was working her way through the worst of L.A.'s rush hour traffic.

They rode in silence through the town, all three stoplights of it, and then Charlotte said, "He's very handsome. Excellent body. And good hands. I like a man with good hands."

"Who are you talking about, exactly?"

"Kevin, of course," Charlotte said innocently. "Why, did you think I was talking about Josh?"

"I thought you were talking about Hugh Jackman, actually. Did I tell you I danced with him last year at that AIDS benefit? He's pretty light on his feet."

"I wonder if Josh can dance."

Ashley wanted to bash her head against the steering wheel. Or maybe do that thing her character did in the last slasher flick, where she'd unbuckled the passenger's seat belt and then rammed them into a tree. The airbag would save the driver, but Charlotte wouldn't be asking any awkward questions for quite a while.

Well, okay, maybe that was a bit over the top. And Ashley might as well get the conversation out of the way before Charlotte said something totally embarrassing in front of Josh. "It's not a big deal," she sighed. "Just a . . . I don't know. A series of misunderstandings, kind of. Most of which involve me acting like an entitled brat, a drunken floozy, or

a petulant bitch." And then, to honor the spirit she'd managed to find earlier in the day, she added, "And *all* of which
involve Josh Sullivan acting like an uptight little princess
with absolutely no sense of humor."

"Sounds like a good time," Charlotte said. "I'd love to hear
some details."

Yeah, Charlotte was all about details. She said it was
because she was an actor and needed to store up ideas for
future characterization, but Ashley was an actor, too, and
she didn't feel like it gave her an excuse for burrowing into
every corner of other people's personal lives. But now that
she'd gotten started with her confession, she kind of wanted
to keep going. Part of her obsession, she supposed. So she
gave Charlotte a short-form version of her interactions with
Josh. The stupidity in the bar with the bet, and Josh refusing
to go home with Ashley because she was drunk. . . .

"Okay," Charlotte said. "So far, this is, like, a totally
romantic story. I mean, maybe he was a bit paternalistic, but
you were drunk, so you needed to be taken care of. Right?
I love this guy. He doesn't sound like a little princess at all."

"No," Ashley admitted. "You're right. He was a gentleman. In the real sense of the word. And then . . . that morning on the dock . . ."

"Sounds lovely," Charlotte said carefully. "What happened?"

So Ashley had to explain how Josh had found out about
the bet. Charlotte squirmed around in her seat. "If the roles
were reversed, you'd have been mad, right? You'd have
thought he was an asshole for dragging your body into his
stupid game. Right?"

"Yeah. I would have. But I didn't even take the bet. Or . . .
I don't know, maybe I kind of did? I wasn't actually . . . I
don't know." Shit, this all sounded even worse as Ashley
explained it to Charlotte. She wasn't sorry for the topic

change when she was able to say, "Oooh, a church! It looks abandoned, right?"

"Looks condemned."

"Okay. So we turn here. And now we're looking for . . ."

"The top of a hill."

"There are street signs up here. He could have given us street names!"

"Maybe he's hoping we get lost."

"Yeah," Ashley said. She supposed she couldn't blame him if he was.

They drove in silence until they reached the top of a hill. "Right, here?" Ashley asked.

"Hopefully."

"There's the first driveway," Charlotte said absentmindedly. When Ashley had heard the word "driveway" in the directions Charlotte had recited, she'd thought of something suburban, or maybe the two- or three-acre lots like she was staying on by the water. But up here, she was in the forest. A real forest. The driveways were dirt paths leading into darkness that made her feel like she'd travelled through time, or at least a couple hours ahead to when the sun would be setting.

"Second driveway," Charlotte said after they'd driven a while. Then, "So, that's all? You met, he was sweet, you screwed it up with a stupid bet?"

So Ashley had to explain about the dinner-that-wasn't.

Charlotte was mercifully silent for quite a while. The she said, "Jesus, we are getting deep into the back country, here. You don't think he's luring us out for some sort of *Deliverance*-style revenge, do you?"

Ashley snorted. "He wouldn't give me the satisfaction of acknowledging that I'd done anything that deserved revenge," she said. "He's made it pretty damn clear. I'm nothing. Just a shallow little Hollywood idiot with my plastic friends and my stupid ambitions."

"You've talked to him about your ambitions?"

Well, that caught Ashley a bit off guard. "No," she admitted. "I mean . . . not in so many words. But I could tell how he felt, just by the way he looked at me."

"He does glower pretty well," Charlotte said. "But maybe you were projecting a little bit, too? Maybe he doesn't have any feelings about your ambitions at all, but you've imagined the most negative reaction you can think of and—"

"Third driveway!" Ashley announced triumphantly. "Also, *two episodes*. You are not a therapist!" She turned the car onto the rutted dirt road. It was like driving through a tunnel of trees, and when she leaned forward to look up through the windshield she could only see occasional glimpses of surprisingly blue sky. It should have felt claustrophobic, probably, but it didn't. She felt safe, as if the forest were giving her a hug.

"We should be leaving a trail of bread crumbs," Charlotte grumbled.

But Ashley ignored her and rolled down her window to let the magic of the place wash over her.

JOSH sat on his front porch with his feet up on the railing and cracked the cap of his second bottle of beer as he watched the car bounce up the driveway. It should have felt like an invasion. In a way, it did. He was nervous, almost jittery, and despite his resolution to only clean the bathroom, he'd ended up taking half the afternoon off so he had time to go over the whole damn house. It wasn't that big of a place, he told himself. And it had needed it. He was just being polite.

Then she stepped out of the car and his brain lost its ability to form excuses. He could only stare. She was so beautiful, and she was at his home, looking around her as if she liked the place, as if she understood that things didn't have to be sunny and polished to be beautiful. *This* was the woman from the dock, the woman who'd seemed like a mermaid then but who might be a wood sprite now. He'd thinned the trees around the cabin enough that she was standing in dappled shade; the light filtered through the trees and danced across her face as the wind shifted the leaves. She looked up at the porch and she smiled at him, genuine and open and warm, and he couldn't stop himself from smiling back at her. For a moment, it was just the two of them, without all the rest of it, and they were perfect.

But then a car door slammed and a horse nickered and Daisy the Demon Dog came barreling in from the forest and charged at the new arrivals with a big show of barking and raised hackles, and the moment was gone. Daisy was a black-and-brown terrier-type with mismatched eyes, one brown and one blue; mismatched ears, one straight up, one folded down; and an innate suspicion of almost all humans. A good dog for a man like Josh to have around, really. Josh made himself look away from the people earning her attention and took a long drink before he kicked his feet down from the porch railing and heaved himself upright. "Settle, Daisy," he said, and he stared at the dog until she lay down. Then he made himself walk toward the car.

"You weren't joking about the beer," Charlotte said lightly as he approached.

Josh was wishing he had something a little stronger to numb his brain, but he just nodded and raised the bottle in a little toast. "I'm a country boy. If I'm not driving or working, chances are pretty good I've got a beer nearby."

"Well, at least it hasn't given you a beer gut," Charlotte commented, then looked down at his belly. "Yet."

"Something to look forward to," he replied. With Charlotte, there was none of the instant burst of attraction there'd been with Ashley, but he still wanted to keep himself from liking her. She was just passing through, and nothing that happened on holidays was going to have any effect on her. Being forgotten by a friend didn't hurt as bad as being forgotten by a lover, but it still wasn't a sensation Josh was looking to feel any more often than he had to.

"Kevin's at the barn," he said, nodding his head to the building. He liked to keep his horses outside in all but the very worst weather, so the barn wasn't big. And it wasn't glamorous. These two had said they had English riding experience, so they were probably used to one of those horse palaces like he'd seen on the Internet. Places with fancy flooring and soaring ceilings and skylights, matching blankets and halters for all the horses, shower stalls and . . . He made himself stop thinking about it. His hay and tack were dry, and his animals were healthy and happy. That was all that mattered.

He led the way along the short path to the clearing where the barn was nestled, Daisy trotting happily beside him. Horses wanted grass and grass wanted sunlight, so Josh had spent a long time clearing the trees away from the pastures. This part of the property felt like a regular farm, if you could ignore the outcroppings of stone and the dense forest that surrounded the fenced areas.

"That's Sunny," he said, pointing to a palomino mare tied to a fence post, "and that's Rocky." He gestured to the other horse tied nearby, a dingy brown creature with donkey ears and the sweetest nature Josh had ever encountered. "They're both old-school quarter horses, big feet and big hearts. They'll take care of you."

Kevin came around the corner then, picking bits of hay off the front of his shirt. Josh had to admit that his cousin had been working hard, doing chores around the place to make up for this imposition. Now Josh supposed it was time to give the guy a break. "You want to ride, too? You've already got these two brushed. You want to go get Casper while I show them how to deal with Western tack?"

Kevin looked torn. Show off his riding or stay close by and earn points by being helpful. A tough choice. Or it would have been if Kevin were a better rider. As it was, he was probably better off on the ground, but it was too late for Josh to take his suggestion back.

Luckily, Kevin seemed aware of his limitations. "Maybe I'll ride next time," he said. "I could show them the trails. But this time I'll just watch."

"Just watch? No. You can still be useful. Go get the saddles for Sunny and Rocky."

As soon as Kevin headed off, Josh regretted being so cantankerous. Not for Kevin's sake, but for his own; by making Kevin run errands, Josh had stranded himself with the movie stars. But damn it, he was an adult, and he wasn't shy. Not usually. "You guys care who takes which horse?"

"Can I ride Rocky?" Ashley asked. Josh realized that they were the first words she'd spoken since she arrived, and the sound of her voice affected him more than he would have liked.

"Ooh, good!" Charlotte said. "I get the pretty one."

"Rocky's pretty," Ashley protested. "Look at those beautiful eyes!"

"Look at those enormous ears," Charlotte retorted.

"All the better to hear me with! I bet he's going to be super obedient."

"They're both super obedient," Josh interjected. It was time to get them all back to business. "They're both well-trained and sensitive and submissive to humans. So if you ask them to do something, and they don't do it? You didn't ask them right." He wasn't the sort of person who liked giving speeches, but if these two had come to him to learn, he'd do his best to tell them what he knew. "I don't know shit about English riding," he said. Possibly not the best place to start, not if he wanted to inspire confidence. But it was too late to change, so he charged on anyway. "But from what I've seen, it's mostly about forward movement. Racing around a track, going over jumps, whatever. That's why the stirrups are so short—so it's easy for you to go up and forward, and just trust that your horse is going to go up and forward, too." They were both listening to him, at least, although he had no idea whether they thought he was making any sense. "Western riding is different. More like dressage, maybe . . . but I don't know shit about dressage, either, so I can't say for sure. But Western stirrups are longer, so you're more balanced in the saddle. Your horse should be able to go in any direction—front, side, diagonally, back—and you need to be able to go with him. Okay?"

They both nodded, and then Kevin was back, carrying a saddle and Navajo blanket on each hip, with the bridles trailing over his shoulders. It wasn't exactly a dignified look and Josh let himself enjoy it for a moment. He finally stepped in when he realized Kevin was about to drop at least one piece of valuable tack onto the gritty, rocky ground.

Josh rescued the closest saddle from Kevin's precarious grip and tried not to take it as a punishment from above when he realized that it was the one he used on Rocky. It had been a fifty-fifty chance, after all. Just his bad luck that he got stuck with the horse Ashley wanted to ride.

"Can I do it?" she asked hesitantly, holding her hands out, offering to take the saddle from him. "I want to learn as much as I can. I want to feel authentic. My character would have been saddling her own horse, for sure."

"Knock yourself out," he said, and he let go of the saddle. He realized as his fingers were just done releasing it that he'd made a mistake. All summer he'd been trying not to touch her; he didn't want one more detail to obsess over, and he knew that the feel of her skin against his could keep his stupid brain busy for days. So he let go of things before she could take them from his hands. It was fine if he was handing her a drink or giving her a set of keys, but quite a different matter when he was dropping a bulky forty-pound saddle on her.

He tried to fix his mistake, grabbing wildly at the falling leather. She'd seen what was happening and shifted forward, twisting a little. He grabbed the saddle, but only after firmly brushing the back of his hand against the front of her warm, soft breast.

He stared at her and she stared back. It should have been nothing. The contact had clearly been innocent, they were both adults, neither one of them was anything close to virginal . . . it wasn't a big deal. Except that it was. Because he wanted to drop the damn saddle into the dirt, and he wanted to grab her and touch her and kiss her and probably throw her over his shoulder and carry her somewhere that he could get rid of that stupid baggy shirt she was wearing, somewhere he could slide her jeans off her perfectly curved hips . . .

"Sorry," she gasped.

His mind was blank. He couldn't imagine what she was apologizing for.

"I almost dropped it," she said.

"It wasn't your fault." And she wasn't staring at him because she was sharing his arousal. She was just worried that she'd pissed off the grumpy local who had agreed to give her something she really wanted.

"I'll be more careful," she promised.

And he would be, too. This time he grabbed the saddle by the horn, extending it out in a way that made him worry his wrist might snap in two from the strain but that would definitely keep his hands the hell away from her body. "Try again," he muttered.

She took the saddle and sagged under its weight, and he tried not to notice. He certainly wasn't going to help her with it; if she wanted authenticity, there it was.

He stepped back and tried to collect himself, then remembered his bottle of beer, resting in the shade of one of the fence posts, and gratefully scooped it up for a long swallow. He just needed to calm down, and he'd be fine.

But he knew his brain was going to be reminding him of the feel of her breast against his hand for a long, long time.

❧ *Nine* ❧

"I CAN'T BELIEVE this place doesn't have a hot tub," Charlotte groused as she limped toward the kitchen table. "I need a long soak."

Ashley smiled sympathetically as she filled a mug with coffee for her friend. "And we signed up for more torture on Friday. Our legs are just going to be getting back to normal, and we're going to jump back on and do it all again."

Charlotte took a careful sip from her mug, then squinted in Ashley's direction. They'd both just woken up, but, as usual, Charlotte's brain was working faster than Ashley's. "You seemed to have fun, though. Seemed like it was a good time."

"It was hard work," Ashley retorted. She didn't think she was ready to talk about the rest of it. Not yet. The peace that seemed to have sprouted between her and Josh was still too fragile to withstand full daylight, or the withering heat of Charlotte's examination. Better to keep it quiet and safe, somewhere she could protect it. Obsess over it. "But Josh is a good teacher. And Kevin was a lot of fun. You and him . . . you're thinking about doing something?"

Charlotte shrugged. "Thinking about it. He's a good guy, for sure. And cute. He hasn't got that whole brooding thing that your guy's working, but—"

"He's not *my guy*!"

Charlotte smiled into her mug. "So it'd be okay if I made the trade? 'Cause Kevin's fun and all, but Josh . . . there's just something about Josh." She didn't say anything more, just looked over, saw the strained expression on Ashley's face, and started laughing. "Relax, Ash, I'm joking. I'm just looking for fun, not a big, emotional . . . whatever. Mister Grumpypants is all yours."

"No, he's not," Ashley said. There was no point denying the truth. "And he's made it completely clear that he doesn't want to be mine. He doesn't even want to be near me."

"Yeah, okay," Charlotte said. "If you say so."

Ashley felt like a teenager, and she knew she should let it go, but she couldn't. "Why do you say it like that? Do you think . . . Did you see . . . I mean, you sound like you think he *does* want to be near me. Do you have a reason for thinking that?"

"Woman's intuition."

"That's it?"

"Yup. Take it or leave it."

"Well, if you haven't got any actual proof—" Ashley started, but she broke off when she saw Josh's familiar pickup appear through the opening in the trees. He'd said they'd be over to do some more work on the place that morning, but somehow she'd expected them a little later. For the second day in a row she had to resist the temptation to run inside and put on a little makeup.

"We should go shopping this morning," Charlotte said quickly and quietly. "We can get some good stuff and make them lunch. To thank them for the riding lesson."

Ashley cringed, and Charlotte saw her do it. "What? You don't want to cook for your man?"

"After the surprise dinner? I really don't think he'd want to eat with me." And then it was time for the hard part. "And he's right not to. I've been treating him like a piece of meat instead of a real person."

"Why on earth have you been so stupid?" Charlotte's voice was louder than it should have been considering how close the men were.

Ashley made a shushing gesture with her hands before whispering, "I'm an idiot. That's why."

"But, you're *not* an idiot." Charlotte frowned thoughtfully. "Not usually. Now you two are a mess, and it's ninety percent your fault. Any other stupid things I should know about?"

"Nothing big. I think I've got myself more or less under control, at least for the moment."

"I admire your discipline." Charlotte smiled at her. "You've never just asked a guy out, have you? You've been a movie star your entire dating life. You don't really know how normal human beings relate to each other."

"I'm not a Martian."

"Might as well be, from the sound of things." Charlotte leaned forward a little. "Want to see something neat?"

"Probably not—"

But Charlotte was already on her feet. "Kevin!" she called. "Josh? We're going into town to get groceries this morning, and we were hoping you'd let us make you lunch. Would that be okay?"

There was barely a moment's hesitation before Kevin called back, "Sounds great! Thanks!"

Charlotte sank back into her chair and looked at Ashley triumphantly. "Huh. Simple communication between Earthlings. Not that difficult, really."

"You only got Kevin to agree," Ashley protested. "Kevin's easy. It's Josh who's the problem."

"Josh isn't a problem," Charlotte said mysteriously. "He's a solution." And then she sprang back to her feet and said, "We should get cleaned up and go shopping." There was a teasing gleam in her eye when she added, "I don't suppose you happen to know where we could hire a chef and a server at short notice?"

JOSH Sullivan's life usually made sense. He usually felt like there was a rhythm to things, a pattern. It was how he liked it. But that all went to hell every time he ran into Ashley Carlsen.

He felt like a fraud, sitting there on the deck. Kevin was laughing and chatting, chugging his lemonade like he didn't know it had been homemade by a woman who was used to sipping champagne on yachts and jetting all over the world for her vacations. A woman whose annual income was probably more than Josh and Kevin would make, combined, over their whole lives. But Kevin was letting the stars serve him like it was totally natural, like it made sense for them to be asking him whether he wanted extra pesto on his grilled chicken sandwich.

It was a game. A charade. Like kids making a big deal out of serving their mom breakfast on Mother's Day: it was only fun because everything was reversed every other day of the damn year. Ashley and Charlotte were enjoying the novelty of their experiment, but this wasn't something they were interested in making a habit of.

And it wasn't something Josh *wanted* to be a habit. Not with Ashley, but not with anyone else, either. He didn't expect women to serve him, and didn't even want it, not really. He mostly just didn't want to be part of Ashley's experiment. Didn't want to be a damn novelty.

But Kevin was beaming like a man who'd just won the lottery, so Josh ate his sandwich and stabbed at his salad and kept his mouth shut when he wasn't putting food in it. Let Kevin have his adventure. Maybe things would turn out better for him than they had for Josh.

Unfortunately, Charlotte didn't seem interested in leaving Josh to his meal. "So, have you two worked together for long?" she asked. It was a question Kevin would have been happy to answer, but Charlotte was looking right at Josh.

"Off and on," he said. "For a while." Well, maybe that was a bit more curt than he should be to someone who'd just made him a really good sandwich. "About five years, I guess?" He looked at Kevin for confirmation.

"Almost six," Kevin said. "But like he said, not full-time. When there's work, I work. With Josh, or a couple other places. Busy in the summer, slow in the winter." He shrugged. It was the reality of living in an area with a lot of seasonal visitors. When the cottages were full, business was booming. When the summer people went home, things slowed right down.

"So what do you do all winter when it's slow?" Charlotte asked, her voice just slow and lazy enough for the invitation to be felt.

Kevin grinned at her. "We find ways to keep warm," he promised.

Josh turned away, looking toward the lake and forcing himself to stay seated. He couldn't leave without messing things up for Kevin, and that meant he had to sit there and listen to the two of them as they started flirting. He realized that Ashley was just as quiet as he was but he didn't dare to look over and see what she was doing.

"How about in the summer?" Charlotte asked. "Do you give all that up in the warm months? Too busy to have any fun?"

"Oh, we still manage to find time for a little fun," Kevin said.

"Like what? If someone was visiting from out of town and you decided to show them a good time, what would that look like?"

Josh hadn't realized he was going to stand up until he was already on his feet. "I'm going to get measurements on those screens that need replacing," he said to Kevin. "It's a one-man job, so if you want to finish up your lunch, that's fine. We should probably hold off on staining the railings until the place is empty, though—we can do it on a warm day in the fall." He should get the job done and get the hell out of there. A couple hours that afternoon, a couple hours on Friday with the horses, and that was it. He'd have done his duty to his cousin, done his time with the movie stars.

But Kevin seemed to have different ideas. "I was hoping you'd help me out with this," he said with a smile. "It kind of sounded like a challenge, didn't it? Showing them a good time? Sounded like she's not sure we can manage it."

Josh was out of patience. "I'm sure you'll be fine," he said. "If you want to take the afternoon off, go for it. But I've got some work to do." He nodded as politely as he could while refusing to make eye contact with anyone at the table, then headed for the truck to get his clipboard and tape measure.

He didn't realize he was being followed until he grabbed his tools, turned around, and almost ran into Ashley. "Sorry," he said quickly.

"No, I'm sorry." She looked miserable.

"Wait. For what?"

"For making you uncomfortable. For all the stupid stuff I've done. You know. For making it so you can't even sit there and eat lunch with us."

"I ate lunch," he protested.

"Yeah," she conceded. "I guess you did. But you sure didn't enjoy yourself. And that's because I've been an idiot, and I'm really sorry about that."

Damn it, he did not want to have this conversation, especially not dead sober. "The world doesn't revolve around you," he said. He knew the words might sound harsh, but he hoped his tone made it clear that they weren't meant that way.

And when she glanced up at him she seemed curious rather than insulted. "What do you mean?"

"There's lots of reasons I don't like hanging out with summer people," he said. "You being an idiot is only one of them." She looked so confused, and so sweet, that he found himself giving a little more away than he really wanted to. "And me reacting to the stuff you've done? It's not just about you. Not you as a person. I just . . . I don't get involved with summer people. That's all."

She stared at him. "What, like we're not good enough for you?"

"It's not a question of good or bad. Just not what I'm looking for."

"Oh," she said. It was pretty clear that she was acknowledging that she'd heard the words rather than that she'd understood them.

But it wasn't Josh's job to spell everything out for her. "So I'm going to get those measurements done," he said, hoping she'd take the hint.

She nodded, then glanced back toward the cottage. The lunch table was on the other side of the building, facing the lake, so neither of them could see what Kevin and Charlotte were up to. "Your cousin doesn't share your preferences," she said carefully.

"No, I guess not."

"I'm going to feel like a third wheel."

This shouldn't be his problem. It wasn't his job to entertain one movie star in order to allow a different movie star to seduce a local in peace, not even if that local was his cousin.

But Ashley wasn't saying it like it was his problem. That was the part that got to him. She was just saying it. She was sharing a piece of herself with him, however small that piece was. Even movie stars felt like third wheels sometimes. Even Ashley Carlsen sometimes felt out of place.

"You could write down the measurements for me," he suggested. It was strange to feel as if he was doing her a favor by turning her into his assistant. "I'd do the measuring, you'd write it down. It'd save me a bit of time." And mean he'd get the hell away from her that much faster. That was the part he should focus on. He wasn't being soft, he was being efficient. Wasn't giving in to temptation, just taking a long view to avoiding it.

"Sure," she agreed. "Happy to help!"

So she took the pencil and clipboard from him and they worked their way around the cottage, assessing the screens and measuring those that needed replacing. They didn't talk about a single thing that wasn't screen-related, and it was actually kind of relaxing. There was a moment of embarrassed tension when they reached the lake side of the cottage and found the eating area abandoned, but a whoop from the lake made it clear that the other two had gone for a swim, not for more intimate pursuits.

It was a big cottage and it took a while to do all the measuring. The sun was warm, even filtered by the trees, and when Ashley handed the clipboard back to him at the end of the job, Josh noticed a gleam of sweat on her neck. He wanted to lick it, and then follow its path down beneath the fabric of her shirt. He wanted to know if her breasts were channeling the moisture, if there was a trickle running down toward her belly button. He wanted to know if her bra was damp, and then, of course, his mind started thinking about other damp undergarments. . . .

"Kevin!" he bellowed. Ashley jumped, and he stepped a little away from her and peered down toward the lake. "I'm done," he yelled. "If you want a ride, it's leaving now!"

There was a moment in which he could see their two heads bobbing in the water, facing each other, discussing it all, then Kevin yelled back, "Come for a swim! Ashley wants to know where the waterfall on the other side of the inlet is—you could kayak over and show her."

Josh took another few steps toward the lake. "Ashley's up here, asshole. How do you know what she wants?"

"I have a spy. Come for a swim."

Seeing Ashley in a bathing suit, warm and smooth in the sun, her skin slick from the water? There was no way he could expose himself to that; he was still trying to forget the sight of her from that morning on the McArthur dock. "It's the middle of the afternoon. I have work to do. If you want a ride, let's go."

Another brief conference on the dock below, then Kevin raised a hand and waved Josh off. "I'll catch up with you later," he called.

Yeah. How much later and how messed up Kevin would be by then remained to be seen, but Josh wasn't surprised by the answer. The siren was singing and Kevin hadn't learned how to block his ears.

"Looks like you're back to being a third wheel," Josh said as he turned toward the truck.

"I'm going to find that waterfall," Ashley said. "I can kayak over on my own."

The waterfall wasn't too big in the dry summer months: enough to tantalize with its sound, but not enough to disturb the water beneath it after it hit the lower rocks. And the sound echoed strangely against the cliffs, so it wasn't too surprising that someone would have trouble finding it if they didn't know where to look.

"Just west of the point, there's a grove of cedars with their branches stretched out over the water," Josh said. He felt like he was giving away a local secret. "If you can make it past their outer branches, there's a sort of cave closer in to the trunks. Not a real cave, just a hollow in under the branches. You can see the waterfall from in there."

She beamed at him as if he'd given her something worth having, which made no sense. This woman had travelled the world. She'd probably seen half of its listed wonders, had almost certainly been shown huge waterfalls that would make the little trickle across the lake look like someone's leaky faucet, and she was this excited about it? Was she just acting?

Maybe. It was her profession, after all. But it felt real. Real and bewildering.

Josh didn't like being bewildered. "Good luck with it," he said, and he got the hell out of there. He hadn't been lying about having lots of work to do, and he knew he was doing the smart thing by staying away from Ashley. Just because she was appealing didn't mean he should spend time with her. In fact, it was the main reason he knew he needed to stay the hell away.

❧ Ten ❧

ASHLEY BROUGHT AN apple for Rocky on Friday. Actually, she brought him two apples, two carrots, and a bag of special horse treats she'd ordered on the Internet and had arranged for the store to express-courier to the cottage. Josh eyed the bag full of goodies skeptically.

"After you ride," he said. "And not all of that!" His voice softened a little. "You don't really need to bribe him, you know. He likes being around people. You can scratch his neck for him and that's all the thanks he needs."

"They're not for him, they're for me." She saw his expression and grinned. "I mean, he's the one who should eat them. But I want to give them to him because *I* want to. But I won't if you say no. He's your horse." She wasn't sure she should push it, but she shrugged and said, "I guess if you want to deprive him, it's your business."

"One apple, one carrot, a couple of whatever the hell those things are, and all of it after you ride." His frown wasn't as sincere as it usually seemed. "That's the kind of deprivation my horses have to endure."

Charlotte swooped into the conversation then. "Sunny can have the leftovers, right?"

"You two are going to leave me with two fat, spoiled horses," Josh grumbled, but he didn't say they couldn't feed them the treats.

He also didn't stalk off, stare angrily into space, or swig his beer as if it were poison and he was hoping it would carry him away from the frustrations of his world. He just leaned against the wooden railing, watching them as they groomed their horses, and only looked a little put out when Kevin led a light grey horse in from the field. "You're riding?" Josh asked.

"You said I could," Kevin retorted. Then, as if realizing that he sounded a bit like a rebellious teenager, he added, "Is it a problem?"

"No," Josh said. But he ducked under the railing and headed for the gate Kevin had just closed.

"So where are you going?" Kevin asked.

Josh didn't answer because he didn't have to. A gorgeous chestnut horse was galloping toward them across the field Kevin had just come from. They all watched the chestnut as he approached, and when it seemed as if the horse wasn't going to stop, Ashley took a step forward in alarm, as if her movement would make any difference. He was going to charge right into the gate, right into Josh. . . .

But he didn't. The horse skidded to a stop, his whole body moving back over his haunches so it looked like he was almost sitting down, then straightened up and waved his head over the gate, his eyes rolling and showing white around the edges.

Then Josh touched him. A calming hand on his neck, a few murmured words, and maybe most significantly, a halter slipped over his head with a lead rope attached under his chin. Ashley drew a little closer, near enough to hear Josh saying, "Did you think you were going to be all alone, Ember? Did you think they'd all left you?"

He glanced over when he realized she was watching, and shrugged. "My horse is a bit of a baby," he said. Not apologizing, not embarrassed, just speaking the truth. "And a drama queen," he added, this time apparently speaking to the horse. Then he looked back at Ashley. "And clueless. He wanders off, away from the others, and doesn't keep good track of them. So we'll go to get them and he won't know about it. Sometimes it takes him half an hour before he figures out he's alone, and he's still just as panicked as he was this time."

Josh led the horse to the side of the gate and swung it open wide enough for the animal to fit through. "I'll just hang on to him until his buddies come back."

"You should get him a goat," Kevin suggested. "Goats are good company for horses."

"But then I'd have a goat," Josh replied. He turned toward Ashley and quietly told her, "Goats creep me out."

"Their eyes," she agreed. She wasn't sure what this new dynamic was, couldn't quite remember how she'd come to be standing next to Josh instead of grooming her own horse, but she wasn't complaining. She liked being on Josh's side of things. Given the amount of time Charlotte and Kevin had been spending together over the last couple of days, she figured neither one of them was too hungry for her companionship, so she could spend time where she pleased. Which apparently meant right next to Josh. "You'll just hold him? You don't want to ride with us?"

"He's still young; he's not much good at standing still yet. And I have a hard enough time thinking of things to teach you guys when I've got my full attention on the job."

"You have a hard time? My God, Josh, I feel like every time you open your mouth you're teaching me something super useful and important!" She wasn't just flattering him. She'd taken riding lessons before, but her instructors had focused mostly on the what and the how. What she should be doing, how she should be doing it. Josh was all about the why. Why the rider might want to do something, why the horse responded the way it did . . . It was fascinating. She was pretty sure she could have a useful riding lesson from Josh somewhere far from any animals, just sitting in a couple chairs talking about why horses behaved the way they did.

But he didn't look convinced. "Well, your lesson for right now is that Rocky's really good at untying knots and it looks like he's getting started on your lead rope."

"Rocky!" she scolded, and headed back over to the animal she'd been neglecting.

She managed to tack him up without any help, even recalling the arcane knot for the girth—no, the cinch and the latigo—without prompting. She was pretty proud of herself, and was tempted to give Rocky a contraband carrot as a celebration, but she managed to hold back. Rocky wasn't her horse, and she hadn't even figured out a way to pay his owner for letting her use him.

Which was a conundrum she had time to think about, since Charlotte and Kevin were apparently tacking up together, with lots of giggling and groping and other annoying behavior that slowed them right down. She snuck a glance at Josh, who seemed to be working on Ember's ground manners, and tried to figure out how to thank him for his reluctant cooperation.

No grand gestures, she reminded herself firmly. No surprise dinners and no drunken advances. No stupidity of any sort. She shouldn't buy him a new horse. She definitely shouldn't buy him a goat. Probably she shouldn't *buy* him anything, which made the whole problem a good bit trickier.

"Do you need help in the barn?" she blurted out.

Josh stared at her for a moment, then turned and looked at the building. "I don't think so," he said cautiously. "Is something wrong with it?"

And then she remembered the secret strategy that had worked so well for Charlotte at the cottage. She was going to try it. Honesty. "No, of course not. I'm sure the barn is fine. I was just hoping to find a way to repay you for your help. The part I'm trying for, in the movie? I really want the part. Really a lot. And I need every edge I can get. Char and I are going over the lines like crazy women, and I've talked to my agent and manager and I've got them lobbying hard, but I really think it'll give me a leg up if I can go in there and tell them I know a bit about Western riding, too. And it's good for me. It helps me get into the right mind-set. So, you know . . . I really owe you. I know you didn't want to do this, and I totally understand why." She caught herself. "Well, I understand why you wouldn't want to spend time with me, as an individual. I'm still figuring out why you don't like summer people in general. But I figure I've done enough stupid stuff all by myself to make it totally natural for you to not want to do this. But you did, and I just . . ." She knew she'd said far too much, but it was too late to take any of it back, so she closed with, "I'd just really like to thank you."

He looked completely unsure of himself. Possibly he looked like someone who thought he was in a conversation with an alien. But he managed a tentative smile. "How about if I just say 'you're welcome' and we leave it at that?"

"That's where things get frustrating!" Again, she knew she was oversharing but didn't seem able to stop herself. "Because a 'thank you' should be about 'you,' right? And you've made it pretty clear that the thing you'd like best is getting rid of me. So the best way to thank you would be to disappear, clearly. But I'd feel like I was being ungrateful if I did that, even though I know it's what you want, so the only reason for me to try to do something else is so that I don't feel ungrateful, so that means that just by trying to find a way to thank you I'm actually being selfish, which seems totally wrong emotionally, but intellectually I'm pretty sure it's right. . . ." She finally managed to stop speaking.

Josh was staring at her. So was Charlotte. And Kevin. Hell, even the horses were giving her the eye. But Josh was the one who mattered. She had to lean forward a little to be sure she heard him when he said, "I don't want you to disappear."

She was pretty sure it would come across as obnoxious, but she couldn't help herself. She wasn't trying to rub anything in, she just really needed to hear that again. "I'm sorry," she said, her voice almost as quiet as his had been. "Could you just . . . could you say that once more?"

His raised eyebrow made it clear that she was walking a fine line. "I don't want you to disappear," he said. And for one perfect, glowing moment, they were back where they'd been when they'd first met, back when they were just discovering each other, before everything had gotten in the way and ruined it all. Then he added, "But it would be great if you'd get a bridle on your horse so we could get this 'lesson' started."

She wanted to push for more. Hell, she wanted to grab him by the hand and drag him into the barn and tear that ratty T-shirt right off his hard, broad chest. But she managed to control herself for a change. "Okay," she said quietly. "A bridle. Right. That'd be useful."

And she tried to pay attention to poor, patient Rocky, who'd only been trying to untie his lead rope because he was lonesome, not because he was bad. Yeah, she tried to focus on her horse, but it didn't do her any good. There wasn't an animal in the world that could distract her from the man she knew was standing only a few paces away. Standing there just as remote as he'd always been, but somehow not angry anymore.

Josh had forgiven her, she was pretty sure. It didn't mean they were best friends, didn't mean she could push for anything more from him. But at least she'd fought her way back up to neutral. Now she was just another annoying summer person, someone to be avoided because of the group she was a member of, rather than for anything special about herself. It probably said quite a bit about how messed up she was that she was treating that slight advancement as a victory.

ASHLEY was born to ride Western. Charlotte was doing okay, but her default was always to go for the reins, to worry too much about the horse's forward motion, or lack of forward motion, and treat that like it was all that mattered. Ashley understood, seemingly instinctively, about riding from her seat. A cowboy needed at least one of his hands free for working, and sometimes he needed both of them. A good Western horse was trained to respond to the rider's weight, to his legs and his voice, even without any backup from the reins. It felt like giving up control, Josh figured, for someone trained English to start trying to ride Western. But they had to give up the light, false control of the reins in order to gain the real control of riding from their seats.

Maybe he was being too poetic. Too philosophical. He was in a weird mood, that was all. But he was starting to like the "teaching riding" business. It gave him a great excuse to stare at Ashley, after all, and that was pretty much the biggest reward he could imagine.

"Okay," he called out to the riders who'd been loping

around him, trying to adjust their horses' speeds without changing gaits. "I think that's good. That's about all I know, I think. It's just about feeling the horse and sending the right messages back. That's all."

"So we can go for a ride?" Kevin suggested. "We've got half an hour before it's totally dark and the horses need to cool out anyway. Can we go back to the creek?"

"The creek's twenty minutes away," Josh said. He was speaking to the women, not to Kevin. "And when we get there, Kevin's going to want to swim. There's a couple places that are deep enough, but just barely." He didn't bother to mention that if the creek had been deep enough for serious swimming, rich summer people would have snapped up his property before it had ever hit the market, at a price he'd never have been able to pay. "Then twenty minutes back. Which means we're coming back after dark."

"Is that safe?" Charlotte asked.

"Fairly. The horses see pretty well in the dark, and they know the way. And it's a clear night, with an almost-full moon. But it's not as safe as riding in daylight."

"You do it?" Ashley asked.

"Yeah," he admitted. "But sometimes I do stupid things."

"So do I," she said firmly. "And I'd love to go to the creek. If it's okay with you."

Put that way, Josh couldn't really object. So he clipped an extra lead rope to the far side of Ember's halter and moved the first one from under his chin to up on the side of his jaw, then pulled himself onto the horse's back. He could tell everyone was watching him, and he didn't like it. "It's your show," he said to Kevin. "We going?"

So Kevin and Casper led the way, with Daisy the Demon Dog enthusiastically scouting ahead. Ember didn't like being at the end of the line, of course, but that was good. Teaching the horse to be patient was useful training, and more importantly, it gave Josh something to think about other than Ashley.

Except that she ended up right in front of him as they fell into single file at the edge of the forest. Right where he could watch her most easily, and without having to pretend he wasn't. It felt almost dirty, like he was spying on her, but where else was he supposed to be looking?

At the trees, probably. She obviously was. The forest was darker than the open field had been, so she couldn't be seeing much, but she was peering around herself with clear delight. At least, he was pretty sure she was delighted. He could only see her face in occasional profile and it always seemed to be smiling, so that was good. And her back was straight but not strained; she looked relaxed, but interested.

"We should have brought bug spray," Charlotte said from her spot behind Kevin. She was windmilling one of her arms, clearly trying to ward off mosquitos.

"Think of it as feeding the forest," Ashley suggested. "We need to make a little blood sacrifice in order to be admitted."

"The little bastards can have all the blood they want—I'll cut my arm open and they can come drink from it if it'll stop them from biting me. It's the itch I can't stand!"

"And the malaria," Josh said quietly.

Ashley twisted around in her saddle to stare at him with a raised eyebrow. Her expression clearly asked, *Malaria? Really?*

He grinned at her and shook his head. *No. No malaria.*

Her frowned response was a teasing rebuke, and he almost turned Ember around right then. He almost sent the horse galloping back to the barn, hell, maybe past the barn, farther away, somewhere Ashley Carlsen would never be able to find him. He wanted to get away because he knew what was happening. He hadn't been careful enough. He'd thought he'd built up enough resistance to handle a little casual contact like this, but obviously he'd been wrong.

There was something about the woman that made its way through his best defenses, and the only reason he didn't turn the horse around and take off was because he knew it was already too late. She'd made it past his best barriers and she was inside him now. There was nothing he could do to get her out, not until she decided to leave. And when she did, he'd be left with a gaping hole in all the spaces she'd inhabited.

He stared at the back of her head and a part of him hated her. Because she was going to hurt him. Bad. And she'd just skip back down to Hollywood, not a care in the world, laughing about her summer fling with the handyman. Yeah, she'd been slumming, but he'd been convenient. Handy.

It didn't mean she was thoughtless. Well, yeah, probably it did. But just thoughtless, like she wasn't thinking about it. Because why should she? She wasn't cruel, just . . . one of them. She was a summer person. That was what he needed to remember.

He watched as she ducked down to peer under some overhanging branches, trying to understand the forest beyond the path, and the tiny bit of hatred washed out of him. He couldn't be angry at her for this. It was all his fault. He'd known better, and he'd let it happen. It was only fair that he'd be the one to suffer the consequences.

She turned around again, a vague shape in the dim light until she smiled and her teeth gleamed white. "I can hear the water," she whispered.

She was exploring, having an adventure. She'd managed to keep that part of herself alive, and he envied her. But maybe he didn't have to keep holding back. He was already totally screwed, so it wasn't going to hurt him any worse if he let himself have a little fun. Let himself enjoy whatever time they did have together.

So he allowed his memory to go back to his first discovery of this creek, and he remembered the sense of wonder he'd felt. She was open and willing to share that with him, and he should let himself enjoy it with her. "Wait 'til you see it," he promised, and this time when she smiled at him, he let himself smile back.

❧ *Eleven* ❧

ASHLEY KEPT LOOKING for elves. She knew it was stupid, and if someone had asked what she was doing she would have lied. Well, no. If most people had asked, she would have lied. But she was pretty sure she would have told the truth to Josh.

After all, it was his forest. And the way he maintained the trail suggested that maybe he wasn't immune to the elf-wishing himself. The trees were trimmed back far enough that it was comfortable to ride, but the forest wasn't denuded and sanitized like some of the parks Ashley was used to back home. There were moss-covered logs for the horses to step over, loose rocks and roots on the trail itself—obstacles that probably should have been cleared in the name of safety, but that made it all feel much more organic and magical when they were left behind. They made it seem like Josh wanted visitors to his forest to step carefully, avoiding the obstacles, the fungi . . . the elves?

She didn't notice the horses in front of her coming to a

halt and probably would have ridden Rocky right into Sunny's yellow butt if the horse hadn't hesitated enough for her to start paying attention.

"We're there," she heard from somewhere around her left thigh, and she looked down to see that Josh was already dismounted, looking up at her curiously.

"I was somewhere else," she said apologetically.

He stepped back as she slid off Rocky's back, then said, "He ground ties. Just drop his reins and he won't go anywhere."

She stared at him. "Really?"

Josh shrugged. "Well, if a dragon came, he'd probably run. But he won't just wander off."

"The elves would protect us from the dragon," she said before she realized it made her sound insane. Then again, he was the one who'd brought up dragons, so how bad was it for her to counter with her own mythical creatures?

Apparently not too bad, because he just nodded. "That'd help. So as long as Rocky knows that, he won't go anywhere."

Apparently Sunny and Casper could also be trusted to stay put, but Josh used his lead-rope reins to tie Ember to a sturdy tree. "He's still young and stupid," he explained.

By the time that was taken care of, Kevin and Charlotte were out of sight. Josh didn't seem too surprised. "There's a bunch of little pools," he explained. "None of them more than four or five feet deep, at the most. So don't kick too hard or you'll scrape your feet on the bottom. And the water's pretty cold." He frowned. "And we've got to make the ride back to the house, and then you'll have a drive home. This is really a pretty crappy place to go swimming, especially when you're living right next to a great lake."

"I like it," she protested. It felt strange to be defending the forest against the criticisms of its owner, but she charged ahead anyway. "I've gone swimming in pools and oceans and lakes and rivers. But I don't think I've ever gone swimming in a forest stream."

"You've probably never gone swimming in a sewer, either, but that doesn't mean it's something you should put on your bucket list."

"Wow. You're determined to be grumpy about this?"

He looked at her for a moment, then shook his head. "No. Sorry." He reached over his shoulder and grabbed the back of his T-shirt, then dragged it up and over his head in one casual, almost dismissive gesture. She supposed he must have dropped the fabric on the ground when he was done, but she didn't really notice because she was too busy staring at his chest.

She'd never seen him shirtless before and it was frustrating that this first glimpse was only lit by the sparse moonlight filtering in through the branches overhead. Even in the dim light she could see enough to know that this torso deserved to be warmed by the most brilliant rays of the sun. She'd known Josh was fit, but he was more muscular than she'd expected, with enough definition to make a Hollywood trainer feel insecure about his job prospects. The trainer probably wouldn't approve of the hair dusting over Josh's chest and then trailing down in a thin line to his jeans, but Ashley found herself wanting to reach out and touch it. Well, she wanted to touch *all* of him.

He didn't seem to notice her attention. He was moving around . . . pulling off boots and socks, she realized, and then he was unbuttoning his jeans and her mouth was suddenly dry. She looked away, strangely frantic, then let her gaze return. She felt like a virgin, apprehensive but tempted, and it made no sense that a woman of her age and experience would get this worked up over a little . . .

Oh. Not actual nudity. He was leaving his boxer briefs on. She should have known that.

He glanced over at her and she managed to tear her gaze away from his ass quickly enough that she was pretty sure he wouldn't have noticed. "You chickening out?" he asked gently.

"No." Her assertion probably would have carried a bit more weight if there were any evidence she was getting ready to go swimming. But Josh was polite enough to not point that out. Instead, he turned and walked carefully toward a large rock that jutted out into the stream.

He was giving her a little privacy, she supposed, and she quickly pulled her shirt over her head, letting the cool night breeze dance along her too-warm skin. She felt stupidly shy. Josh had seen her in a bathing suit, and her underwear was no more revealing than a bikini would be. And she'd done topless scenes, too. Being half-naked on a soundstage full of virtual strangers should surely have inoculated her against any concerns related to one man and a moonlit night.

She tried to relax as she tugged off her boots and then wriggled out of her jeans. It was just swimming. Kevin and Charlotte were . . . Well, it wasn't totally clear where they were, but probably not far. Close enough to count as chaperones, as if Ashley had any reason to need supervision. She grinned to herself. Based on past behavior, it was Josh who needed to worry about protecting his virtue, and he seemed okay with it all.

That realization helped, and she picked her way toward the water, stepping carefully in her bare feet.

Josh was already in, his hair wet and gleaming dully in the moonlight. The water came up to the middle of his chest. Too low for someone who was treading water, so he must be standing on the bottom. He was looking casually downstream; he could see her with his peripheral vision and was close enough to help if she needed it, but he wasn't staring at her. The etiquette of underwear-swimming, she supposed.

"The rocks there are almost stairs," he said, gesturing vaguely toward the overhanging boulder. "Easiest way to get in and out."

She followed his advice, shivering as the cool water hit her knees, her thighs, her tummy, and finally her breasts. She was determined not to complain, but she knew she was breathing more quickly than she should be, almost gasping each breath into a chest tightened by cold.

"It takes a minute to get used to it," he said calmly, turning to face her now that she was mostly submerged. "The cool will take the itch right out of any bug bites, though."

"Excellent," she said with only a slight shiver in her voice.

"You enjoying the experience so far?" he asked with a smile.

"I'm glad I've done it once," she said, leaving it unsaid that she probably wouldn't be looking for a repeat visit.

"Look up," he said softly, and as soon as she did the cold didn't matter anymore.

She'd never seen stars the way she saw them when she was in Vermont. The clear air combined with the lack of much light pollution to make the distant lights seem impossibly vivid. There were more of them than made any sense, and a glowing white band that made her understand how the Milky Way got its name. As she looked up from the water, the branches overhead framed the view, making it all seem more remote, and more perfect.

"Lie back," Josh suggested quietly. "Let yourself float."

She hesitated, then did it. She shivered as new areas of her skin were exposed to the cool water, but her feet bobbed easily toward the surface and she kept herself in place with only the slightest movement of her wrists.

When she felt the first gentle touch on her ankle, she kicked and pulled her head out of the water; Josh pulled his hand away quickly. Then he slowly, carefully brought it back. "Trust me," he said, and she did.

He wrapped his hands around her ankles, his index finger extending halfway up her calf, and slowly guided her body farther into the pool. She didn't understand what he was doing, really, but she let herself go with it.

It was almost startling when she felt herself caught by the current. But Josh's hands were still firm on her ankles and as the water tried to catch her and carry her away it pushed her down toward him until her feet were braced on the middle of his chest.

It was like artificial gravity, the force of the water making her feel as if she was standing on his body, but the stars were still in front of her and that only made sense if she were lying down. For a moment her senses rebelled and she felt absolutely dizzy. Then she let go of her attempts to sort it out and just let herself feel, and it was perfect. The water was cool but his chest and hands were warm, and her ears were underwater so there were hardly any sounds, just a dull rush. Her hair tickled her shoulders and she was weightless. She felt like she was floating in space instead of in a stream, except she was anchored to Josh and he was more earthy and real than anyone else she'd ever met.

How could someone so determined to keep his own feet on the ground give her the freedom to fly?

IT all felt strangely anticlimactic. Kevin and Charlotte had eventually reappeared from wherever they'd been, and Josh and Ashley had climbed out of the water and fumbled into their clothes. They'd all been quiet on the ride back to the farm, and Josh had thought about inviting them into the house for a drink but decided against it. They'd just given the horses a quick brushing and turned them out into their pasture, and then the women had climbed into their car and Kevin had climbed into his, and they'd gone.

So Josh was left alone on his porch, his underwear soggy and cold beneath his jeans. Daisy the Demon Dog stared at him like she, too, was expecting something a bit more exciting to round out the evening.

"Did I call Ember a drama queen?" Josh asked the dog.

"'Cause maybe I should have been talking about myself." He'd been the one thinking about it like it was a done deal, a foregone conclusion that something was going to happen between him and Ashley. "She just wanted something quick and easy," he told the dog. "And I turned that down. It's done. It's over."

Daisy stared at him for a while, then stood up and trotted down to the tree line, coming back with a stick. She dropped it at his feet and when he threw it she chased it obligingly, although of course she didn't bring it back. Demon dogs might chase things if the mood struck them, but they didn't retrieve on command.

He stayed on the porch, watching the night, while he drank a beer and then another. He was trying to decide between going to get a third and going in to change out of his damp jeans when he saw the headlights on the driveway. Daisy came tearing in from wherever she'd been and for a moment he thought she might actually throw herself at the car, but she swerved enough to just chase alongside it, her gaze locked on the person in the driver's seat.

Josh was looking at the exact same place. He stood up and stepped down off the porch, wishing that he'd gotten changed at some point so he'd look a bit less like someone with bladder control issues.

But when Ashley got out of the car her shirt was damp along her breasts and he knew her jeans would be clammy, too, and he decided it was good that they matched.

She stood by the door of the car, not even closing it, and she stared at him while Daisy sniffed her and then trotted off. He supposed it was up to him to say something, but he was afraid it would be the wrong thing. What words would make her get back in the car and what words would make her stay? And which of those things did he want anyway?

So he stood at the bottom of the porch, and she stood by the car, and they both stared. Finally, she shook her head as if waking from a dream. "I didn't want it to be over," she said, just loudly enough for him to hear. "We don't have anything else planned. You're done working on the cottage, and you said only two riding lessons, and that's totally fair. More than fair. It was really generous of you. But that meant there's no other reason for me to see you, and I felt like . . . I felt like it wasn't finished. Or maybe just that I don't want it to be finished."

He moved then. All the way to the car, but somewhere around the back wheel on the driver's side he ran out of steam and stood there, one big stride away from her, and he couldn't trust himself to go any closer. "You can have another lesson," he managed to say. "If you want. Or we could do something else. I could make you dinner." Which was a stupid suggestion, because he was a pretty terrible cook. "You could break something at the cottage and I could fix it."

She shook her head at that, embarrassed. "If I did that, would you trust me not to have a big fancy dinner set up to surprise you?"

"I'd come over in the morning," he said, shuffling a little closer to her. "And I wouldn't give you an exact time, so you wouldn't be able to plan a brunch or something."

"Crafty." She wasn't looking him in the eye. Her attention seemed caught by something else, and he wanted to wipe his hand over his face to check if there was something stuck to his skin. But then he licked his lips, unconsciously, nervously, and he saw her eyes widen. Oh.

It gave him his confidence back. This wasn't the part he was supposed to be insecure about. She'd made it clear that she wanted him, physically. Abundantly clear, on multiple occasions. And he'd spent enough time around summer women to learn that they were no different from anyone else, not when it came to their desires. He knew what he was doing, for this part at least.

And maybe the confidence made him a little cocky,

because instead of moving forward and letting himself finally touch her warm, soft body, he stepped back. "Would you like a drink?" he asked, raising the beer bottle he'd almost forgotten he was holding. "I have beer, or Scotch. Red wine, but no white, I don't think."

She looked disoriented, and he liked it. "A beer would be good," she finally said, but she didn't sound convinced.

Of course she wasn't convinced. She hadn't driven out there for a beer. She'd come for the same thing she'd wanted from him every other time. This time, she'd won, and she was going to get it. But he could at least make her wait a while. He could drag it all out, torture her with anticipation and frustration. Sure, he'd be torturing himself as well, but he'd rather have this kind of suffering than the one he was facing down the line.

"Come sit," he said quietly, starting toward the porch. He didn't let himself turn to check, but he could hear the gravel crunching as she fell in behind him.

"You going to be cold?" he asked when they reached the top of the porch steps. He turned and nodded briefly to her clothing, with its damp spots.

She looked down at herself, then back at him. It was hard to tell in the dim light filtering out from inside the house, but he was pretty sure she was blushing. When she spoke, her voice confirmed his suspicion: the movie star was embarrassed. "I'm a mess. I didn't think about . . . I should have cleaned up. God, I should have dried off at least! This is not how I'm supposed to look."

"Not supposed to look real?" he asked. "You're supposed to wear waterproof underwear or something?" He shook his head and gestured to his own jeans. "I'm a little soggy myself. And if you think any guy is ever going to complain about you wearing something that reminds him he recently saw you mostly naked, you're crazy." It wasn't much fun to torture someone who was actually suffering from it. "Sit. I'll get a blanket in case you get cold. And a couple beers."

She did as she was told, and he did as he'd said he would. When he came back from inside she was sitting on the porch swing with her boots off and her feet curled up under her ass, and she looked tiny and delicate, more like someone to be protected than someone to be lusting after. Then she shifted a little and the light shone on the full roundness of her breasts, and that was it for his protective instincts.

He handed her one of the beers and then sat down beside her, the blanket between them. They were quiet for a while, until Ashley said, "Thank you."

He looked at her quizzically, but didn't ask for clarification. He just waited.

She smiled. "For the beer, and the blanket, and the swim, and the riding lessons. But mostly . . . it feels like . . . I don't know. Thank you for letting me be here. For not chasing me off and telling me to leave you alone."

"I've already tried that," he said lightly. "It never seemed to do much good."

She was quiet for too long this time, and he realized that his words had hit too close to home. Or maybe they'd hit exactly where he'd intended them to; maybe he still wanted to punish her, at least a little. But that wasn't fair. "Sorry," he said. The word wasn't quite enough, so he tried to find a few more to go with it. "I'm glad you're here." That was true, on some level, and he should have just stopped talking, but instead he added, "It's a bad idea and I should know better— I *do* know better—but I'm still glad you're here."

She whirled toward him with such vigor that he had to plant his feet to keep the swing from lurching out of control. "I don't get that! What is it about me that's so *poisonous*? Why is it a bad idea for us to spend some time together? I'm a nice person, Josh! I'm not . . ." Her voice trailed off, and her last words were barely audible. "Why am I a bad idea?"

What was he supposed to say to that? He could tell her it wasn't anything personal. That was true enough, but he didn't think she'd believe it, not unless he went into a lot more detail than he really wanted to about it all. "Summer people," he said heavily. He knew what he meant. Any of the other locals would know what he meant. They'd understand that it wasn't just about the amount of time summer people spent in the place, it was everything. Wealth, status, celebrity, arrogance. The way they arrived like a swarm of locusts, sweeping over the quiet wilderness and changing everything in their paths. They assumed Vermont was theirs, that it was one more venue for their enjoyment, like an amusement park or something. They forgot that there were people who lived there year-round. People whose whole existences were anchored to the rocky soil, people who had been born there and were going to die there, just like their parents and grandparents before them. Josh was pretty sure the summer people thought the place was boxed up and stored away once fall came, and the people who'd served them all summer were packed away with it, with no thoughts or emotions or regrets about anything that had happened over the warmer months. "You treat us like we're not real," he said. It was the best he could do.

But Ashley didn't look convinced. "What does that mean?"

"Like we don't matter," he tried again. Then he looked at her and saw how upset she looked. She'd come out for a quickie, and had gotten stuck with a beer and this instead. Not a pleasant surprise. So he added, "Not you." But that wasn't quite right. "Not *just* you. You're not . . . you're not the worst of them."

She stared at him, and he knew there would be more questions. He'd try to answer them, but he wasn't really sure he'd be able to. He wasn't great with words at the best of times, and trying to explain something like this? "It's just not a good idea. Getting involved with summer people. Sometimes it makes you forget who you are, and who *they* are. . . ."

"How do I treat you like you don't matter?" Her voice

was shaky, and for a horrible moment he was afraid she was crying. He looked at her long enough to be sure her cheeks were dry, but he wasn't really sure what he would have done if they'd been wet.

Probably if she'd been crying he'd have had the sense to shut up. Maybe he would have taken her in his arms, if she'd let him, and that probably would have led somewhere a hell of a lot better than this conversation. But she wasn't crying, so, God help him, he kept talking. "Like I'm a piece of meat," he said. "No. Not that dramatic. But you know what I mean."

"The bar," she said. "That was . . . It was a mistake. I was drunk and stupid and I did something stupid."

"Yeah. I've done stupid stuff, too. Lots of it. I just . . . You aren't that sort of person, right? Like, have you ever taken a dare like that before?"

"No!"

"But you did that time. Partly because of Jasmine. I know how she . . ." He stopped there. He didn't want to tell Ashley about all that, and he could pretend to himself that it was because he didn't want her to think less of Jasmine. "But partly you did it because you're on vacation. You're somewhere else, away from your real life. What happens in Vermont stays in Vermont. I get it." He shook his head. He did get it. "But I'm not on vacation. This is real life, for me. You planning a dinner—for you, it's just something funny, a silly thing you did one time on vacation. But for me . . . that was my cousin who saw you treating me like a boy toy. Like someone you'd decided to play with. She told my whole family about it. They laughed, mostly. Not a huge deal. But how would you feel if your whole family knew about some guy treating you like that? Some guy trying to seduce you while your cousin watched?"

"I screwed up that time, too," she said. "I know."

"Look, it's not a tragedy," he started. He might have had more to say, but they both heard the car coming, the low purr of its engine and the crackle of gravel under its wheels, and then they both turned to see its headlights as it approached through the forest.

"Oh," Ashley said. "You have a visitor."

A rescuer. Someone who'd keep him from making a mistake with this woman. But now that escape was at hand, Josh knew for sure he didn't want to get away. He'd chosen this mistake, and now he wanted to make it.

But when the car's lights turned off, taking the glare out of his eyes, he recognized the vehicle, and a moment later, the driver who stepped out, and he knew that he wasn't going to get the chance to make a new mistake that night. Not when one of his old ones was staring at him from the driveway.

⋧ *Twelve* ⋦

ASHLEY HAD NO idea what to say. She remembered what she was wearing, and how ridiculous she must look with patches of dark everywhere her underclothes had soaked through her clothes. She knew her hair was a mess, and she wasn't wearing any makeup. The woman walking toward them was absolutely going to pick up on all that. Then Ashley stopped worrying about that as her brain prompted her with the question it should have been asking from the start. What the hell was Jasmine McArthur doing at Josh's cabin?

Maybe Jasmine had come out to ask him to do a few repairs? But it was Friday night, fairly late, and Jasmine was wearing high heels and a short dress. She was holding a bottle of wine in her hand. Ashley tried to keep her mind from leaping to the obvious conclusion.

"Josh," Jasmine said in her low, sultry voice. "Hope you don't mind me dropping by." Then she squinted a little and said, "Ashley? Honestly, is that you? I barely recognize you, sweetie! Are you okay?"

"I'm fine," Ashley said. Her voice sounded light and stupid next to Jasmine's.

"You know the dare had a time limit, right?" Jasmine sounded amused. "I think it's a little late to try to claim a prize now."

Finally, Josh broke in, and his voice was as cold as Ashley had hoped it would be. "What can I do for you, Jasmine?"

Even in the moonlight, Ashley could see the way Jasmine's eyes flared at Josh's tone. She was excited by it. She wanted him angry. She sashayed a little closer to the deck. "You could fetch us a couple glasses, for a start." She held up the bottle of wine. "Ashley, you'll join us?"

As if Ashley was the one crashing the party. And as usual with Jasmine, the words held a little suggestiveness, the hint of the idea that maybe Ashley would be joining them for more than a drink.

"I should go," Ashley said desperately. Spending time with Josh and the forest had stripped away her protective armor, and Jasmine was too sharp to be around without defenses.

Josh didn't argue. He seemed to have removed himself from the situation almost entirely, just sitting there on the swing and watching the two women as they . . . as they what? As Jasmine toyed with Ashley like a cat would play with a mouse, probably. If Ashley'd had time to prepare, she could have given Jasmine a run for her money in the polished appearance department, but she'd never picked up the woman's conversational fierceness. Yes, Jasmine was definitely a predator, and Ashley was the prey.

Or, more likely, Josh was the prey. Jasmine was just another summer woman making a booty call, treating Josh—what had he said? Treating him like he wasn't real. Ashley was pretty sure she understood what he meant by that now. Treating him like a servant, really. An unpaid gigolo. At their beck and call, ready to perform at their whims. Was that how Josh thought Ashley had treated him?

Yeah, she needed to get out of there. She stood up, wishing it were darker so the others wouldn't be able to see her messy clothes, or her messy face. At least she managed to keep herself mostly turned away from Josh. But Jasmine was watching her with savage glee, taking in every detail of her appearance, and her reaction.

"I'm up for another week at least, and I don't have any guests for the next couple days. We should get together, sweetie." Her smile was wicked as she glanced at Josh and then half whispered, "We could compare notes!"

Ashley wasn't sure if the strange sound she made could count as a reply or not, and she didn't think she had the self-control to clarify anything. She felt like an innocent, blundering around in some game Jasmine and Josh were playing together. Josh didn't have a rule against summer women; he just didn't want anything to do with Ashley. So let them sit there on the porch, let them talk about her and laugh.

But they wouldn't likely be sitting on the porch for long. She refused to turn around, but by the time she'd scrambled to her car and backed it up, she could see them in the rearview mirror and Josh was already standing, he and Jasmine so close together Ashley couldn't see any light between them.

She drove too fast on the way home. She eventually slowed down a little after she saw the eyes of some animal glowing at her from the forest and remembered that her bad night could get a hell of a lot worse if she murdered some wildlife just because she was upset.

By the time she got back to the cottage she was more or less under control, but she still had to keep herself from groaning when she saw Kevin and Charlotte sitting on the porch. They'd been spending every possible moment locked away in Charlotte's bedroom, and *now* they were peacefully enjoying a nightcap in a shared space?

Because they'd expected her to be away all night, she realized as she parked and headed for the house. If there was anything worse than the walk of shame in the morning, surely this was it—the walk of someone who couldn't even manage to do something shameful.

Charlotte's mouth was gaping open as Ashley approached. "He did *not* shoot you down!" she said, clearly waiting for an explanation.

But Ashley wasn't ready for that conversation. Instead, she turned to Kevin. "Josh and Jasmine McArthur. They have a thing?"

His expression made it clear he knew something, but wasn't sure how much he was supposed to share. He looked guiltily in Charlotte's direction, and seeing her glare, made a face, then nodded reluctantly. "They did. That's what I heard, at least. But it was a while ago. I didn't know it had started up again. But Josh is always pretty quiet about that stuff."

"'That stuff,'" Ashley echoed. She supposed she was included in that generic term. Whatever nonsense she'd come up with, it was all just "stuff" that some summer woman had done.

"Sit down," Charlotte said gently. "I'll get you a drink. Wine? Or a cooler?"

Ashley looked at the amber liquid Kevin was restlessly sloshing around his glass. "Scotch," she decided. It wasn't quite right to drown your sorrows in a berry-flavored cooler.

Kevin stood up then. "I'll get a glass," he said.

"And ice," Charlotte added. She and Kevin were drinking theirs straight, but apparently that would be too much for a Scotch neophyte.

Ashley was left with the vaguely comforting notion that the other two were combining efforts to take care of her. She should have been too proud to accept their pity and too strong to need it, but it felt nice to be babied a little.

"I like Kevin," she said when he was safely out of earshot.

"Yeah," Charlotte agreed. "He's a good guy. And pretty

good in bed, too. I mean, not a lot of sophistication, but excellent enthusiasm and stamina."

Ashley wondered what Josh would think about his cousin being described that way. Was Charlotte being dismissive? Treating Kevin as a sex object and nothing more? "Are you thinking it might be something long-term?" Ashley asked hopefully. After all, there was nothing wrong with a woman enjoying sex. Nothing wrong with starting a relationship with a little—

"Uh, no," Charlotte said firmly. "How the hell would that work? We're too different. Noncompatible, long-term." She peered curiously at Ashley, obviously realizing her words weren't what her friend had hoped for. "What's going on with you? Are you getting prudish in your old age?"

"No." Ashley shook her head impatiently, trying to make her ideas make sense. "I'm just . . . When I was talking to Josh, I thought I was starting to understand what he meant. But now I'm talking to you, and everything you're saying makes total sense. I just can't quite figure out how to mix the two together."

The screen door opened and Kevin stepped outside. He'd obviously heard at least the last bit of their conversation, but he didn't say anything until he'd poured Ashley a drink from the bottle stashed behind his chair and delivered it to her. Then he sank into his own seat and said, "Josh does the same thing." He grinned at her. "He thinks there should be one set of rules for everyone, and the rules should be based on what's best for him." He took a sip of his drink, then shook his head a little. "No, not rules. He's not a big fan of rules. Just . . . he thinks everyone's the same, I guess. If it's a bad idea for him to spend time with a gorgeous movie star, knowing it's a short-term thing, then it must be a bad idea for everyone else, too." He smiled at Charlotte, his expression open and affectionate with no hint of angst or worry. "He's wrong."

Charlotte raised her glass in a little toast to Kevin's wisdom. Then she turned to Ashley. "But if he's involved with Jasmine McArthur, you're better off away from him. Messing around with him up here was one thing, but if you mess with her? If you piss her off? That's something that could follow you down to L.A. That woman has a lot of influence."

Kevin nodded. "Even up here, she's not someone to mess with. She's put some pressure on Josh, I know that. Pissed that he dumped her, so trying to punish him through his job."

"So *he* dumped *her*? Why? How long ago? Does David know?" Ashley asked.

Kevin licked his lips. Maybe he was savoring the last drops of Scotch, or maybe he was buying time. "You should ask Josh for details on that," he finally said. "For all of this, really. I shouldn't be gossiping. I don't know any of this firsthand, or even secondhand, because he's never mentioned it to me. I'm just repeating shit I heard around town. It could all be wrong."

Charlotte squinted at him and Kevin refused to meet her eye. Ashley knew her friend would do some digging and get whatever information she could out of the man. But probably he'd been right. If Ashley wanted to know about all this, she really should ask Josh. But she thought back to the scene on the porch, remembered how close Josh and Jasmine had been standing, and she wondered whether she'd ever get the chance to talk to him about it all. And she wondered just how much of his history she really wanted to know.

THE early morning light should have brought clarity, but it really didn't. Josh had no idea what he was doing. Well, he knew exactly what he was doing, but he wasn't sure why he was doing it. Or whether he was going to be able to do it right.

He pulled the truck in beside Charlotte's convertible and climbed out, then hesitated. Not too late to escape. He could take the events of the night before as a lucky break, a way to extricate himself from whatever was going on with Ashley. Everything could go back to normal, if he just let it.

But instead he gently shut the door of the truck and headed up the stairs to the porch. He didn't think he was too early, but there were no obvious signs of life. It was Saturday, a day he generally worked during the busy summer season, but a day off for others. Did people who were already on vacation sleep in extra late on weekends?

He didn't want to wake anyone up, but it seemed a bit creepy to just sit there on the porch and wait. So he headed down the wood-and-stone steps toward the lake.

And that's where he found her. No graceful pose, this time. She was just sitting there on the end of the dock, her feet in the water, her shoulders slumped as she stared down at her toes.

"Getting any bites?" Josh asked quietly.

Ashley twisted her upper body around and stared at him, obviously startled. Then her expression became calmer, and more remote. Less honest. "Fish, you mean? Nibbling my toes? Yeah, a few."

He nodded. That was about as far as he could go with that conversational topic. So he lifted the paper bag in his right hand. "I brought muffins. From the bakery. If you're hungry."

She just stared at him. Apparently he wasn't going to be able to bypass the conversation by offering a baked-goods bribe. There went Plan A.

So he took a few more steps forward, then nodded at the other side of the end of the dock. "Can I sit?"

She had to think it over, but finally, reluctantly, she nodded. He supposed he'd have to count that as a tiny victory.

He was wearing cargo shorts and sports sandals. Maybe it had been arrogant for him to leave his work boots in the truck—it probably seemed like he was planning a day of relaxation rather than a quick apology before going to a job site. But Ashley wasn't looking at his feet, or at any other part of him. She was staring out at the lake, clearly waiting for this human annoyance to go away and leave her in peace.

Another easy escape. But again, Josh didn't take it. Instead, he lowered himself to the dock and stuck his feet in the lake next to Ashley's. "Sorry about last night. You and me were talking, and then . . . not a pleasant interruption, I guess. You and Jasmine aren't still friendly?"

Ashley shook her head. "But obviously you two are."

Josh snorted. "Not really. Just those little visits. She'll see me on the street or at the bar or something. She doesn't usually come out to the house."

"She didn't seem to have any trouble finding it."

"Yeah. I guess she's been there before." He wasn't quite sure how he'd gotten himself in a situation where he felt like he needed to explain himself, but he added, "She left a couple minutes after you did. I could have asked you to stay, but I figured she'd take it better without an audience."

Ashley finally looked at him. "But you've been with her before. Kevin said so, and it was obvious anyway. She somehow managed to get past your 'no summer people' rule, huh?"

Josh had known the conversation was going to go there. And now he was digging up history best forgotten, exposing aspects of himself best kept hidden, in order to repair a relationship that he knew was going to cause him pain in the long run. What the hell had happened to his sense of self-preservation? He looked at the woman sitting next to him and had his answer. Ashley Carlsen had happened to it. "She was the reason I made the rule," he said reluctantly. "Or at least, she was the final straw."

"Does her husband know?"

"I don't think so. I'm not sure. I think . . ." Shit, he hated talking about this. But Ashley deserved a bit of an explanation. "I think she wanted to get caught. I don't know why.

But she sure wasn't sneaky about it, toward the end. But he never seemed to notice. . . . Maybe he just didn't want to know. Didn't want to have to deal with her, you know?" He kicked at the water a little and wished the conversation could end there. But if it did, there wouldn't have been any point to starting it all. "I'd let myself believe in it all. In all the . . ." He tried to find words that would explain without offending. "This isn't a ritzy resort area. The summer people who come here like to think they're not snobs. They think they're 'getting back to basics' and 'exploring the wilderness.' They're building huge mansions for their 'basics' and 'exploring' from their luxury SUVs, but it's what they want to think. And they think they want to hang with the locals. A lot of them even say they're getting in touch with 'real' people."

Ashley was frowning at him now. He couldn't tell whether she was concentrating or getting ready to object. He decided he'd better just keep going and get it all out before she said anything to confuse him. "I used to believe all that. I hung out with their kids when I was younger. Played with their toys. And then I got older and needed a job, and I was good with my hands and I could tell myself that it was . . . I was like a craftsman, or something. I wasn't an employee, because I had my own business. I worked *with* them, not *for* them. When they invited me to their parties, I went, and I had fun. We were all friends."

Yeah, that was what he'd fooled himself into believing. It hadn't been easy to maintain the illusion, but he'd worked hard at it, and he'd managed.

"You dated some of them," Ashley prompted quietly.

"Sure, yeah. Why not? Just casual stuff, but that was fine. That was all I was looking for."

"And you didn't care if they were married."

Now it was his turn to stare at the lake. "That was . . . It was at the end. I was starting to realize I wasn't . . . I don't know. I realized I was a toy, I guess. One more amenity offered by the Vermont hospitality commission. So I was kind of pissed at them all. And you know Jasmine. She's pretty good at making things seem like a good idea, even when you know they aren't."

"So, now you're equating me making a stupid bet at a bar with you having a long-term affair with a married woman? A woman whose husband you work for?"

Josh shot a quick glance at Ashley, then looked away. He didn't want to see her with that mix of anger and disappointment on his face. "I messed up," he said. "They had a party and Jasmine was flirting with me and David saw it and went out of his way to talk to me like the hired help. It pissed me off. So I left, and when Jasmine caught up to me on the driveway . . ." He shrugged defeatedly. "It all kind of started from there."

Ashley nodded slowly. Josh wasn't sure if she'd already known the whole story; he was a little pissed at Kevin for having told her *anything*, but if the bastard had told her all this? That would be way over any line Josh had ever heard of, and final evidence, as if any was needed, that Kevin was getting his head turned around by the Hollywood crowd. But that was something to worry about later. For now, Josh had to wrap up whatever the hell he was doing with Ashley. "So that's . . . I think that's all of it. It's why I don't date summer people, and why I've been trying to avoid you. It's why Jasmine came to my house last night, and why I sent her away."

Ashley didn't say anything for a while. Finally, she turned to look at him, and she waited until he made himself look back at her. "So why are you here now?" she asked quietly. "Wouldn't it have been easier to just stay away? You had to know I'd be gone for good after that scene last night."

"Yeah," he said reluctantly. "I guess I figured you would be. And I guess . . . when it came right down to it, I guess I decided that wasn't what I wanted."

She nodded, and then turned back to the lake. "I've got

to tell you, Josh, I'm getting pretty damn tired of spending all my time worrying about what you want. Especially when you're so totally undecided yourself. You know?"

He did know. He understood. But before he could admit to that, she added, "You know what I'm starting to wonder? I'm wondering whether maybe you just get off on rejecting me. Maybe *you're* the one into revenge, but you're too chicken to go after the people who actually hurt you so you're focusing on me instead. It was fun for you to turn me down, and then it seemed like I was going to walk away, so now you're here, saying whatever you think it's going to take to get me wanting you again, so you can have the fun of shooting me down one more time."

He didn't know what to say. He was on his feet before he'd realized he was going to start moving. He'd opened his soul to her, told her things he'd never told anybody, confessed to his arrogance and stupidity and shameful behavior. On one level, he'd known she'd be mad, but somehow he'd fooled himself into thinking that maybe she'd understand a little, too. One more mistake to add to his long list. "Okay," he said, as much to himself as to her. "Sorry to have bothered you."

He turned and headed off the dock, refusing to let himself run or even walk fast. This wasn't a big deal. It was a good thing, really. His heart was pounding faster than it should be and his stomach was tense and roiling; if he reacted that way to this tiny disappointment, how much worse would it have been if he'd let himself really care about her and then been dumped?

Kevin and Charlotte were on the deck when he walked by, sharing one chair and watching him like two bobcat kittens wondering if the passing wolf was going to notice them. Josh resisted the urge to growl. Or, at least, he made his growl sound like words. "You working today?" he asked his cousin.

"Do you need me?"

"No." He didn't need anybody. "But there's work if you want it."

Kevin hesitated, clearly torn between enjoying himself with his movie star and actually making a living. "Will you have hours for me next week?"

Josh wanted to punish the bastard for squealing to Ashley, but Kevin was Aunt Carol's kid, and that bought him some serious forgiveness for being a loudmouth. The whole thing was too tiring; Josh just didn't have the energy to hold a grudge. "Yeah, probably. I'll see you at The Splash on the weekend, let you know then."

And that was all. He gave Charlotte a courteous nod and got the hell out of there. He'd been planning to work on the Fullers' gazebo, but that would be fidgety precision work. He wanted something that would use his whole body and let him burn off some frustration. The Claymore bush clearing would burn some energy, so he'd do that.

He headed out along the cottage road, trying to find a plan for the day, trying to think about other jobs he needed to get done. Trying to think about anything but the angry, disappointed woman he'd left behind him.

❧ *Thirteen* ❧

ASHLEY'S COPY OF the script was already dog-eared and ragged, but it deteriorated even more when she threw it across the room. She watched it hit the wall and then flutter into a twisted heap on the hardwood floor. The little tantrum didn't do the script any good, and it didn't really help Ashley, either. She was still as frustrated and confused as she'd been all day.

Kevin was in the kitchen working on dinner, but Charlotte was sitting at the far end of the same sofa Ashley was on, and she wasn't the sort to ignore someone else's display of emotion. "You ready to talk about it now?"

Ashley wished she had something left to throw. Instead she flopped her body restlessly to the side. "There's still nothing to say. It's all just too . . . It's supposed to be simple, isn't it? You and Kevin are simple. You like spending time together, so you're spending time together. That's how these things are supposed to go!"

"Do you think it makes sense to compare you and Josh

to me and Kevin?" Charlotte's tone was carefully neutral, but the question was pretty clearly rhetorical.

"Because Kevin isn't a brooding, grudge-holding psycho, you mean?"

"Oh. I didn't realize it was that simple. Yeah, if Josh is a psycho, you're right! There's nothing to talk about. Phew, it's lucky you got rid of him so easily!"

Ashley made a face at her friend. "Not, like, a *psycho* psycho," she admitted reluctantly. "But the brooding and grudge-holding are real."

"Well, that doesn't sound too healthy, either. I mean, life is too short to waste time with someone who gets upset over stupid stuff and can't get over it."

"Yeah!" Ashley looked at the crumpled script on the floor. "Except maybe it wasn't stupid stuff, exactly, that he got upset over. Maybe it was actually some stuff he should have been a bit upset about. Maybe."

"But he's not letting it go. He's not trying to move on, and he came here this morning to yell at you about it all. So screw him! It's over."

Ashley wished Charlotte wasn't quite so good at this. "He is trying to move on, I guess. It's not his fault Jasmine showed up last night. And he came over this morning to explain it all, not to yell at me." She looked down toward the lake. "He brought muffins. From the bakery."

"Muffins? I was unaware of muffins. We could have had them for breakfast."

"No. I threw them in the lake."

Charlotte was quiet for a few moments. Then she said, "That's some excellent diva behavior you're working on. The script, the muffins . . . You just need to throw a cell phone at someone and you'll be a true star."

"I was upset."

"About what? What did he say that upset you?"

Good question. Ashley played back the conversation. She

hadn't really enjoyed hearing about Josh and Jasmine's history, but that wasn't what had made her angry. What had it been, really? "Do you think I treat him like a toy? Like he's one more amenity provided by the Vermont hospitality commission?"

"Is that what he said you did?"

"Not me. Not that specific. Just summer people in general. Summer women, I guess."

"Huh."

Ashley waited for more, but apparently Charlotte wasn't planning to give it to her. "What? What does that 'huh' mean?"

"It means . . . well . . . I've only heard your side of the story. You told me the stupid stuff you did. Would you have done all of that to a guy back home? Taken the dare in the first place, and then refused to take 'no' for an answer? Even with the riding—it was mostly me, I admit, but I wouldn't have been that pushy about riding lessons with someone back home. Up here, it's like, yeah, we're on vacation, so we're being goofy. But they're not on vacation." She made an amused face in the direction of the kitchen. "Well, Kevin seems to be. But Josh isn't." She frowned thoughtfully in Ashley's direction. "But there's more to it than that, isn't there? Maybe? I mean, me being pushy about riding, that was partly because I really, really want this part, but we could have flown back home and gotten riding lessons there, if we'd had to. I think part of it is . . . I think I really couldn't believe that some backwoods nobody would say no to a big star like me."

Ashley stared at her, and Charlotte stared back. "It doesn't sound good, does it?" Charlotte asked quietly. "Makes me sound like a snob, like somebody who actually believes her own publicist. And I wasn't thinking it consciously. But I think maybe there was an element of that involved."

"And you're saying you think maybe that's part of it with me, too?"

"I don't know, Ash. I don't think you're a snob. I don't

think you're full of yourself. But, honestly, when we're working—and when are we *not* working, really, because all the parties and appearances and all the rest of that crap, that counts as work and we both know it—when we're working we're the centers of our little universes, aren't we? It actually . . . Wow, I'd never thought about it before, but the 'star' thing actually makes more sense than I thought. We're not just bright lights twinkling in the darkness of the movie theaters, we're also huge, dense bodies with smaller objects rotating around them! We're the centers of our solar systems."

"I'm neither huge nor dense," Ashley said. She really wanted to deflect Charlotte from the conversational path they seemed to be on.

But Charlotte barely seemed to hear her. "So it'd be pretty impressive if we could just shut that off entirely, wouldn't it? There's lots of self-centered people in the *regular* world, and then we get it all reinforced for us by being around people who actually act as if we're the sun and they're just planets." She took a moment to appreciate her new understanding of the figure of speech, then shrugged. "I don't know about the Vermont hospitality commission bit. But if the only side of the story I've heard is yours, and I still think he's got a few reasons to feel a bit objectified? Then maybe he's got a point."

"By me." Ashley worked hard to keep her voice from being shrill. "You're saying that *I've* been objectifying him."

"I don't know," Charlotte said carefully. "What do you think?"

"It was *two episodes*!" Ashley yelled at her friend. How the hell had Charlotte gotten so good at this after playing a therapist for two damned episodes?

She needed to think, but her brain was racing too fast for anything to make sense. She wanted . . . Oh. Yes. She wanted to lie back in the cold forest stream with her feet braced against the warm strength of Josh's stomach, and she wanted to look up in the sky and float. That was what she wanted, but she was pretty sure she wasn't going to get it. "I'm going for a swim," she told her friend. The lake wasn't going to be as good as floating in the stream would have been, but it was the best she could manage.

"OF course you're coming," Kevin said. He sounded genuinely confused, and not exactly pleased, by Ashley's attempt to beg off his plans for the weekend. "It's The Splash."

"The event of the season," Charlotte said cheerfully. "Got to see and be seen. And you said your potter friend had a stall at the craft fair, right? You want to see that, don't you?"

"Yeah, I'll drive in for that," Ashley said. "But I probably won't stay that long, so we should take separate cars."

"Ash . . ." Charlotte started. Then she turned to Kevin. "You want to go get the car, babe?"

The car was about twenty feet from the doorway; everyone knew Charlotte was just trying to get Kevin out of the conversation. He smiled, happy to escape, but Ashley wished he'd stay and be a buffer.

"You won't be a third wheel," Charlotte said as Kevin headed out the front door. "It's not like the two of us are gazing into each other's eyes and doing baby talk; we're just hanging out. If we're having sex, you're not really welcome, but all the rest of the time, you're good. Seriously." She paused for Ashley to absorb that truth, then added, "And you'd damn well better not be hiding from Josh Sullivan. That's either over with, in which case it doesn't matter, or it's not quite over with, in which case you should get out there and figure it out. Right?"

Ashley sighed. "I just might not be great company."

"You'll be fine. It's already almost dinnertime, so you'll have a hot dog and a beer and you'll be ready for fun. Now get some shoes on."

Ashley let herself be pushed around and tried not to feel like an unwelcome imposition when Charlotte shoed Kevin into the back of the convertible and ensconced Ashley in the passenger seat.

As they drove, Kevin leaned forward and gave them a rundown of what they were heading for. "The Splash is our big summer festival. It's not really in honor of anything. . . . Like, it's not an ice cream fest or a lobster fest or whatever. It's just pro-summer. The golf courses open their doors to nonmembers for the weekend, and there's a fishing derby and a cool triathlon—kayak, mountain bike, and speed-hiking instead of the usual events—and there's the craft festival, but you already know about that, and . . . I don't know, just lots of random stuff. Some of it's cool, some of it's weird. But at night there's a huge barbecue down in the park by the lake, and a dance afterward on the tennis courts. That's the part everyone goes to, so that's why we're going."

Everyone. Ashley resisted the temptation to inquire whether "everyone" included Josh. She wasn't going to get over her obsession by talking about him all the time. "What's a fishing derby?" she asked instead.

"It's just a fishing contest. Certain timelines, and you see who can catch the biggest fish. Usually there's some subcategories—different kinds of fish and different classes of fishermen or whatever. Some people take it really seriously."

"I want to be in a fishing derby." Ashley was surprised by the words as they came out of her mouth, but she took a moment to consult herself and realized that they were true. She looked over to see both Kevin and Charlotte giving her weird looks. At least Charlotte was driving, so she couldn't stare quite as overtly as Kevin. "Not *this* fishing derby," Ashley said quickly. "I've never fished in my life. But someday. A bucket-list thing, I guess. I'd like to enter a fishing derby."

"What's the appeal?" Charlotte asked after a moment. She sounded genuinely curious.

"Just . . . it's just something to try. Something that means something to a whole group of people, and I've never even heard of it, and it just seems like I should give it a try. If they all like it, and they aren't crazy . . ."

"Well, I wouldn't go all the way to saying they aren't crazy," Kevin said. "You should talk to Mr. Ryerson in the place next door to you. He says he's a recovered fish-a-holic, but I think his wife always watches him for a relapse. Some of these guys are pretty intense about their fishing."

"I won't be that intense," Ashley decided. "But I'll take it seriously. It won't be a joke. I'll spend some time figuring out . . . I don't know, I guess figuring out how to fish, for starters, but then I'll learn the right bait or techniques or whatever, and I'll wake up really early on derby day to get a good start, if that's allowed, and I'll really concentrate on whatever it is people concentrate on when they're fishing."

"Will you have an outfit?" Charlotte asked.

"Only if there's a reason for it. Like, a practical advantage. Not just to look cute."

"Okay," Charlotte said with a decisive nod, as if Ashley had been asking permission and Charlotte had decided to grant it. "That's weird but cool. Do you have a timeline?"

"I need to do some investigation first. I'll get back to you."

Ashley felt good as they drove the rest of the way into town. She was being proactive. She was taking charge of her life. She was using her control to make some pretty strange decisions, but that was her right. And she thought she might really like this fishing thing.

WATCHING fishermen weigh their catches for the derby was even more boring than fishing itself. Josh didn't slow down as he walked past the docks.

It wasn't like he had anywhere to go, really; The Splash was mostly just about wandering around and visiting. It was one of the few breaks in the busy summer season, a rare chance to catch up with people who were working just as hard as he was and who wouldn't get another chance to socialize until the last leaves fell and the tourists finally went home.

But he was supposed to be meeting his cousins at the triathlon finish line, so he worked his way slowly in that direction, arriving just as the first kayakers were rounding the point and heading into shore.

"Is that Gil?" Josh asked Theo. He looked up to the five-year-old on Theo's shoulders. "Is that your daddy in the kayak? Can you see?"

The little guy clapped his hands and bounced a little, but Theo just squinted and shrugged. "Might be him."

Gil was Theo's brother, the oldest cousin in that generation, and he'd been training hard for this event. He was a good guy and deserved to win, and Josh should have been spending all his energy on cheering, but he found himself distracted.

Ashley Carlsen was there, only a few yards away, standing with Kevin and Charlotte. She was talking to Sarah, Gil's wife, and the sun made Ashley's hair glow as it was tossed by the wind off the lake. When the kayakers got closer and everyone began to cheer, her voice was raised with the rest of them, and she clapped and jumped with excitement as the racers neared. When Gil crossed the finish line in first place she threw her arms up in triumph and was enveloped in the group hug as if she were . . . as if she were part of the group.

Josh made himself stop staring and let the crowd jostle him forward. Theo saw him and suddenly Josh was holding Andrew, the five-year-old, as Theo went to help his exhausted brother haul the kayak out of the lake.

"Daddy went *fast*," Andrew said, his eyes wide with excitement.

"Faster than anyone else," Josh agreed.

It was a small-town event, the competitors were all total amateurs, some of whom didn't even train, and the grand prize was a free dinner at the barbecue that night. But the smile on Gil's face was as wide and as real as if he'd just won the Olympics. It wasn't a big deal, except for all the ways that it was. And when Josh looked over at Ashley, when he saw her broad smile and genuine excitement, he felt like she somehow understood every one of those ways.

Josh let himself stand close behind her as they waited for the presentations. "I'm retiring," Gil told them all. "We need another Linden to carry the torch." He looked at the crowd. "Theo? Ben? Hell, Josh, you might not have the right last name, but I won't hold it against you. You in for next year?"

"You're only calling out the men?" Emma demanded. She was Gil's much younger sister, and always up for a challenge. "Maybe Sarah and I will do it!"

"Speak for yourself," Sarah said quickly. "Being married to the champ gives me bragging rights; I looked after the kid when he went to train, so I've already done my time!"

It was just another Splash, just another family gathering. Nothing special. Gil's victory would be added to the long list of family stories, just one more event that no one really cared about except for the people involved. And, maybe, people like Ashley.

Josh stayed quiet as the family rolled over to the barbecue pits and continued their celebration. They were used to him not saying much, so it wasn't a problem. He ate, and he paid as much attention as he could to the talent show that was happening in the background, and when Theo left to go set up for the dance, he tagged along. He needed to stay busy and keep his mind off women. Or one woman in particular.

As the sun set, the crowd began to gather. As always they were set up inside the community tennis courts, with long strips of various fabrics hung down to cover the chain link perimeter and thousands of fairy lights strung on top of it all to illuminate the scene. Once the court was full enough so the bright green pavement and sharp white lines couldn't be seen, it was actually a pretty elegant setting. Well, maybe not elegant by some standards. Josh tried to see it through his own eyes and ignore his imaginings about what visiting movie stars might think.

Then he looked over and saw Ashley standing just inside the gate, looking around her as if she'd stumbled into a fairyland. And damn it, that was just too much.

He was walking toward her before he realized what he was doing, but even once he knew, he didn't try to stop. He wasn't sure what his goal was; he didn't have anything to say, but he guessed he wanted to see her close-up. He wanted to enjoy her enjoyment.

But when he arrived, he realized it wasn't socially acceptable to just stand and stare at someone. She didn't seem inclined to complain, though, since she was doing her own awkward staring. Finally she broke her gaze away from his and blurted, "The fabric!" as if she were compelled to name the first thing she saw.

He waited for the words to turn into something he could respond to, then finally echoed them back to her. "The fabric?"

She stared at him a moment longer, and then her grin was quick and sheepish. "Sorry. That was a bit out of the blue. I was . . . I don't know. But, yeah, the fabric covering the fence." She took a deep breath, clearly organizing her thoughts. "Kevin said people donated it and a lot of it is significant. There's supposed to be one strip that's made from a wedding dress and all the bridesmaid dresses from a wedding. Do you know where that one is?"

"No idea," he admitted. But he was so grateful for the neutral topic of conversation that he resolved to share any information he had. "I hadn't heard of that one. I know there's one that's got all the jerseys from the school basketball team the year they won state. And the senior class makes one each year; each kid brings in a chunk of fabric and somebody sews it all together. Some of them are memorials, I know. . . . People bring fabric to the funeral or visitation, something they think would mean something, and the church ladies sew it up. I don't know about the wedding one, though."

"So your high school one is up there somewhere? From when you were a senior? What's your fabric look like?"

"It's just a chunk of blue. I was a bit of a minimalist, I guess." He didn't say that the blue of the fabric had been an exact match for the color of the lake on the day his father had left them for the last time. He didn't say that he checked on it every year, saw how the color was fading, and was glad of it, because the memory was fading, too, and that was just how it should be. Maybe someday he'd tell her about . . .

Wait a second. There was no someday, not for him and Ashley Carlsen. What the hell was he thinking?

Before he had time to figure that out, though, there was a new distraction. Someone roaring his name from across the tennis court, and the crowd parted as David McArthur strode forward. He was dressed for golf and carrying a golf club, and Josh had time to think it should have been tennis before David was right in front of him, red-faced and blustery. "You son of a bitch! Right under my nose? While I was fucking *paying* you?"

It was happening. Here, in front of everybody. In front of Ashley. Josh knew he deserved it, but he wished they were somewhere more private.

But David clearly wasn't interested in making things more low-key. "You've got nothing to say, you *whore*?" He didn't wait long for Josh's reply. He raised the golf club he'd been carrying and he swung, hard.

Josh half turned so the club hit him on the back of his knee instead of the side. He'd take some pain, but he didn't want a permanent injury because of this. He felt the explosion as the club connected and let his knees buckle. He caught himself on one hand and didn't try to stand up. He'd done it. He deserved this.

Another swing, this one catching him on his bicep, then another to his back, then his side, then his shoulders.

He saw the crowd stir, the people who'd been frozen with shock jostled aside as the cousins arrived. But Josh couldn't let any of them fight his battles for him, and he knew they wouldn't just stand there and watch him take a beating.

So on the next swing he reached out and caught the shaft of the club, letting his arm be driven back by the force of the blow while his hand stayed tightly gripped. David tried to pull it away but Josh hung on, twisting the club out of the other man's grip.

The cousins got between them, Kevin and Ben grabbing David none-too-gently and pushing him away. Josh stayed on his knees for a moment, his eyes closed, wishing it would all just go away. But he knew it wouldn't, so he laid the club gently on the green pavement and made himself stand up, ignoring the complaints from his abused body.

And then Aunt Carol arrived, swooping in like an angry eagle, glaring at David McArthur for half a second before turning all her attention toward Josh. "Are you okay?" she demanded.

"I'm fine," Josh said. He raised his voice just a little. "It's not a big deal. I'm fine."

Cal Montgomery had arrived and was helping to calm David McArthur down, which was good; the man was a lot more likely to listen to someone he considered a social equal. And Cal's family name would protect him from any revenge McArthur might have thought was due to people who'd interfered with him. Yeah, Cal could take care of that mess; Josh just needed to get out of there.

"Should you go to the hospital?" Aunt Carol asked. "No, don't bother answering, you always say 'no.' But I think you need to, and I win. Let's go, Joshy."

It was the pet name that made it unbearable. Did she not know why David McArthur had been so angry? Did she think it made sense to call him a child's name after that?

"No, I'm okay," he said. He forced a smile. "Seriously."

"No, you need to get—"

And then Ashley's voice, clear and strong, but with such completely random words that he was sure he'd misheard her. "I'm going to learn to fish." He turned toward her, waited for things to make sense, and then nodded cautiously. She smiled back at him, but he could see a little wildness around her eyes, a little desperation and maybe even confusion. Whatever she was doing, she clearly wasn't sure it was going to work. But she kept going anyway. "I'll be in a fishing derby, eventually. Have you ever been in a fishing derby?"

Aunt Carol was looking at her as if she was deranged, but as Josh caught up, he was pretty sure he appreciated the topic change. "No," he said. There might be a larger audience for their conversation, but he didn't have to pay any attention to it. "I've done some fishing, though. It's not quite as exciting as you might think."

She nodded encouragingly. "That sounds good. I'm not looking for excitement."

"Well, then, fishing's your sport." He winced as he cautiously rolled his shoulders.

She stepped a little closer and lowered her voice. "You're sure you're okay?"

Aunt Carol seemed to approve of the conversation finally returning to something relevant. "You should go to the hospital," she said firmly, her hands hovering over Josh's shoulders as if craving contact but afraid to cause pain. "And we should call the police."

"No police," Josh said. He looked at Ashley, the embarrassment back as he said, "I deserved it."

Aunt Carol's mouth twitched in frustration. "No, you didn't. His wife, she made her own decisions. If he's not going to take a golf club to her . . ." She caught herself. "Well, of course he shouldn't hit his wife! But—"

"It's okay, Aunt Carol." The crowd was starting to fade away and he wanted the whole thing to go away with them. "I'm fine. It's The Splash—shit happens."

Aunt Carol had her mouth open to respond.

Ashley stepped in close so only Aunt Carol and Josh could hear her as she said, "I didn't really want to come to this in the first place. I've been feeling like a third wheel since we left the cottage. If you're planning to stick around, that's great, I can do my thing, but if you were planning on leaving, and if there was any chance you'd want some company? You'd be helping me out if the company could be me."

He knew what she was doing, but he'd be damned if he could make himself care. "Yeah, okay. We could head out, if you want."

"I'd like that." She dodged around him, practically herding him toward the exit, and he pretended not to see her as she mouthed *I'll watch him* at Aunt Carol as she moved. Aunt Carol nodded cautious approval. Josh was making his escape.

They stopped briefly by Kevin and Charlotte as they left, Kevin squinting at Josh while Charlotte assessed Ashley, and then they were free.

"I think people who enter fishing derbies should also drive pickup trucks," Ashley said as they reached the parking lot. She held her hand out for the keys.

"You're pushing it," Josh warned. But she'd helped him escape, so he dug in his pocket and handed over the keys.

"So, that was The Splash," she mused as she carefully drove over the potholes of the makeshift parking lot.

"A bit dull this year," he said. "Usually there's some pretty good drama."

She laughed, a low, easy sound he was sure he'd be happy to hear on a constant loop for the rest of his life, and he closed his eyes and let himself dream, for just a moment, of a world where something like that would be possible.

❧ Fourteen ❧

THERE HAD STILL been a little twilight at the lake, but by the time they reached the cabin it was full dark. Daisy the Demon Dog came roaring out toward the pickup, only briefly illuminated by the headlights, and Josh watched Ashley sit up straighter, peering around to try to be sure she didn't run over the animal. "She's smart about cars," he said. "Don't worry."

Ashley relaxed and pulled the truck into its usual spot by the cabin door. "Thanks for letting me drive. It was fun."

"Almost as fun as fishing is going to be." He pushed the door open and swung his legs around, his muscles protesting the movement. They'd seized up a little during the ride in from town, and he didn't want to think what they were going to feel like in the morning. Daisy danced over to greet him and he inhaled and then stared at her. "Holy Christ, Daisy, what the hell did you roll in?"

Daisy tossed her head and danced a little more, clearly thrilled with her new perfume. Ashley came around the bed of the truck and took a cautious sniff. "Oh my God," she said, her hand flying up to cover her nose. "What *is* that?"

"I don't . . . It's like . . . It's got some skunkiness, but . . . Daisy, did you roll in a dead skunk?"

Daisy didn't answer, and Josh couldn't blame her. The stench spoke for itself.

He groaned as he turned to Ashley. "Thanks for driving me out here. If you want to take the truck to the cottage—"

"Your aunt would kick my ass if I left you out here on your own."

Well, that was true enough, but Josh could clearly remember Ashley's attitude the last time they'd been together, on the dock, and there was no way seeing the wronged husband appear would have made her less disgusted with his behavior. "She doesn't have to know."

But Ashley shoved the truck keys into her purse and looked down at Daisy. "She gets a bath? You're not going to enjoy that, with your bruises and all."

No, he wasn't. But he deserved the punishment, and Ashley sure didn't. "I'll be okay."

"I think people who enter fishing derbies and drive pickups are pretty good at washing dogs," she said.

"You haven't actually entered a derby yet, have you?"

"There isn't a rigid chronological order to my achievements," she said archly. "Now that I've mastered pickup driving, I can work on dog washing. I'll move on to fishing later." She was pretty good at smiling while still looking like she wasn't going to take any of his crap. "So, do you have special dog soap or do you just use shampoo or something?"

"Horse shampoo," he admitted. "And I've got baking soda and peroxide, in case that *is* skunk." He was an asshole for letting her do this, but damn it, he hurt, and he didn't want her to leave. "She likes baths. I can do most of it. But yeah, if you don't have anything better to do . . ."

"It sounds like a good time," she assured him.

He let himself go with it. Every step to the barn hurt, mostly his leg but his shoulder as well, and he really didn't think his right hand was going to be much good at scrubbing a squirming dog. "I could have just locked her outside for the night," he said apologetically. "But she's used to sleeping inside. She would have barked. . . ."

"No problem." Ashley followed his gesture toward the trunk where he kept the shampoo, then called the excited dog out to the hose in the stable yard. "A *bath*!" she exclaimed in an excited voice, and Daisy jumped up in the air, clearly anticipating the fun. Ashley looked at Josh. "Aren't dogs supposed to hate baths?"

"Daisy's defiant," he said. "If she's supposed to do something, she does the opposite." He stood and watched as Ashley figured it all out. She squirted shampoo onto the dry dog, realized it wouldn't foam without water, and then used the hose to soak the dog, washing most of the shampoo away in the process. "Harder than it looks," she said with a grin in Josh's direction. "But it's good. I've got this."

"I can—"

"You can stay still," she replied, aiming the hose at him in a threatening manner. "This is my life experience. You can go get your own!"

So she sudsed and scrubbed and rinsed and added baking soda and peroxide and laughed, and Daisy shook herself and then came back for more, and Josh stood and watched, trying to ignore the ache in his chest that had nothing to do with a damn golf club. When Daisy was finally rinsed clean and Ashley's sniff test confirmed that bath time was over, Josh stepped a little closer and said, "Thank you. Really. That would have been pretty rough for me to do."

"And it was pretty fun for me to do. What's next?"

"What?"

"Are you just going inside? Do you want me to—you had dinner at The Splash, right? What else do you need done?"

"I'm good. I just have to see to the horses—"

"I can do that."

He squinted at her. "Do you even know what it means?"

"They live outside, right? So I assume you feed them? They have that big water trough, I guess you check that it's full. And then you . . . sing them to sleep?"

"Yes. Exactly. All of that. They like eighties rock ballads."

"Well, they're in luck, 'cause I like eighties rock ballads, too!"

She started humming as she headed around the side of the barn toward the horses. She looked back over her shoulder. "You coming? Or should I just throw some hay at them and hope for the best?"

"I'm coming," he said, and he pushed away from the wall that had been offering him much-needed support. There was no way he was letting her out of his sight, not for as long as he could manage.

He followed Ashley around the corner of the barn and showed her how to put just a little sweet feed in a bucket and then rattle it around until the horses came for a snack. "They don't actually need the feed," he explained. "They don't work that hard, and they're all good keepers. But I like to check on them every night, and this brings them in so I can do it."

"And 'check on them' means . . . ?"

"Just watch them move," he said, and he eased in behind her so they'd both have the same view. "In the morning, when it's light, I can check for scratches or whatever, but at night, as long as they're moving smoothly, I figure they're okay."

He crouched down to bring his eyes closer to the same level as Ashley's, both of them still staring out at the horses.

"See the way Rocky's ears are moving? It's just a silhouette, but it's all you need to see. Those are relaxed, curious ears; they belong to a healthy horse."

"Okay," she said. That was all, just one word, but there was a breathiness to it, a quality that was the complete opposite of the practical tone she'd used while washing the dog. He realized how close they were standing, how his breath must be tickling her cheek, and he let himself inhale, just gently, just enough to get a scent of her skin after a day in the sun.

"Josh," she whispered, and she turned slowly toward him.

It was natural. Inevitable. She stretched up and he leaned down, and their lips met, just a light brush of skin. It could have passed for a casual greeting if either of them could breathe properly, or if either had pulled away. Instead, they stayed there like that, for several moments too long, and then just as Ashley swayed one hairsbreadth closer, he pulled away. All the doubts, all the certainties about why this was a bad idea washed back over him even though he had new ideas now. There had been so many times when this woman had been more than what he'd expected, but . . . it was too much. His brain was spinning and he didn't want to make a mistake, so he pulled away.

"I should get some sleep," he said gruffly. "Rough day. You can drive the truck back to the lake, if you want; I can get Kevin to pick me up tomorrow."

Her nod was shaky. "Right," she said, sounding as if she wasn't at all sure. "Okay. Yeah."

So they finished up with the horses and walked back to the house, and Josh handed Ashley the truck keys and walked her outside. He needed some time to cool off and think about all this, he was pretty sure.

She climbed behind the wheel and he headed inside. He was going to go to bed and get some sleep. And maybe things would make a bit more sense in the morning.

*   *   *

ASHLEY sat behind the wheel of the truck, not moving. She didn't even have the ignition turned on. She just kept replaying the kiss over and over in her mind, wondering what it might mean, and what it meant that he'd pulled away, and what might have happened if he hadn't.

She saw the lights turn off in the house and imagined Josh laying his head down on the pillow. What did he wear to bed? Did he sleep on his back or his side? If she were in bed with him, would they snuggle or give each other space?

She was still daydreaming about it when she saw the headlights shining through the trees. A moment later she heard the purr of the approaching car's engine through her lowered window.

Daisy bounded off the porch, growling fiercely as the familiar car pulled up in front of the cabin and the engine shut off, and the dog's objections got a little louder and angrier as Jasmine stepped out of the driver's side.

Ashley was out of the truck and heading for the car before she gave it any thought. "He's asleep," she said. "You should leave him alone."

"He's okay?" For the first time since Ashley had known her, Jasmine looked almost frazzled. "I didn't . . . honestly, Ashley, I didn't mean for this to happen. There was some reporter sniffing around, trying to get an update on you after the breakup with Derek. He asked around, heard about Josh, and then I guess he heard about me. And the son-of-a-bitch went running to David with the news." Jasmine seemed dazed, but almost pleased as she added, "I honestly thought David already knew. I thought he just didn't care."

"He seemed to care," Ashley said. She knew this was none of her business and she knew it was dangerous to her career to get involved, but she couldn't keep from adding,

"Josh has moved on. Whatever you guys had, you need to let it go."

Jasmine fought to control her expression, and she won, coming up with a calm, almost haughty face as she said, "He's moved on to you?"

"Probably not," Ashley admitted. One kiss didn't cancel out all the rejections. "I think I managed to screw that up. You helped a bit, if that makes you feel any better."

Jasmine somehow made her snort sound sophisticated and ladylike. "No. It doesn't, really." She was quiet for too long, looking at the stars, the dog, anything but Ashley, and then she finally whispered, "Does he hate me?"

Ashley knew what she was supposed to say, but instead she told the truth. "I have no idea." The expression on Jasmine's face made her add, "If he does, it's not because of tonight. Tonight was . . . He said he deserved it. And even if he didn't, that was David, not you."

Jasmine nodded slowly. "And he's really okay?"

"He'll be fine." Ashley stepped a little closer. "But, Jasmine? He's done his penance, okay? This has to be over."

Jasmine nodded slowly. She looked up at the stars again, took a deep breath as if gathering strength, and then said, "David will fire him, of course. And some of our friends probably will, too. I don't think there's anything I can do about that. I need to focus on my marriage, and fighting for the financial security of my ex-lover will not help me with that."

Ashley nodded. "I assume he's figured that out for himself."

"I'm sure he has." Jasmine straightened then, and looked down at Daisy standing by Ashley's side, still growling. "That damn dog never liked me."

"You should have given her a bath."

Jasmine raised an eyebrow at the absurdity of that suggestion and just like that they were back to where they'd been before the visit.

Well, not *quite* where they'd been, Ashley mused as she watched Jasmine's taillights disappear into the forest. That one brief moment of connection, of humanity—that would be what Ashley would try to remember when she thought about Jasmine.

She headed back to the porch and looked down at Daisy. "There's a guest room, right? I could sleep in there. Would that be okay with you? It just doesn't feel right to leave."

Daisy wagged her tail in cheerful agreement and followed Ashley into the house.

JOSH woke up disoriented. Where the hell was he, why did he hurt so much, and what was that smell? In his own bedroom, he realized, but on the wrong side of the bed. A small difference, but apparently enough to throw him off. And he hurt because . . . Oh. Yeah. He hurt because David McArthur had clearly *not* known about his wife's affair before, but obviously did now. But that was something to be depressed about later, because the smell . . . He sniffed carefully, then rolled off the bed onto his feet. He was still wearing his jeans and T-shirt from the day before, but he was barefoot. The smell was coffee. And maybe bacon. And was there something sweet mixed in with it all? Something that smelled like baking?

He staggered into the bathroom, tried not to look toward the mirror as he peed, then washed his hands and splashed some water onto his face. All his bruises were beneath his clothes, except for the wide black-and-blue stripe on his right palm. He flexed his fingers carefully; it hurt, but everything was functioning.

He made his way to the kitchen and stood in the doorway, bemused. Ashley was there, and she was cooking. It was a bit hard to understand, but somehow it felt right. Well, it felt right that she was there, but it felt wrong that she was doing all the work. "Can I help?" he asked, and Ashley jumped in surprise and whirled around, spatula raised in an aggressive manner. He grinned at her. "You going to flip me to death?"

"If I had to, I would," she responded once she'd collected herself. She pointed the spatula at him and said, "A woman who can drive a pickup and wash a dog and who's planning to enter a fishing derby can absolutely flip a man into submission."

"Damn, somehow you're making it all sound kind of sexy."

She grinned at him and waggled the spatula a little. "There's coffee. And I've got bacon frying, and cinnamon buns in the oven, and we can have eggs, too. And toast."

He raised an eyebrow. "I didn't even know I had ingredients for cinnamon buns. And is that a movie-star-approved breakfast?"

"That's my breakfast calories for the week, at least," she admitted. "I'm splurging."

He wanted to ask what the occasion was but somehow that felt like he'd be pushing too far. So he shuffled to the counter and poured a coffee, then lowered himself into a kitchen chair and watched her as she worked. Daisy trotted over and laid her head on his knee, inviting an ear scratch, and he frowned down at her. "What happened to you last night?" he asked, but he was pretty sure that he already knew. He glanced over at Ashley and caught her hiding a guilty smile. "Did you sleep with my dog, Ashley? Did you seduce her with your sudsy, watery fun and then drag her into bed with you?"

"Oh, there was no dragging," Ashley retorted. "That bitch was begging to get into my bed."

He wanted to kiss her. He wanted to wrap himself around her and not let go, not for a long, long time. He knew his bruised body wouldn't appreciate it, but he was pretty sure the pleasure would be worth the pain. If he could taste this woman, if he could claim her, even if it was just for a little while . . . that would be worth a lot of pressed bruises. And maybe even worth the bruised heart he was sure to suffer later on.

But Ashley was still working on breakfast and he didn't make a move, just sat there and rubbed the dog's ears with his unbruised hand. Eventually Ashley said, "I think that was the first time I've heard you say my name. Just then, when you accused me of seducing Daisy. I don't think I've ever heard you say it before."

He thought for a moment. "Did I mispronounce it or something? I mean, there can't be that many ways to say 'Ashley.'"

"No," she said slowly. "You said it just right." She was pulling the bacon out of the pan and mopping the fat off it with paper towels, and she kept her eyes on her task as she added, "I liked hearing it. From you. I liked the way it sounded."

He wasn't sure how far he could push his luck. "So you're not mad at me anymore?" Her quizzical look made him say, "The other morning. On the dock? You were mad at me, right?"

But she shook her head. "Not really."

"You said I was trying to get revenge on people and I got my kicks out of shooting you down."

She looked at him as if he were speaking another language, then nodded slowly as her words came back to her. "Yeah. Okay. I was a little mad at you. But I got over it." She stepped away from the counter, just a little closer to him, and he felt the hairs on his arms rise and strain toward her. "Even before last night, I was over it. I want . . ." She frowned. "I was going to say that I want the same thing I always wanted. I'm pretty sure I was going to paraphrase *Pride and Prejudice*, that scene where Darcy tells Elizabeth that his 'affections and wishes are unchanged.'" She looked at him and clearly realized he had no idea what she was talking about. "Okay, you should read that book, or at least watch the movie! But the thing is, I'm pretty sure my affections and wishes *have* changed. I think. . . ." She sighed and half turned as if the bacon was calling her, then turned back to him. "I think you were mostly right. About me treating you like a . . . I don't know. A prize. I played games, and I stopped thinking about you as a person with your own life and started treating you like a—like a satellite, or something."

She trailed off and stared at him, waiting for a response, and he said the only coherent thing that came into his head. "I don't really understand the satellite part."

"You should talk to Charlotte about that," she replied. "But the point is, I don't think I feel that way anymore. Spending time with you, even with you trying to get away from me through it all, and fighting with you on the dock and worrying about you last night . . . you're real to me, Josh. A real person, someone I value, someone I care about. You're not a prize anymore. You're you, and I'm me, just like that first night at the bar, and the morning after on the dock. And I really think that if we could just keep it that way—" She broke off and frowned at him. "What?" she demanded, clearly not pleased with his expression.

He had no idea what his face looked like. Which probably meant he needed to use words. He felt like he'd already used up more words on this woman than on anyone else in his life, ever, but if she wanted more he'd try to find them. "Okay," he said. And when she was clearly waiting for more, he added, "We should try that. It sounds good. Being real, and being just us. That sounds good."

"Even though I'm a summer person?"

"Summer people don't drive my truck," he said. "They don't feed my horses or plan to enter fishing derbies. And they sure as hell don't wash my dog."

"So I had to prove myself to you?" she asked, and he could see her starting to get irritated again.

"No," he said. But again, she was waiting for more. Damn it. "What were those lines? From the book, or the movie, or whatever? My affections and wishes . . . yeah, they're unchanged. I wanted you that night in the bar, and I've wanted you ever since." Scary to say it, but even scarier to not say it and maybe see her walk away. "I managed to keep a lid on it for a while, but the lid's off now. You didn't have to prove anything. I came to see you on the dock, remember? Before any of this happened?"

"You did," she agreed thoughtfully. She turned back to the bacon, then reached over and turned off the oven before asking, "How sore are you?"

"Pretty sore," he admitted, and then his addled brain realized why she might be asking. "But not that bad. Bruised, not broken."

She nodded, then waited. He took his time. If this was really happening, after all the false starts and stupidity, all the angst and doubt, then he wanted to make sure it was something he'd remember. Something *she'd* remember, but he couldn't think too much about that without getting nervous. So he focused on himself. He stood up, trying to ignore the complaints from his bruises, and stepped slowly toward her. She turned so she was facing him full-on, and he raised his hand and let his fingertips hover over the smooth skin of her face. Finally, slowly, he brought his hand down until he saw her eyes jump at the first touch, the touch that sent a small shockwave through his whole body. And that was just from his fingertips on her temple.

He let his hand relax until the palm cupped her face, his thumb skimming along her cheekbone and then down to trace the outline of her lips. No makeup, just her own beauty shining out at him. Her eyes were big and round, her lips soft before they quirked into an encouraging smile.

He smiled back at her. How could he not? But they both grew more serious as he lowered his head and she raised

hers, and when their lips finally met it felt like a new beginning, as if all the misunderstandings and confusion were
washed away by the sincerity of this connection.

He pulled away before anything could happen that would
ruin things, and she didn't try to follow him. She just stood
still, then slowly licked her lips and smiled at him, as if she'd
tasted him and found him delicious.

"We should eat some breakfast," he made himself say.
"You made a feast."

"If you like carbs and fat . . ."

"I do like carbs and fat," he said sincerely.

She nodded. "So do I. On special occasions." Then she
smiled at him and turned around, reaching for the plates to
serve their first breakfast together.

❧ *Fifteen* ❧

EVERYTHING SEEMED BRIGHTER. Better. The bacon was saltier, the cinnamon rolls sweeter, the coffee more invigorating and aromatic. And Josh himself? Clearly the sweetest, handsomest man on the planet. His smiles turned her insides to mush, his gentlest, most casual touch made her ache for more contact. She knew she was being silly about most of it, but she had the sneaking suspicion that her reaction to Josh was going to be a little more permanent.

They ate their breakfast with goofy smiles and a fair bit of unnecessary touching, and Ashley was torn between wanting to jump on Josh and drag him to the bedroom and wanting to stretch the perfection out as long as possible. When they were done eating, Josh said he'd do the dishes. Ashley challenged him to hold a plate in the hand bruised by David's golf club, and he almost growled at her and then looked so abashed she wanted to wrap him in blankets and snuggle him forever. "I'm not establishing a pattern of behavior," she said. "I'm not always going to cook and clean up. But when you're not at your best? I can do it. Okay?"

He looked like he wanted to argue, but finally sank back in his chair and let her work. Then she insisted on them going to check on the horses, and they were just coming back from the barn when Charlotte's convertible appeared in the driveway, Kevin again relegated to the back as his mother rode shotgun. Ashley felt Josh groan beside her and she realized that he was letting her in, letting her understand his reluctance, because in his mind she was finally on his side, and it was the two of them together facing whatever challenges might come.

As it was, the challenge wasn't too serious. Aunt Carol fussed a little, Charlotte and Kevin smirked, and Josh tried his best to change the subject away from himself and any health concerns he might be experiencing.

They ended up all sitting on the front porch as the day heated up. They would have been more comfortable, objectively, at Ashley's cottage, with the cool breeze coming off the lake, and the wider porch and more abundant seating. At the cabin, Josh ended up on the wood floor, leaning his bruised body back against the post at the top of the short flight of stairs, because all the other seats were taken.

But Ashley knew better than to suggest a change of venue. This was Josh's home, and he relaxed here in a way he never had at the lake house. He still didn't say much, but he listened to the conversation and interjected occasionally, and his smiles came easy and often. He was home, and Ashley was welcome. She wasn't going to push for more.

JOSH was content. He knew it was just temporary, but he didn't care; he was going to enjoy it while he could. And everything got a little bit better when Ashley squeezed past Kevin's long legs and crossed the porch to settle onto the floor next to Josh. She was just in front of him, and there was a question in her eyes. He knew what she was asking. If they'd been alone, it would have felt totally natural to pull her in next to him, finding a nest for her in the space between his legs, her back leaning against his chest, her head resting against his shoulder. It would have been perfect.

But they weren't alone. Kevin and Charlotte and Aunt Carol were pretending to be absorbed by their conversation, but they weren't blind. If Josh and Ashley . . . if they *cuddled*, out there on the porch in front of everybody, that was a declaration of sorts. An admission. Josh didn't think he could touch Ashley without being tender, and if everyone saw that, it would make it a hell of a lot harder for him to pretend he wasn't hurting after she left. Kevin and Aunt Carol were family. They might tease, but for something like this? Something bigger? They probably wouldn't. They'd probably sympathize, and that would be even worse.

Josh knew better, but apparently his body didn't agree with his brain, because he let his legs relax a little, let his eyes answer Ashley's question in the affirmative. Then he didn't have to pull her in because she was moving on her own, scooting over and nestling and burrowing and nudging until her Josh-shaped backrest was molded to her satisfaction.

It was like being back in high school and holding hands in public for the first time. A simple action, but with so many consequences. And Josh's stomach was dancing the same way it had back then, a mix of dread and excitement and, of course, a good helping of lust. He was letting this happen. Later, maybe he'd actually *make* it happen. And now everybody, everybody who mattered, knew he cared.

"Oh my God," Ashley whispered to him. "Relax! I feel like I'm leaning against a brick wall!"

Relax. Because for her this wasn't a big deal. She wasn't declaring herself in front of her family. She was just trying to find a comfortable place to sit.

Josh winced and forced his body to comply with her orders. His muscles relaxed, and after a short battle his brain surrendered as well. It was too late to worry about it, so he might as well enjoy. He let himself smell her hair, and savor the way her skin felt against his hands, and appreciate how warm she was, how flexible and pliant and strong. He was holding her, and as scary as it was, it felt right. So he focused on that, and went back to ignoring the conversation the others were having.

He didn't realize his eyes had closed until he was startled by a gentle touch on his cheek. He opened his eyes and saw Ashley twisted around and frowning at him. "You okay?" she asked. "Were you asleep? You're looking kind of grey."

"I figured I'd be looking black and blue."

"The parts of you that show are grey. You probably didn't sleep well last night if you couldn't get comfortable."

"I'm fine," he said.

"You should go lie down."

"Come with me." He surprised himself with the words, grateful that he'd at least said them quietly, and even more grateful that she didn't seem offended by them.

"You need to sleep," she said with a smile.

"A nap, maybe. But when we wake up . . ."

Aunt Carol's voice broke into their little flirtation. "Okay, then, let's go." There was an uncomfortable moment before Josh realized she was talking to the whole group and referring to whatever she and the others had come up with. Maybe Josh had been asleep, because the conversation certainly seemed to have shifted at some point. "Josh, I'm assuming you're done with The Splash for the year? You don't want to come back in with us this afternoon?"

"Not really," he admitted. Then he looked down at Ashley. "But you should go. You didn't get to see that much yesterday. And you were interested in the fishing derby—the big measurements happen tonight."

"I don't think I want to see someone else derby-ing, not when I'm not doing it myself." She raised her head proudly. "The derby is not a spectator sport."

Kevin stood up then, Charlotte with him. "We came out in one car," he said, nodding to the parking area. He looked at Ashley with an annoying little smirk. "You want to hitch a ride home, or you going to babysit?"

"Babysit," she said, then turned to Josh. "If that's okay. If you can give me a ride back in later."

Hopefully by "later" she meant the next morning, but Josh figured he didn't need to press for a commitment on that, not quite yet. "Sure. Okay."

And that was it. Everything was taken care of. Aunt Carol frowned at Josh and said, "Take it easy today," and she sent a look in Ashley's direction that probably meant something in woman-ese, but was nothing Josh could interpret.

Then they all piled in the convertible and left, leaving Josh and Ashley standing on the porch, both of them suddenly a little shy. But Josh had waited too long to let them slip backward now. So he stepped forward and brought his hand to her cheek, gently angling her compliant face toward him. He leaned down for a short, sweet kiss, one that teased of more to come.

Ashley kissed him back, then slipped two fingers through his belt loops and tugged gently. "Come on. You said you'd have a nap. And the sooner you go to sleep, the sooner we can wake up."

He liked the sound of that, and followed her into the bedroom. This time instead of pushing him under the covers and abandoning him, she gave him another questioning look. He lifted the covers and let her spoon in next to him, then whispered, "For future reference . . . I'm on the wrong side. We'll need to switch, eventually."

"No. This is *my* side." She smiled and rolled over onto her back, edging her leg in between his so she could keep it straight while his stayed curved. His hand felt completely right, absolutely natural as it rested on the curve of her ribs, his thumb tickling in just under her breast. He supposed it was still bruised, but he really didn't notice. "Nonnegotiable," she said, and she stretched up to kiss him.

He managed to resist for about a second before the temptation of her lips was too much. "We could take turns," he suggested, and leaned down for the kiss.

"Maybe," she conceded, and she rolled back over onto her side, nestling her ass back into his crotch in a way that made it clear to him that he wasn't going to be winning many arguments with her, not if they took place horizontally. "Maybe I'll let you earn this side of the bed."

"I'm ready to start working," he started, but she shook her head and gripped his hand, bringing it up to nestle under her chin, his forearm tight against her soft breasts.

"We're sleeping," she said firmly, her face turned so he could see her profile. "You need some rest." Another tiny wriggle of her ass, combined with a grin that made it clear she knew exactly what she was doing, and then she added, "You'll need your strength. Absolutely."

❧ Sixteen ❧

BEING AT THE cabin was like being in another world. Ashley tried to fit the experience into the real/unreal pattern they'd been worrying about, but couldn't make it work. It was real, she was sure of that. The bugs buzzing outside the window screen, the heat of the morning promising a muggy afternoon with no air conditioning and no convenient lake or swimming pool for cooling off, the smell of the manure pile she'd noticed the night before when they'd gone down to visit the horses. That was all real.

But the way she felt? Like a fairy-tale princess who'd found her way to a hidden kingdom where no one could ever find her? There was no palace and no fancy gowns, but there were trusty steeds and a dog that may as well have been designed by Disney, with all her mock ferociousness and secret snuggling. Maybe Ashley hadn't slayed a dragon, but she'd tamed a demon dog, and surely that was something worth celebration.

Most of all, of course, there was Josh. She couldn't really fit him into her real or unreal classifications, either. The bruises on his body, and the reason he'd gotten them? Too real, and too tawdry for a fairy tale. But the warmth of his smile? It seemed unreal. The way her body reacted to his touch, her ears to his voice, her nose to his scent—it was too powerful, beyond anything she'd ever felt before.

He stirred, his arm tightening around her and then relaxing, and she cautiously turned her head, then rolled over onto her back, keeping his arm tucked under the side of her body that was farthest from him. He had to lean forward to let her move and ended up hovering over her, looking down with a bemused expression as if he wasn't sure how he felt about what she was trying to engineer. "I just dozed," she said confidently. "Not a deep sleep. No morning breath to worry about."

He moved his jaws and she could imagine his tongue roaming around his mouth, exploring and assessing. "You want me to go brush my teeth?"

"No. I want you to kiss me."

"You've got me all self-conscious now," he started, but she wrapped her hand around the back of his neck and pulled herself up until her mouth found his, and whatever shyness he'd been experiencing was gone as she slipped her tongue between his unresisting lips and tasted him for herself.

"Not bad at all," she decided. "You must take good care of your teeth."

"I floss every day," he said, and then he was kissing her again, pressing her down into the mattress as he shifted over on top of her. He had one leg between hers, taking most of his weight, and his arms carried a lot of the rest, but he was a big man and even a fraction of his weight was enough for her to notice. It made her feel not trapped, but safe. Cherished rather than imprisoned.

When his lips left her mouth, working their way along her jaw and down to her neck, her body arched involuntarily, pushing up into him, demanding more of whatever he had to give. She'd never been so inflamed by a kiss, and when he nibbled and kissed his way down to her breast, pushing her tank top down so he could suck her nipple through the thin fabric of her bra, she was pretty sure she was going to explode from just that sensation.

"Too many clothes," she gasped, and she felt wanton until he looked up at her and she saw his eyes, already dark with excitement and desire. He pulled off his shirt with the same casual ease he'd shown the other night at the pond, then reached down and slid his hands under her top with the care she'd expect of someone unwrapping a delicate treasure.

But she was too distracted by the unnatural colors on his side to pay much attention to his hands. "Oh, Josh," she whispered, trailing her fingers down over the bruises. She just ghosted over them, feeling his skin pebble and tighten beneath her touch. "We don't have to do anything. You must be really sore."

"I have no idea what you're talking about," he said firmly, then grinned at her before adding, "I feel good. Really, really good."

Well, she wasn't sure about that, but decided not to argue. Instead, she shoved him over onto his back and saw him wince as he landed but then smile encouragingly. "I'm good," he said again, and she threw a leg over his so she was straddling him. He looked up at her with frank, honest appreciation, and she rewarded him by pulling her tank top up and over her head, one tantalizing inch at a time. Tantalizing for him, but for her as well. She wanted to be naked, wanted him inside her, and wasn't quite sure why they were stretching it out. Surely there would be time for long, lazy mornings down the road? Couldn't their first time be fast and desperate?

She pulled her top the rest of the way off her head with a quick tug and reached behind her to unhook her bra. Josh caught her hands and held them still for a moment, and she tried to read his thoughts. He wanted it slow, she realized. And then he released her hands and she knew that he was giving in. He'd give her what she wanted, do things her way, even though he wanted something else.

"You think this is a one-time deal," she said as the thought came to her. "You want to make it last because we may not do it again."

He looked away from her, focusing on some spot on the ceiling, and sighed. "It's an uncertain world. That's all."

"No, that's *not* all!" She lifted her hips up and shifted her weight forward so she could push down on his shoulders, pinning him with all her might. She knew he could still get up if he tried, but at least she'd make it crystal clear that she wanted him to stay put. "What the hell, Josh? You still think I'm being casual about this?"

"You're not the only person involved, you know. Maybe I'll decide it's not worth the trouble."

"Bullshit. I mean, if this was a wham-bam-thank-you-ma'am quick fuck, fair enough, maybe you would. But taking it slow? Treating it like it's a . . . like a holy ritual or something? No, that's not because you think it might not be worth the trouble."

"Depends how you define trouble, I guess."

Well, that was cryptic. And he didn't seem inclined to explain himself, either. "I'm here, Josh," she said quietly. "I'm right here."

He looked at her and slowly nodded. "Yeah. You are."

Then he twisted around and kissed her, and he wasn't taking his time anymore. His lips were hard and demanding, his tongue twining around hers ferociously. He pulled her to him and when she tried to brace herself so she wouldn't crush his bruises he tugged her in tighter. Her bra disappeared like magic and they were skin to skin, their chests heaving as they both gasped for air between kisses. He flipped them over and peeled her underwear away at the same time he tugged off her jeans, and this was what she'd wanted. Hard and fast, all desire and desperation. He shuffled to the side just long enough to drop his own jeans and underwear and grab a foil packet out of the nightstand.

This was what she'd wanted, but now she wanted to slow it down. Oh, not because her body wasn't ready. She was wet and aching for him. But he was so beautiful, so raw and naturally perfect, and she wanted to stare at him and memorize him. But then he was touching her again, his mouth hot as it travelled down her body, and she decided she could stare at him some other time. Maybe when he was asleep. Sometime when his mouth wasn't . . . Oh. When his mouth wasn't being put to such good use.

She let herself get lost in the sensations. The warmth of his tongue and his lips, the scratch of his stubble against her thighs, and then his strong fingers slipping inside her, finding the perfect spot so he was tantalizing her from inside and out. She could feel her climax building and tried to hold it off so she could enjoy it all just a little bit longer, but there was no denying his insistent mouth. She let herself go with a ragged cry, arching into him, finding him strong and gentle as he worked her through.

He kissed his way back up her body and smiled when he reached her mouth. "You'd better stick around for a while, because I want to be able to do that a lot more times."

She grinned at him and said, "I wouldn't argue," before kissing him.

SHE was so beautiful. Inside and out, body and soul, she was strong and beautiful and perfect. He had no idea how the universe had allowed him to spend even this tiny moment with her, but he was past the stage where he was asking any questions.

He was pretty much past the point of thinking coherently about anything. He had enough presence of mind to find the condom, and she mercifully took care of rolling it onto him, and that was it. His brain shut off, leaving his body to do what it wanted. She moaned and lifted to meet his first thrust and he rocked back so he was sitting on his heels, dragging her warm, responsive body with him. Without his weight on her she was free to move however she wanted, and he soon found the angle that had her writhing and gasping, her pleasure almost more significant than his own as he worked toward his climax. So beautiful, so lithe, so uninhibited and natural. She hooked her heels around his back and pulled him in harder and faster, and he added "greedy" to his list of her perfections.

He knew he should take his mind away, start thinking about sports scores or math problems or ways to fight mold in damp basements, but he couldn't make himself do it. He couldn't think of anything but her, and if that meant he wouldn't last as long as he should, it could be one more item to add to his long list of flaws. "Come on, Ash," he urged, although he wasn't quite sure what it was he wanted her to do. "Come on, come on." His brain wasn't working, he had no control over his mouth and very little over the rest of his body. All he could do was move, drive into her warmth, feel her rising to meet him, and finally, blessedly, feel her shudder and clench around him as she threw her head back and found her release. He followed her, chased her, and finally joined her in a warm, spent tangle of sweaty limbs and smiling mouths.

"I want to do all of that again," Ashley said, burrowing her face into Josh's neck.

"Not . . . not immediately, right?" He could feel her lips curve into a smile.

"As soon as possible," she whispered, and she kissed him, then nipped a little along his collarbone.

He grinned at her and let his head flop back onto the pillow, ignoring the complaints from his bruises. He wasn't going to think about the end of things, not while he was still having so much fun with the beginning.

❧ Seventeen ❧

THEY STAYED IN bed all day. Well, there were brief excursions to the kitchen for food, and to the bathroom for a shared shower, and finally down to the barn to check on the horses before it got dark.

They'd just returned from that trip when the phone rang. Josh looked at it reluctantly, then sighed and reached for the handset.

"If it's bad news," Ashley said, "hang up on them."

He grinned at her, then listened to the caller and frowned. "Wait a second," he said, and put his hand over the mouthpiece. "Someone named Adam Wagner. Says he's your manager? He says it's important that he talk to you, and Charlotte told him where to find you."

Ashley made a face. She didn't want to talk to her manager. She didn't want to think about her manager, or her career, or anything other than the gorgeous man standing in front of her, holding the phone out with a questioning look on his face.

"Want me to take a message?"

"No," Ashley said reluctantly. Adam really had seemed to understand that she needed some time to recharge, and Charlotte certainly wouldn't be giving Josh's number to anyone if there wasn't an excellent reason for it. So she reached out, took the phone from Josh, then lifted it and said, "Adam. Hi. What's up?"

"How's your vacation going, Ashley? Making new friends?" The question was too pointed to be casual.

"Why do you ask?" she said carefully.

"I just got a call from TMZ—the same parasites who broke the news about Derek's little friend. Apparently they've got some new photos."

"Of Derek?" Ashley asked. But the tightness in her stomach wasn't fooled by her attempted optimism.

"No, Ashley, not of Derek. They've got shots of David McArthur going after some guy with a golf club. And they've got you leaving the place with the beat-up guy, maybe driving his truck?" Adam paused to let her catch up, then added, "And of course they got the backstory from whoever sold them the pictures. I think they're just going with a lot of 'rumored' and 'alleged' right now, but they'll be looking for confirmation."

Ashley wanted to hang up the phone and pretend it wasn't happening. She wanted to go back to bed with Josh and forget all about L.A. and gossip websites and anyone named McArthur. But she was supposed to be a responsible adult, so she said, "It's not that bad, is it? I mean . . ." She frowned. It wasn't that bad for her. So she was involved with someone who used to be involved with Jasmine McArthur. Not a big deal. But for Josh? She tried not to look at him as she asked, "Is the story already out? Already posted?"

"Not the last time I checked. But it'll be a matter of minutes, probably. They were ready to go when they called me for your comment."

"I don't think I want to comment, do I?"

"I told them you were on vacation and unreachable."

"Good. Thanks." She was vaguely aware of Josh, putter-ing around in the kitchen, unaware that his indiscretions were about to be splashed all over the Internet. She stepped out onto the porch and whispered, "There's no way to stop it, is there? I mean . . . if I gave them something else? It's not that big of a story. Just a little bit of gossip for them. But for people up here . . ."

"What else do you have to give? They don't want in-depth stories or interviews or anything, Ashley. And even if they did, it would hurt your career if you were seen to be working with them."

"My career can take care of itself."

"You think that's how it works, do you?"

She sighed. "I know you do a lot, Adam. I know you work hard. I just don't want an innocent person dragged into our stupid celebrity bullshit."

"Well, based on the stories I heard, I don't know that 'innocent' is the right word."

"Private," Ashley said fiercely. "A *private* person, not someone working in the industry and playing the game. There must be something we can do."

There was a long pause, and then Adam said, "I'm sorry, Ash. I just hit refresh, and the post is there. Several pictures, and enough text to make the reason for the attack clear."

"This is my fault," she said softly. "Isn't it? If it was just the McArthurs . . . Jasmine used to act, but she's been out of the spotlight for a decade at least. And he's a producer. Hollywood people care about him, but the people who read that site? They'd barely recognize him. This got publicized because of me. Right?"

Adam didn't answer right away, but finally said, "Prob-ably. Yeah. You know the game, Ash."

She did. She didn't only know the game, she played it,

using the media to keep her face in front of moviegoers and build publicity for her projects. This little invasion was nothing to her, but she was pretty sure it was going to be something big for Josh.

She hung up the phone and wandered back into the house. Josh was standing at the kitchen counter, cutting a ripe tomato, but he turned and faced her when she arrived. "Everything okay?"

She knew she had to tell him, but she didn't want to do it yet. She wanted to keep things simple and happy for just a little bit longer, long enough to convince him she was worth all the trouble she was going to cause. "Just work stuff."

"All the stuff you were trying to get away from when you came up here," he said sympathetically.

He was right. She'd wanted a vacation from all this. Needed a vacation. But he was wrong, too. "I wasn't running away. I mean, I wanted a break, but I love my job. The acting part of it, at least. Getting to be so many different people, exploring so many different lives. I really do love the acting. All the rest of it . . . you were right, that night in the bar, that putting up with assholes shouldn't be part of anyone's job. But it's kind of part of mine, and that's what I needed a break from. But mostly, I was running *to* somewhere. I mean, maybe I was looking for an escape when I first came, but I stayed because I love it here."

He nodded as if he appreciated her words. "You should get a job with the tourism department."

"Oh yeah? Any perks with that job? Maybe a visit from a representative of the Vermont hospitality commission?"

"I don't think that's a real thing," he said with a smile.

"Oh. How disappointing." This was more like it. Much better to stay in the moment and enjoy herself with Josh than to worry about things she couldn't control. "I guess private citizens need to step in and fill a gap like that, huh? Everyone has to do their part to make the tourists feel welcome?"

"There's so many different ways to make 'fill a gap' sound dirty, I don't think I can pick just one of them." He stepped forward and stretched his arms around her, resting both of his hands at the small of her back. "But I'm definitely willing to do my part."

His hands slipped lower, cradling her ass and lifting her like she weighed nothing, and she wrapped her legs around him and held on tight. "Take me to bed and show me your natural wonders," she ordered.

"I'll make you see stars," he promised, and he carried her to the bedroom.

MORNING came. Josh woke around dawn and lay there watching Ashley sleep as the room grew brighter and brighter. He shifted his body to shade her eyes from the direct rays of the sun so she wouldn't be wakened. He was only delaying the inevitable, but that was hardly a new behavior for him.

When she finally stirred, he watched her wake up, saw her disorientation, saw her remember where she was and who she was with, and saw her smile.

It made it all worthwhile. Right there, right then, she was happy to be with him. She didn't care that the cabin was small and a bit ragged, didn't care that he was battered and bruised. She was happy.

"I'll get coffee," he whispered, and slipped out of bed before she could protest. It was stupid, he knew, but he needed a moment on his own, a bit of time to process and appreciate the wonder of having her in his bed. So he pulled on a pair of sweatpants that he'd been wearing the day before and headed to the kitchen. When he'd made the coffee and fixed her mug the way she liked it he returned to the bedroom and she was sitting up, wearing his T-shirt, her hair messy and perfect.

She smiled at him. "I don't know if I want coffee," she said quietly. "It'll wake me up, and I don't think I want to wake up."

"You can sleep more." He thought about it. Maybe he could crawl back into bed with her. Sure, he had work to do, lots of it, but this was absolutely a special occasion. Maybe he could tell himself he was still too sore to do any work. None of the houses he looked after were actually on fire or anything, and if the McArthurs carried through on their threats, his list of projects was probably about to get a lot shorter.

"No," she said resolutely, reaching for the mug. "I need to get in gear. Charlotte's going back to L.A. later this week and we want to get some more work done on the script before she goes. And . . . I need to talk to you about something."

He didn't want to hear the last part of that. Didn't want to wonder what she needed to talk about. So he said, "Charlotte's going back? Does Kevin know?"

Ashley shrugged. "I guess so. Probably. I don't think it's a secret."

Not a secret. Just not a big deal. Charlotte was leaving. No drama, no need for alarm. Her real life was calling, so obviously she had to respond. He made his voice level when he asked, "What do you want for breakfast?"

"After yesterday's feast? I guess just coffee." She didn't sound regretful, just matter-of-fact. "I don't know what body type they're looking for on the Western, but I figure I'd better go in at my fighting weight, and they can always tell me to gain if they want. If I go in fat, they might assume I'm undisciplined."

He nodded again. He didn't know a thing about Hollywood expectations, but obviously she did, and she had a plan for how to meet them. She'd been with him for one day and was already starting to work her way back home. He wasn't surprised, exactly. But he'd hoped he'd have a little longer.

"I'm going to shower," he said. "If you change your mind

and want some fruit or something, help yourself to whatever's in the kitchen."

She smiled at him and stretched languorously, but he made himself look away from the way her breasts arched against the thin fabric of his shirt. Then he let himself look back. One more memory to torture himself with after it was all over. But she saw him watching, grinned wickedly, and looked down at herself. "Oh, this is your shirt, isn't it? I should return it . . . or maybe you should come get it."

Damn it. His feet were moving before his brain even kicked into gear, but who was he kidding? His brain wasn't going to get in the way of this, not anymore. He crawled up the bed, bracketing her quilt-covered body with his arms and legs. His senses seemed enhanced and he could smell not only her coffee but the sweet sugar in it; not only her natural fragrance but the scent of her growing excitement. The quilt was softer than he'd ever noticed, and when he got past it and slid his hands under her shirt, her skin was so warm he wondered if she might be fevered.

"You're okay?" he whispered as his lips hovered over hers.

Her eyes were wide. "A hell of a lot better than that."

His control was gone. This was going to end, but right now, he had her. She was in his bed, in his shirt, at least for another couple of seconds, and he was going to take advantage.

He pulled the front of the shirt up over her head, lowering his mouth to her breasts almost absently as he dealt with the fabric behind her back. Not taking it right off, but leaving her arms in the sleeves, then knotting the fabric in the middle tight enough that her wrists were bound. Enough slack so that she could bring her hands to either side of her body— he didn't want her to be uncomfortable, lying on her hands. He just wanted her to stay there with him, at least for a while. She'd be leaving soon enough.

But not right then, he reminded himself. Right then, he had an incredible woman in his bed, and her eyes had widened when he'd restrained her arms, the same way she'd responded the night before when he'd held her wrists. Not a sign of anything, he reminded himself. They were on compatible sides of the same minor kink: it didn't mean they were fated to be together forever. But it damn well meant they could have fun right then.

He trailed one finger down the soft skin between her breasts, then flattened his hand over her rib cage. She arched her back, pressing up into him invitingly, but he just grinned at her. He'd be a little late starting work that day, and that was just fine. He'd have plenty of time to make up for that later, after she was gone.

He pushed himself up onto his knees, hovering over her, the hardness jutting out of his sweatpants so close to its ultimate target but separated by layers of fabric. She was staring at him; not his face, but lower, and he dipped his fingers beneath his waistband and wrapped his hand around himself. She licked her lips unconsciously, then grinned at him and raised her eyebrows.

"Got anything I could help you with?" Her voice was husky, and this time when she licked her bottom lip, then bit it, he knew she was doing it on purpose.

"I can take care of it," he said casually, running his fist along his hard length to demonstrate.

"You had better not, you asshole!" She was laughing, her eyes dancing, her breasts jiggling just right as her chest moved. He couldn't tease this woman for long; he didn't have the self-control.

So he leaned down and kissed her, ground his hips down to meet hers, and he wasn't sure which of them was moaning and which was gasping, but he was pretty sure it didn't matter. He slid a hand under the quilt and found his target, then kissed her as her body responded.

The early morning sun streamed into the room, Daisy the Demon Dog flopped to the floor beside the bed, disgusted at her humans for apparently planning to waste even more of their time indoors, and Josh knew things would never be better than they were right at that moment. If he'd been able to freeze time, he would have done it.

But he couldn't, and Ashley seemed completely unaware of how fragile their happiness was. She leaned up to him, murmured encouragement and dares and threats into his ear, kissed him until he couldn't think, couldn't control himself, couldn't resist the temptation to strip down the covers and let her roll over on top of him.

"Condom," she ordered. "Right now."

Obedience was a virtue. And there was something hot about having her arms restrained behind her back and her still being in charge and bossing him around. So he found the condom and she sank down onto him with a satisfied moan.

"Perfect," she whispered as she started to move, and he looked up at her, and he absolutely agreed.

❧ *Eighteen* ❧

ASHLEY LEFT HER sweater in Josh's bedroom. It wasn't deliberate, exactly, but it wasn't accidental, either. She liked the idea of establishing a beachhead, making it clear that the full invasion into his life and home would soon follow. But he frowned at her as she was heading out the kitchen door, jogged down the hall, and came back with the garment in his hand.

"Oh," she said. "Thanks."

He nodded an acknowledgment, but didn't say anything. They were quiet as they walked to his truck. Ashley clambered into the passenger seat, shut the door, and looked out at the property. The horses had come down to the front of their pasture and were watching the humans, and Daisy was sitting near them. They felt like an audience, but Ashley wasn't sure just what kind of show they were going to see. "Uh, Josh . . . I didn't want to tell you last night. I don't really want to tell you now, but I guess I have to."

He stared at her for a moment, then said, "You're going back to L.A. with Charlotte?"

"What? No. No, it's not about me, really. Well, a little bit about me, but mostly . . ." She sighed. She wasn't going to be able to sneak up on this, wasn't going to find any magic words that would make it all okay. "Last night when my manager called, it was to warn me that somebody sold some pictures to a gossip site on the Internet. Pictures of . . ." Damn it. She didn't want to do it. But he needed to be warned. "Pictures of you. And David McArthur. At The Splash. And I guess whoever sold the pictures gave a pretty good idea of why David was hitting you."

He stared at her. "On the Internet?" He didn't sound upset, exactly. More stunned.

"Yeah. On a gossip site. A pretty popular one."

He kept staring, then asked, "Why? Why the hell would anyone care?"

"Because the McArthurs are big players in Hollywood." She didn't want to add to that, but she made herself say, "And because you've been seen with me. I guess they got a shot of us driving out of The Splash parking lot. Maybe a few other shots. I don't know."

His nod was too jerky, too forced. "Okay," he said.

"I'm so sorry—"

"It's not your fault," he said. His voice was louder than it needed to be, but he quieted it before he added, "I'm the one who made the mistake. Not you."

"But the mistake is being publicized because of me—"

"Not your fault," he repeated, and he turned on the engine and drove just a little too fast down the driveway.

Ashley had no idea what to say. She didn't think he was ready to joke it off, and she doubted he'd appreciate any sage advice about how the first time in the gossip-go-round was the worst and it would only get better from there. But changing the topic felt fake. So they drove in silence until they pulled up in front of the lake house. Charlotte and Kevin were on the porch, and it was clear from their cautious expressions that they'd already heard the news.

Josh's smile looked forced as he turned to her and said, "It's not a big deal. Don't worry about it."

She knew he was lying, but didn't think there was any point in calling him on it. She wanted to lean over for a good-bye kiss, not worrying about their little audience, but something about the way Josh was holding himself made her wonder if he'd push her away. She didn't think she was brave enough to take that chance, so she pushed her door open and slid down to the ground. "You want to come over for dinner?" she asked.

"I'm not sure. Business might be . . . Things might be a bit hectic today. You know. Tidying up, trying to contain the damage. I might end up working late."

"Call me," she said. She supposed she was a cliché, the desperate girl trying to hold on to a man who just wanted to escape, but she could remember his gentle touch, his sweet smile, and she knew he was worth sacrificing a little pride. "Whatever time you finish work. Even if you don't want to come by, just . . . call me. Okay?"

He nodded, then turned to look at her and his expression slowly softened. "Yeah. Okay." He leaned over then, and she stretched back into the cab and the angle was awkward and impossible but the kiss was still sweet. "I'll call."

It was all she could ask for, so she made herself pull away and then watched as he backed up and drove off. It shouldn't have felt like such a final departure.

She waited a bit to make sure he wasn't going to turn around, then groaned in frustration, stalking up the stairs to the porch and sprawling onto one of the padded wooden chairs. "What a mess," she said.

Kevin grinned at her. "Yeah, that's how people tend to react after spending too much time with Joshy. He's a pain in the ass, huh?"

"He's lovely," she countered. "None of this is his fault."

Kevin looked at her skeptically. "Really? You don't think so?"

"None of the publicity is his fault. And the rest of it? Josh wasn't cheating on anyone. It maybe wasn't totally honorable, but I know how Jasmine is. She can make you do the stupidest things."

"Interesting to hear you defend him like that," Charlotte said. "You sound very . . . enthusiastic about him."

Ashley snorted. "You're acting like you're some sort of genius because you've noticed I'm crazy about him? I've been telling you that since you got here! I've been practically broadcasting it to the whole state for half the summer! You noticing that I've got a thing for Josh Sullivan is not evidence of you having super-psychologist powers."

"You've had a thing for the *idea* of Josh Sullivan for half the summer," Charlotte said. "But you haven't actually spent much time with him until recently. I was wondering how the real thing was going to compare to the fantasy. But apparently physical Josh is just as good as dream Josh?"

"Better," Ashley said with a meaningful look at her friend. "That man can do things—"

Kevin threw up his hands. "No! Okay, no. If you guys are going to have a conversation about the things my cousin can do, when you're using that tone of voice? I do not need to hear it."

Ashley ignored him. "I swear his tongue is, like, prehensile . . ."

Kevin looked disgusted, then confused. "Wait. Prehensile. What does that even mean?"

"Go look it up, babe." Charlotte patted Kevin's shoulder and eased by him, crossing the room to take Ashley's hand

and pull her toward the living room. "And take your time. We have some girl talk to do."

Kevin squinted at them. "Seriously? This is—you're going to talk about—while I'm *right here*?"

"You can go inside if you want," Charlotte said generously.

"I have to go inside or I'll hear about my cousin's tongue?"

Ashley pulled her legs under her and curled up in the corner of the big chair. "You're going to hear about a lot more than just that if you stick around," she warned.

"I'm going!"

And he did. They sat quietly for a while, then Charlotte said, "This is what Adam called you about last night? He said it was really important, so I was hoping . . . well, when I saw the Internet this morning I figured out what it was probably about. But last night I was hoping you got an audition for the Western."

"No," Ashley said. The movie seemed strangely distant. Still something she wanted; something she wanted more than anything. But she'd somehow managed to almost forget about it over the last couple of days. "I don't know if they've even set up auditions yet."

"They have," Charlotte said quietly.

Ashley frowned. "They have? Who'd you hear about it from?"

Charlotte made a face before admitting, "My agent. That's what I'm flying down for. They're going to let me read for both parts."

Ashley let herself feel the disappointment, but not for too long. As soon as she could be sure it would be honest she said, "That's great, Char. I'm really happy for you."

"I didn't want to tell you." Charlotte looked miserable. "It makes no sense, them looking at me and not you! I'll tell them how great you are, okay?"

"Oh my God, Charlotte, don't be stupid! This is the

business! We both know how it works. You win some, you lose some." Ashley was pretty sure that if she said it often enough she'd remember that it was true. "We need to focus on getting you ready! Did they tell you what scene they want you to do? Are you reading with someone else, or on your own?"

"You're really okay with this?"

"I'm a tiny bit jealous and a big bit disappointed, but mostly I'm happy for you, Char. Really."

Charlotte exhaled a breath she'd clearly been holding for too long. "And you don't mind working with me a bit more? Until I have to leave, you're okay working on the script a bit more?"

"Of course. I want to." It was mostly true. And hopefully the part that wasn't true would go away if Ashley just ignored it hard enough.

JOSH was at the Washburns' when he got his first taste of life after pissing off David McArthur. Larry Washburn didn't seem apologetic, exactly, but there was something hopeful about the way he said, "You understand, right? I mean, I've done a bit of business with David McArthur and I'm hoping to do a lot more. It just—it really wouldn't look good." He forced a smile and added, "And from the way my wife's been looking at you ever since you started, I think maybe I'd feel safer with a little distance, too!"

It was supposed to be a joke, but it wasn't funny. Not to Josh. Hard to be offended by it, though, given that he'd earned the reputation fair and square. Just because he'd reformed didn't mean everyone was supposed to just forget what he'd done in the past. So he forced his own smile in return and said, "Do you want me to finish up this job?" He was repairing the rustic lattice around the base of the Washburn deck, so it wasn't exactly an emergency job, and he wasn't too surprised when Larry made a face and said, "I guess not. You've already bought the materials, right? If you could just leave those under the deck. And bill us for them, of course! And then when we find someone new he can just take over where you left off." Larry looked down toward the lake, then cut his eyes back to Josh's and quickly asked, "I don't suppose you could recommend anyone, could you? Anyone looking for work?"

Josh thought about recommending someone he knew would overbill and do poor work, but he managed to resist the temptation. "Everyone's pretty busy at this time of year," he said instead.

He gathered his tools and drove away, wondering whether Larry would actually pay the bill he'd urged Josh to send. It was hard enough getting money out of summer people when Josh could threaten to withhold his services until he was paid. If they didn't *want* his services anymore, he'd lost a pretty valuable bargaining chip. But he'd worry about that when the time came.

The next project on his list was tiny, just trimming some branches away from a short path in the Balfours' backyard. It wasn't easy with his sore hand and aching shoulders, but at least he got through it without seeing the homeowners. He was pretty sure they were back in the city, so he probably wouldn't be technically fired from the job until they got back up to the lake and heard the gossip.

Or maybe they'd read about it on the damn Internet. He'd forgotten all about that. He pulled out his phone and thought about searching for the gossip site, but then shoved the phone back in the glove box and resolved not to worry about things that were out of his control.

Which was a pretty good philosophy, considering just how much of his life seemed to be out of control just then. He made it to the next site and had barely got the truck door open before the man of the house was running outside and waving his arms to stop Josh from going any farther.

He spent most of his morning driving around and getting fired, and only completed one billable hour of work. Then he went into town for lunch and everything was just as bad.

It started with the staring. He'd more or less expected that, and had even considered driving back out to the house and finding something to eat in his cupboards, but there wasn't much food there, town was closer, and he'd be damned if he'd hide. He wasn't really sure which of those reasons was the most significant.

The bell over the door at Abi's café felt like a trumpet signaling the beginning of a play, and Josh was stuck with a starring role. He tried to ignore the other players, focusing his attention on the feet of the person in front of him as they waited, but the audience demanded a show.

"I can't decide if I should be calling Kevin up and trying to get my twenty bucks back or not," was the opening line, delivered by a smirking Scott Mason. "I mean, maybe your threesome didn't happen that night, but—"

"Watch your mouth," Josh said as levelly as he could. He tried to make the warning sound like an expression of concern, not a threat. "You can talk about me, but you don't want to drag other people into it."

"Is that what they like?" Scott leaned in a little as if inviting a confidence, but his voice was loud enough for the whole café to hear. "The chivalrous thing?"

"You should probably fuck off now, Scott." Josh turned away and willed Abi to make her damn sandwiches a little faster.

"Don't be so touchy," Scott said, and he clapped a hand onto Josh's bruised shoulder, pressing just a little too hard to make the contact feel like an accident.

Josh refused to wince, or to reply. Scott had always been an asshole. This level of hostility felt like part of something more, but it wasn't clear what the bigger picture might be. Josh didn't want to get involved in something he didn't understand.

"What's she like?" It was a female voice now, younger and sweeter than Scott's. Josh turned to find Emma, the cousin he'd taught to ride, standing with a friend he vaguely recognized. Emma had just graduated from high school, but she sounded younger as she gushed, "She's so beautiful, Josh. Does she spend a lot of time making herself look so good?"

Josh shook his head. "I don't know."

"Are you guys, like, *going out*?"

Josh almost wished Scott would start talking again, but the asshole was just standing there smirking instead. "Sorry, I need to order," Josh said, and then turned hopefully toward the counter. Abi was still working on the other order but she gave him a sympathetic smile and then said, "We did good business this weekend. Lots of hungry tourists."

It should have been a good topic change, but Scott had apparently decided to get back into things, saying, "Celebrity scandals must make people hungry."

"Are you done eating, Scott?" Abi raised her eyebrows and looked toward the door. "We don't encourage loitering."

Scott snorted in disbelief but Abi stared him down. And Scott finally turned, grumbling, and headed out the door.

"Thanks," Josh said when Abi turned to him.

She just made a face. "What did you expect?" She reached for his favorite multigrain bread. "You're the talk of the town, until something else comes along. Suck it up." She slapped some cheese on the bread and slipped it in the toaster oven while she sliced the avocado. "And Josh? If you and Ashley . . . I mean, she seems really nice. I like her, I think. But if you and her keep going? You'd better get used to this stuff. You know?" She softened her words by giving him extra turkey and bacon without making him ask for it.

He ate his lunch on the way to his next job, and was relieved to find no one home to fire him. He mused about planning the rest of his week that way; he could do work on all the empty homes and put off getting fired by the rest of his clients for as long as he could. But it would just drag out the pain, he figured. He didn't want to spend the whole week waiting for the other shoe to drop.

The entire thing would have been easier if there was anyone but himself to blame for it all. But there wasn't. He'd made his mistake, and now he was facing the consequences.

Mindful of his near-useless morning, he worked late, right through the heat of the afternoon into the cool of the evening. As his bruises complained, he let himself think about Ashley. Her smile, her warm body . . . and the way he'd frozen her out that morning. At least he'd salvaged a bit of that with the kiss good-bye.

He wanted more kisses. And more of everything that might come after kisses. It was time to pack up his tools.

He knew he should go home and get cleaned up and then call her as she'd requested, but instead he pointed the pickup toward the lake house. Maybe they could go for a swim and let the cool lake water cleanse him of his sweat, if not his sins.

There were two people walking down the side of the road as he neared the cottage and he slowed to make sure he didn't startle them, then recognized them and felt his stomach tense. After everyone else, it would be too much to have one final rejection. Especially from the Ryersons.

But they smiled and waved as he drove past. It made him wonder whether they'd heard about it all, and then he decided not to think about that anymore. They were okay with him right then. And Ashley was waiting for him right then. So he'd live right then, and not worry about the next day.

That positive attitude got him all the way up Ashley's driveway, parked, and heading for the front door. And it blossomed into something strong and buoyant when he heard a peal of her laughter from inside the cottage. He'd had a hell of a day, but he was about to be with Ashley. Everything would work out.

❧ *Nineteen* ❧

"THEY FIRED YOU? I mean, the McArthurs . . ." Ashley combined her shrug with a sort of burrowing movement, snuggling her way further into Josh's warm, strong chest. "That's not exactly a shock. But other people did, too?"

"You heard them making the threats," Josh said. He sounded exhausted, but even in that state it had taken Ashley almost an hour to drag the story of his day out of him. They'd driven out to the cabin after he'd stopped by the lake house; he'd needed to get home to look after the animals, and she hadn't minded the prospect of a little privacy. Now, stretched out on Josh's sofa with Daisy curled up at their feet, Ashley was almost completely content. If only Josh wasn't having such a bad time, and if only Ashley had gotten the same chance to audition that Charlotte had. But she was focusing on Josh right then, not herself. His voice was resigned as he said, "If they make me, they can break me. That sort of thing."

"But they didn't make you!" Then Ashley realized that

she wasn't exactly sure that was true. "I mean . . . did they? You worked hard, right? You do good work at a reasonable price? That sort of thing?"

Their fingers were twined together, their joined hands resting on Ashley's stomach. He'd squeezed hers just a little as she spoke, and she knew it was meant as a gesture of gratitude. "I'd like to think so," he said, and he kissed the top of her head. For a man who'd started off as prickly as a hedgehog, Josh was surprisingly snuggly once she'd reached his soft underside.

"So they're just being bullies, then!"

Ashley could feel his chest rise and fall as he sighed. "They *did* give me a lot of referrals. I guess they're just taking them back now."

"That's not what referrals are supposed to be, though! I referred my cleaning lady to Charlotte, but that was a favor to Charlotte, not to my cleaning lady. I had a friend who was looking for someone to provide a service, and I knew someone who could provide that service. That doesn't mean Charlotte has to fire my cleaning lady if I get mad at her!"

"What if your cleaning lady did something really bad? What if she stole from you?"

Ashley shook her head vigorously, even though the motion temporarily disturbed her snuggling. "That's not what happened here! Jasmine McArthur is not something that can be stolen. She was the instigator in all this—you told me that yourself. If I hired a cleaning lady and then I . . . if I planted some of my jewelry in her purse, and then beat her up over it, and *then* told Charlotte to fire her? What would I be?"

"Totally psycho," Josh said. He shifted a little, sliding down so he was stretched out a bit more on the couch, making their bodies line up in an interesting new way. "But I don't really know what you're talking about, anyway. All this stuff about people getting fired? That's stuff that happens out there, right?" He kissed her as his hands began to roam with a little more purpose than they'd had thus far. "But we're in here. And in here, none of that matters. Right?"

She smiled into his next kiss and then squirmed around so she was lying mostly on top of him. "Right," she said. "We're in here. And this is all that matters."

Those were the words she said, but later, lying in the darkness of the bedroom and listening to Josh breathe beside her, she decided the words weren't exactly true. The whole thing with Jasmine had flared up because Ashley had come to town and gotten involved with Josh, so the results of the flare-up were Ashley's fault. And as bad as it was to think of Josh hurting, it was even worse to think that he was hurting because of her.

She might be powerless in her own career, but that didn't mean that she had no influence whatsoever. Maybe she couldn't help herself, but she could damn well help Josh. And she damn well would.

JOSH figured he'd lost about half his clients in the space of three days. Not bad, he told himself. Or, at least, it could have been worse.

And there was a bright spot on the work horizon: the Ryersons had spontaneously come up with a plan for a sort of pavilion on a big rock above the lake and wanted Josh to build it.

"It's for storm watching," Mrs. Ryerson explained. "Both of us love a good storm, but we're a little too old for standing out in the rain and getting soaking wet. We figure if we wear raincoats and have some shelter, we can still get a good view of it all."

"I should look into a lightning rod or something," Josh mused. "And we'll have to make sure that the path up there is nonslip. But still, you could get hit by lightning on the way from the house, couldn't you?"

"That'd be a hell of a way to go," she replied almost wistfully. "But take whatever precautions you think we need, if there's something you think would make it safer. There's no point in being a fool about it."

Josh was up on the site measuring and checking the slope when Mr. Ryerson made his way up and sat down on the bench that had always been there. "We were lucky to get you for this job," he said after looking out at the lake for a while.

Josh knew what the old guy was getting at. "I guess so," he said. "I've got a lot more time than I thought I would, all of a sudden."

And apparently that acknowledgment was what Mr. Ryerson had been waiting for. "I'm sure it's a bit uncomfortable for you," he said slowly. Then he looked out at the lake again, long enough that Josh finished up his work and began to wonder if it would be rude to leave. Finally, Mr. Ryerson said, "We used to have a Sheltie. You know the dogs? Like Lassie, but a quarter the size."

Josh nodded in general agreement, and Mr. Ryerson said, "She was afraid of thunder and strangers. And cats. Any sort of machinery." He shook his head. "She wasn't much of a dog, really. But you know what she was good at? We took her to a farm once, visiting a friend, and she saw a herd of sheep and took off after them like she was possessed. Herded them up together, ordered them around the farm from pillar to post. No reason for it, of course. The poor sheep were just supposed to be eating grass. But the dog just did it because she could."

Mr. Ryerson smiled at the memory, then turned to Josh. "I think those sheep liked being herded. They wanted someone to tell them what to do, even if it was just a yippy little dog who was afraid of her own shadow."

Josh was pretty sure he was getting the point of all this but he didn't think he could really go along with it. "David McArthur isn't afraid of his own shadow. He's . . . I don't know what the hell he is, but he's a powerful man. Rich and successful."

Mr. Ryerson didn't object to Josh's interpretation of his little dog story, but he didn't seem impressed with Josh's rebuttal, either. "So just imagine how those sheep would have reacted if a real dog had been chasing them around. If it had been Lassie instead of Yippie."

"Your dog's name wasn't actually Yippie, was it?"

"Might as well have been." Mr. Ryerson shrugged dismissively. The dog's name wasn't important. "I'm just saying, don't take all of this personally. You know? The people who are firing you are sheep, that's all. It shouldn't be something you worry about, not deep down."

"Mr. Ryerson . . ." Josh didn't want to say it, but he also didn't want this kind old man laboring under false impressions. "I was sleeping with David McArthur's wife. *I* did that. I snuck around with her, doing something I knew was wrong—"

"If it's any consolation, I don't think you were nearly as sneaky as you thought. Seems like the whole town heard about it long before David McArthur found out." He raised one of his over-bushy eyebrows. "And nobody had a problem with you until the sheepdog started yipping."

"*I* had a problem with me!"

"Well, that's different. That's something to worry about." He looked out at the lake for a while, then said, "Were you unhappy because she was married, or because she was just using you and you let her?"

Jesus, when had this innocent measuring session turned into whatever the hell this was? Josh was tempted to leave, but Mr. Ryerson looked so kind, and so gently expectant. Josh thought about the question. "More because I let her use me," he admitted.

"Good. I've always thought it was the responsibility of the people in the marriage to look after it, not everyone else."

He looked at Josh for a long moment, then slowly said, "At least, that's what I told myself when I started wooing Mrs. Ryerson, even though she was married to another man."

Josh froze, then slowly turned to look at the old man on the bench. Mr. Ryerson nodded slowly. "I'm a homewrecker," he said. He didn't sound ashamed, exactly, but he wasn't laughing, either.

It took a moment for Josh to collect his thoughts. "You really love her, though," he said.

"I do. So I fought for her. I didn't let anything get in the way."

Josh didn't want to admit that he'd barely even liked Jasmine McArthur. "I don't think it's quite the same thing," he managed.

Mr. Ryerson nodded. "Nope. Not the same. I'm just saying, there's always going to be people ready to judge other people. Ready to jump on any bandwagon. I think it's best to just ignore those people and consult *yourself.* Your own conscience. And your own sense of compassion."

Josh probably didn't want to know the answer, but he found himself asking the question anyway. "So this shelter I'm building, is this your sense of compassion at work? You throwing some business my way to help me out?"

Mr. Ryerson looked out at the lake again, and when he turned back he was fighting to control a smirk. "This shelter is purely selfish on my part. Mrs. Ryerson? In a storm?" The smirk broke free for a moment. Then he managed to curb himself and add, "A little electricity in a marriage is a good thing, Josh. A little extra excitement, even if it's externally provided—"

Josh held up his hands in quick surrender. "Okay. I get it." He gave his head a shake to clear the images, then made his voice businesslike. "So I've got two possible footprints laid out here. You want to take a look and decide which one's best?"

"Well, I'd better call Mrs. Ryerson up to get her opinion, too." The old man stood and headed for the path, then looked over his shoulder. "A little electricity in life is a good thing. Remember to enjoy it."

He shuffled down the hill, and Josh took a moment to check his phone messages. There were two waiting for him. The first was from a client who'd called two days earlier to say he didn't think he really needed the boulders along his driveway rearranged after all. Now, apparently, he'd changed his mind and hoped Josh could get the work done as soon as possible. The second was from Larry Washburn, saying he'd reconsidered the latticework for his deck; since Josh had started the job, probably Josh should be the one to finish it.

It made no sense. Josh had considered the possibility that some of the lost clients might come back, eventually, when they got tired of being outraged and realized how hard it was to find a good handyman in the busy summer season. But two days was nowhere near enough time for that to have happened.

So what was going on?

The Ryersons arrived then, and Josh was distracted by their decision making. But as he was pulling out of their driveway half an hour later, he got another call, this one from a New York stockbroker who'd been one of the first to call and tell Josh his services wouldn't be needed anymore.

Josh knew the rule about looking a gift horse in the mouth, but he wasn't going to be able to just sit back and accept this good fortune. "I appreciate the interest, Sebastian, but I need to ask. Why'd you change your mind?"

Josh's stomach tightened as he listened to the answer. And as soon as the call ended, he turned the truck toward Ashley's lake house.

ASHLEY was in a good mood, and seeing Josh's truck pulling into the parking area at the lake house only intensified her feelings. But the happiness shifted to apprehension when she saw him stalking toward the door, a dark scowl on his face.

She heard Charlotte and Kevin greet him on the porch, heard him growl something back at them, and braced herself. "What's wrong?" she asked as he pulled the door open.

He stared at her for a moment, then demanded, "You been busy?"

"Busy? Char's leaving tomorrow morning, so, you know . . . running lines . . ."

"But you found time to make a few phone calls, right? Make a few invitations?"

Oh. She'd known he'd find out, eventually, but she hadn't anticipated it happening quite so fast. Still, it wasn't a big deal. "Yeah, a few. I mean, it was my fault you lost the clients, so, you know . . . I thought I should even the playing field. David McArthur isn't the only person with some pull." He was still just staring at her, and she started to get nervous.

"It's not a big deal, Josh. And I'm sure it didn't work for everyone. If they're actually in the industry, they probably care more about David. He's big on the production side, and I'm just an actor. But for some of them? The ones who aren't in the business? They care more about actors than producers. And at The Splash, I noticed that people were interested, but they were too shy or too polite to actually come up and talk to us. I know it's weird, but . . . I'm a celebrity. I'm not saying it makes me a better person or important or anything, but it can be a useful tool. So yeah, a barbecue. It's, like, three hours of my time! That's all. I made a few phone calls, said I was thinking about putting something together for you and some of your clients, and would they be interested?" She'd been pretty proud of her smoothness, at the time. "That's all. Seriously, it's not a big thing."

"Not a big thing." He nodded as if the words were sinking into his brain. "Yeah. Just a barbecue. Just a game you're playing. Is there a reason you didn't mention it to me?"

"I wasn't sure it would work!" She'd done a good thing, done him a favor, and he was getting mad at her about it?

"I thought it would be a surprise if it worked, and I could just forget about it if it didn't. My God, Josh, what the hell happened? Why are you pissed about this?"

"Why am I pissed about you trying to take over my business?"

"Are you mental? You think I'm trying to take over a handyman business in backwoods Vermont? Seriously?"

The hurt only showed on his face for a split second before the anger came back, but that tiny glimpse was enough to drain Ashley's resentment completely. "I'm sorry—" she started, but Josh was already backing away.

"My life isn't your hobby, Ashley. Stay out of it."

And that was all. He turned and strode back to the truck, climbed in, slammed the door, and was gone in a swirl of gravel. Ashley walked to the door and stared after him. It took her quite a while to notice that Kevin and Charlotte were still sitting out there, and they were both watching her through the screen.

"You want to come sit down?" Charlotte asked carefully.

Ashley had no idea what she wanted. Less than five minutes earlier, everything had been good. Now? It was like her life had exploded, and she was definitely feeling shell-shocked. She stumbled out onto the porch and collapsed into one of the big wooden chairs. "You heard that?" she asked.

Charlotte nodded. "Hard not to."

"Did it make any sense to you? I mean, I was doing him a *favor*!"

"Without asking him." Charlotte sounded sympathetic rather than judgmental, but it still stung to hear her pointing out the same thing Josh had.

"What if I'd asked him, and then it hadn't worked? I would have gotten his hopes up for nothing!"

"I doubt it," Kevin said. When Ashley stared at him, he shook his head. "I don't think he'd have wanted you to do it."

"What? Why?"

"Because it's his business." Kevin looked at her, then at Charlotte, and he sighed. "It's partly the man/woman thing, I guess. I mean, macho pride or some shit. I know it's not the way we're supposed to think, but it's pretty hard to avoid the attitude. A guy like Josh, working his ass off for every penny, and a woman like you, rolling in cash? And money you made, not something you married into or inherited. It's probably a bit hard on his pride."

"Not you, though," Ashley said. "You and Char, that's okay for you?"

"Well, I'm totally shameless. It makes things a lot easier."

Ashley had to agree that it would. "So, what, he's supposed to work his ass off, and then lose a lot of business because of a reporter chasing *my* stupid story, and I should just sit back and knit or something? Just ignore the whole thing?"

Kevin glanced at Charlotte as if trying to decide how much further he wanted to go. She apparently either gave approval or gave nothing, because he sighed and then said, "You really want that part in the movie, right? That cowboy thing?"

"Cow*girl*," Ashley corrected as soon as she'd caught up to the topic shift.

"Okay, whatever. So you complain to Josh about it, and he agrees that it's unfair that people aren't even giving you a chance. Right?"

"Okay," Ashley said cautiously.

"So then, say, you got an audition, and you went down and you got the part, and then you found out that Josh had pulled some strings—just for clarity, understand that Josh has no fucking strings to pull, but pretend that he did—to make that happen." Kevin watched her for a moment, then asked, "How would you feel about that?"

There were reasons it wasn't the same. Her career

frustrations hadn't come about because of anything Josh had done, after all, so there wasn't really any justification for him to try to rebalance an equation that he hadn't thrown off in the first place. But maybe Ashley needed to argue less, and find the truth from the parts of the story that *were* the same. "I'd be disappointed," she confessed. "Hurt, maybe, that he didn't have enough faith in me to let me do it on my own."

Kevin nodded slowly. "And the thing is—" he started. Then he looked at Charlotte and stopped talking.

"No," Ashley said. "Keep going. I might as well take all the medicine at once."

Charlotte slowly nodded her permission toward Kevin, and he said, "The thing is, it's not even a long-term solution. It'll work for now, maybe. While you're around to offer barbecues or whatever. But after you leave, Josh doesn't have those bribes anymore, and he'll have lost a lot of his credibility, you know? He won't be an honest handyman who does good work at good rates; he'll be the guy who got a lot of clients because he was sleeping with an actress."

"That's bullshit. He'll do good work for them and they'll want to keep him!"

"He did good work for them before, and they fired him quick enough."

Ashley tried to marshal her thoughts. "But why does it have to . . . I mean, I know I can't stay here forever. But—"

Kevin's voice was unforgiving. "You'll go home. That's what summer people do. You come, you stir shit up, and you leave. We spend the winter tidying up your messes, and then the weather gets warm and you all come and start it all over again."

Ashley wanted to argue, but she couldn't think of what to say. When her phone rang, she grabbed it, hoping to see Josh's name on the call display, then smiled sadly and lifted the phone to her ear. "Hi, Adam."

"I just had lunch with Aliyah Bentham, the casting director for the Lauren Hall project." Adam sounded triumphant. "I showed her the pictures you sent me, you looking all grubby with that ugly brown horse. I told her how hungry you are for the part, and she wants you to audition, Ashley. She wants to give you a chance."

She should have been elated, totally over the moon. Instead, she felt sort of numb. "That's great," she said, because she knew it was what he wanted to hear. "But I thought they'd already set up auditions?"

"They did. I put some pressure on for you, persuaded them to add one more name to their list. But you need to get your ass down here fast. They're sticking you in early, tomorrow at four in the afternoon. I called the airlines and got you on the first flight tomorrow morning. You need to be at the Burlington airport at six thirty local time."

"Thank you. But . . . is there any chance of . . . does it have to be so soon?"

"I thought you were working on the script up there? Aren't you ready?"

"Yeah, I'm ready. It's just not a great time. Personally."

"*Personally?* Shit, Ashley, you said you wanted this. I put myself on the line for you. I told them you were ready to try something more challenging, said you were completely in love with the part—"

"That's all true," she said quickly. Miserably. "Okay. Yeah. I'll fly out tomorrow. Thanks, Adam."

"No problem. I'll e-mail you the flight details, and I'll meet you when you land. We can go to your place and figure out wardrobe, or shop if we need to."

They hung up, and Ashley lowered the phone. It was all catching up to her. Everything she'd wanted to leave behind when she came up for her vacation was back. "You're on the six thirty flight tomorrow morning, right?" she said to Charlotte.

Charlotte nodded. "He got you an audition. Ashley, that's great. I know this is—it's not great timing. But, come on, Ash! Lauren Hall! This script! It's incredible."

Ashley made herself smile. "Yeah. It is. I'm excited, really. It's just . . . I'm just tired."

They didn't argue with her, which was nice, and they didn't try to keep her on the porch when she said she wanted to go inside.

So she went to her bedroom and had to talk herself out of making the big gesture. Josh needed some space. She'd screwed up, again, and this time it was worse because she really, really should have known better. Good intentions were important, but common sense would be nice to have, too. In its absence, she supposed she'd have to keep muddling along as well as she could; she'd just have to try to be honest with him, and see where that got her.

☙ Twenty ❧

JOSH DIDN'T GET the message until the next morning. He supposed he'd been outside the night before when the call came, and when he'd come inside he'd been . . . well, he wasn't going to say he was wallowing in frustration, but he hadn't followed most of his usual nighttime routines, like checking messages. So he saw the blinking light in the morning and made himself a cup of coffee before pressing the play button.

It was hard to stay calm when he heard Ashley's voice. "Hi, Josh. I have no idea if you want to hear this. If you want to hear anything from me. But I wanted to give you a call. I've got to go back to the city for a few days. I'm leaving in the morning, pretty early. But I wanted to . . . I don't know. Before I left, I wanted to . . . to apologize, I guess." She sounded sad, not defensive. He set his coffee down and just stood there in his kitchen, listening to her voice.

"I understand what I did to make you angry. I had good

intentions, but I should have checked with you. And if you'd said no, I should have respected that.

"So I don't know where to go from here, really." She paused for so long that he checked to be sure the message was still playing. Then he heard, "I'm coming back. If you don't want to see me, that'll be hard. I'll—" She laughed a little, sadly. "I'll try not to make a fool of myself again, but no guarantees of that, Josh, because I really, really like you. I want to . . . I don't know. I want to see what we can be. Together. I want to make all this up to you and make you not be mad at me and help you the way you want to be helped, not the way I think you should be helped. Yeah, I want all that. So . . . I guess I don't know whether you care what I want. I don't really know whether you care at all. But I want to find out."

Another long pause, and then her voice was more businesslike. "So I'm going to try to keep myself from calling you while I'm in L.A. It's going to be hard, but I guess I need to give you some space, right? But if you wanted to call me, that'd be . . . that'd be great, Josh. Otherwise, I'll get in touch when I come back. A few days, probably. Okay." Another long pause. "God, I want to say something else, even though I know it's stupid. Like, the words are right there, trying to come out. But I think I've got myself under control. So, yeah. Bye."

The message ended and Josh stared at the machine. What had she wanted to say? Not— No. *Way* too early. Plus, like she said, stupid. That wasn't what this was about. Nobody was falling in— No. This was a summer thing. That was all.

The rest of the message had been almost as . . . what? What the hell was he feeling about it all now?

He shook his head, trying to clear it of confusion. He needed to work. Ashley was gone. She was planning to come back, but last he'd heard she'd been planning to stay at the lake for the whole summer, so her plans didn't always mean too much. And there was nothing he could do about any of it. To stay sane, he needed to focus on the things he could control.

His phone rang and he felt a stir of excitement, almost hope, but when he looked down it was displaying Kevin's name. He hit the button to answer and growled, "You ever planning on working again?"

"That's what I'm calling about. Charlotte's gone. They both are." He waited as if expecting some response to that, but Josh was pretty sure there wasn't much to say about it. Eventually, Kevin said, "So, yeah. If you've got hours, I want them."

"Good. I want some help with the Ryersons' storm-watching thing. Meet me there when you get back up here."

Josh hung up. The stars were gone. Everything was back to normal. Well, his business was blown to hell, but that was a problem, not a crisis.

Yeah, things were calming down. It was good, really. Time to get back to work, back into the summer routine. If he felt a little empty, that was just because . . . whatever. It was just how things were. It could have been worse if Ashley had stayed for longer.

He wouldn't call her, he decided. What was there to say? It was better to have a clean break, not drag it all out.

He'd gotten off easy. He was fine, and it was good to be back to normal. He wondered how many repetitions it would take until he believed his own words.

ASHLEY was exhausted, but she refused to pull over. Six days in L.A., auditioning for the role of a lifetime, meeting with people who might help her get the part, calling in every favor and activating every connection she had, and all she'd wanted the whole time was to get back to Lake Sullivan. Get back to Josh Sullivan. She'd caught the last flight into Burlington, picked up a rental car, and started driving. She'd told Charlotte she'd spend the night at an airport hotel and had even thought she might do it, but as soon as her feet had touched the ground she'd known that the pull was too strong.

And as she approached her destination, she felt the tug even more. It wasn't the lake that was calling to her; it was Josh. He hadn't phoned her while she was away, and she hadn't phoned him, but surely six days was enough time for him to have cooled down a little. Or warmed up, she supposed, considering his cold reception before she left. Surely he'd be happy to see her.

But what if he wasn't? Maybe she should give herself one more night of hope instead of going over and having her dreams crushed right away.

The lake or the farm? Quiet peace, or—or what? That was the problem. She had no idea.

And she'd get no sleep until she found out. She turned quickly, heading out of town toward the farm. She needed to know. She needed to see Josh's face, and let him see hers. It would work. It had to.

Her conviction carried her all the way to the junction of Josh's driveway and the road and then abandoned her entirely.

No, damn it, she wouldn't chicken out.

She turned off the main road and headed down the driveway. She realized how late it was when she saw the darkness of the house. No lights on. If Josh was home, he was probably asleep. Did she really want to wake him up with this?

Yes, she decided. She did. She'd flown across the continent for this man and she wanted to see him, even if it was only to give him the privilege of dumping her in person rather than over the phone.

She sat in the car for a moment, gathering her courage, then pushed the door open and pulled herself outside. The first breath of the night air reminded her of everything she'd missed about the place, and when she looked up and saw the wide band of stars overhead, she knew she was where she should be.

But she wasn't confident enough to pull her overnight bag out of the trunk, she decided. She headed for the stairs empty-handed, then heard a strange snuffling noise from over beside Josh's truck. She took a curious step in that direction and then froze as something moved in the shadows. Something big.

A bit more movement. The bulk of it, the shuffling movement—

It was a bear. A huge damn bear. Ashley's brain froze. The bear moseyed toward her as if it shared her earlier curiosity and hadn't been terrified out of it like she had.

Jesus. What was the rule? Freeze? Play dead? Run away? Be silent? Be loud? She was pretty sure it depended on what kind of bear you were dealing with, but how the hell were you supposed to tell bears apart? The one thing she knew was that the strangled yelp that came from her panicked throat was not on any of the approved response lists.

The bear was about five feet away from her when there was a squeaking sound from the direction of the cabin. The bear turned its head to stare at the opening door.

Josh's voice was calm, but serious. "You don't see any cubs, do you? Just the one bear?"

"Just one." Ashley's voice was trembling, but at least she managed to form words.

And Josh still sounded calm. "I'm going to let the dog loose, Ash. When she distracts the bear, you hustle up here, okay?"

Ashley made a sound that Josh seemed to interpret as agreement.

Things happened fast after that. Josh said, "Okay, get him," and a dark blur roared toward them. Daisy was making sounds Ashley had never heard before, a strange mix of barks and growls and near-howling that was almost as frightening as the bear.

But not quite. Ashley managed to take a couple steps toward the cabin and then Josh was there, stepping between her and the animals, and he was banging two pots together like a low-rent New Year's celebrant, and Ashley managed to peek around his shoulder to see the bear racing for the forest, Daisy hot on its heels.

"Daisy!" Josh yelled after her, but he didn't seem too concerned. "She's pretty quick," he said as if he thought Ashley needed to be reminded of it. "She's chased a lot of bears and she's never come back hurt."

Ashley staggered a few steps to the stairs and sank down onto them, trying to collect herself. "She's chased a lot of bears?" she managed to ask.

Josh sat down next to her. "Vermont hazard, remember? They're good animals, but it's best for everyone if they stay away from humans. They're just looking for snacks or entertainment, usually, so a bit of noise is all it takes to get rid of them."

"I thought . . . play dead?"

"For grizzlies, maybe. Or if there'd been cubs. Cubs change everything."

Ashley felt freezing cold on every part of her body that wasn't pressed up against Josh. She leaned in a little harder and he wrapped his arm around her. "You're okay," he said softly. "I'm sorry you got scared."

"It was a *bear*, Josh."

"Yeah." He kissed her temple. "There's people who come up here their whole lives and never see one. You got lucky."

She hoped her huff of breath would be considered a laugh; it was the best her still-tight lungs could produce.

"You're cold. You want to come inside?"

She nodded. This wasn't quite the arrival she'd been planning, but at least she wasn't being turned away. "What about Daisy?"

Josh cocked his head and listened, so Ashley did the same. They heard nothing and Josh shrugged. "If she's not barking anymore she probably figured she got the bear far enough away. She'll be on her way home now, or else standing guard in the forest. Or maybe finding something disgusting to roll in."

Ashley let herself be herded inside and accepted the glass of Scotch Josh poured for her. She'd just taken her first sip when Josh pushed the kitchen door open and Daisy came racing in, full of triumphant energy. Now that the bear was dealt with, she was ready to greet Ashley properly and check Josh out to make sure he was in one piece and just generally celebrate having two of her favorite people in the kitchen. And if there happened to be some treats in that magical white box that kept things cold, she'd be happy to indulge in a few of those, too.

"Not too much or she'll puke on the bed," Josh warned as Ashley scoured the fridge for dog snacks.

"She saved my life! She gets treats!"

"Puking isn't a treat."

"You won't puke, will you?" Ashley asked the dog, and Daisy licked Ashley's chin in reply. Not the clearest message, maybe, but Ashley figured it was good enough.

"You look tired," Josh said when Ashley had given the dog a final cold cut and shut the fridge door. There was something he was trying to say, but he was right, Ashley was tired and she wasn't sure she was up to breaking through his code. "And you're still a bit shaky. You shouldn't drive. Stay here, okay?"

"Okay," she said quietly. But she'd been the one to leave, so maybe she should be the one to take a bit of a chance now. "I can use the guest room, if you want. But I'd rather sleep with you."

"I'd rather that, too," he said quietly. The small victory washed over her like a warm wave, and she felt much steadier as he took her hand and led her down the hall.

❧ Twenty-one ❧

JOSH WANTED ASHLEY to wake up so she could smile at him, but he also wanted her to stay asleep so he could think about her all snuggled up, warm and safe in his bed. And so he wouldn't have to hear anything unpleasant she might have to say. The conflicting desires ended up making him vaguely restless, but unable to pick any job to spend his energy on. He wiped half of the kitchen counter, washed a few dishes, made coffee but didn't pour any for himself, and then heard stirring in the bedroom.

He snuck toward the door, reluctant to make noise in case Ashley wasn't actually awake, and heard her sleepy voice say, "How's your tummy, hero pup? Ready for some more treats?"

Josh snuck a peek through the crack between the half-open door and the wall and saw Daisy and Ashley both on the bed where he'd left them, with Daisy snuffling into Ashley's neck for kisses. It was a bit sad that he was jealous of his dog.

"I think I saw some bacon in the freezer," Ashley said. She was waking up now and her voice was becoming more dynamic; Daisy's tail wagged in response. "You think we should fry some of that up?" Now Daisy's entire back end was wagging. "And then maybe some broccoli!" Ashley suggested in the same tone of voice, and Daisy almost fell off the bed she was so excited. "You don't speak English, do you, pup? No, no English!"

Daisy barked, a little yip of excited agreement, and Ashley grinned and swung her legs over the side of the bed. "Okay. We'll find good snacks. Lots of vegetables, hardly any meat. Right?"

Josh couldn't stay out of the room any longer. "You ready for coffee?" he asked as he stepped into the doorway. "Or do you want to wake up a little more slowly?"

"Hmm . . ." She stretched languorously, her borrowed shirt riding up in interesting places. "I think coffee would work. But I'll come out to the kitchen for it."

"I can bring it in here if you want."

"No. Daisy and I need to start looking for her morning snacks."

"She's already had her breakfast."

"Kibble. She says kibble sucks. She says bear-chasing dogs need bacon to keep their strength up."

"She's chased bears before and hasn't needed bacon."

"She felt the lack. Go get the frying pan ready."

"I was hoping to watch you for a little longer."

Her smile was almost shy. "Yeah?"

"Yeah." As if there could be any doubt.

But apparently there was, because she made a face and said, "You didn't call me. I was away for six days, and you didn't call me." She didn't sound petulant, exactly—just unsure.

Josh had been hoping to put this conversation off until at least after coffee, if not forever. But if they were going to talk about it, at least he could try to be honest. "I should have called probably. But I was . . . I don't know exactly.

Still trying to figure things out. Waiting to see if *you* called, or if you were going to come back at all."

"I said I was coming back."

"You said you were staying the whole summer. You said you weren't going to hang out with Hollywood people. Said you were taking a vacation."

"Things changed!" she protested defensively.

"Yeah," he said. "I didn't mean you lied or anything. Just, like you said, things change sometimes. So you might have planned to come back, but then when you got to L.A., maybe you'd have figured out that you shouldn't."

"Why would I have done that?"

"I don't know. I mean, you live there. Your life is there. It's not that weird to decide to stay at home instead of flying across the country."

She nodded slowly. "I guess. Yeah. But, listen, Josh, that honestly never occurred to me. I'm sorry if you weren't sure, but I knew I was coming back. I *knew.*"

He let himself believe her. "Okay. Good."

She slid off the bed and padded toward him on bare feet, his shirt falling to the middle of her thighs and then leaving a lot of skin for him to obsess over. "You were mad at me before I left. Is that . . . Are we okay? Is that over?"

"Yeah." He saw her waiting for more and tried to find the words. "I wish you hadn't gotten involved with the business. I appreciate the thought, but I've got my pride, Ashley. You know?"

"I do. I'm sorry. I wanted to help, but I guess I just got caught up in the grand gesture again. I'm learning, though. I promise." She looked up at him, her eyes wide and sweet. "You're sure you're not mad anymore?"

"I was almost done being mad when I listened to your message," he said quietly. "And then if there was a tiny little bit left, it dissolved completely when I saw you standing there facing down a damn bear."

"I can handle bears," she said bravely. "But . . . I wish you'd called me. I wanted to call you, but I said I wouldn't."

"Yeah. I'm sorry."

"You can make it up to me," she interrupted with a sly, suggestive smile.

His body responded to just the hint. "Really?" he asked cautiously.

"Yup. You can apologize with bacon. Daisy and I want bacon, and maybe eggs and definitely toast. Do you have tomatoes? We might want to make BLTs."

He smiled at her, only a little reluctantly. "Daisy doesn't want tomatoes. But, yeah, I might have one. Enough for you."

"I'll share," she promised, and she kissed him lightly. "I want coffee and breakfast, and I want a shower, and I want to brush my teeth. And then I want to climb right back into bed with you and you can show me how much you missed me. Sound good?"

"Yeah. Sounds perfect." He meant it. He'd missed her, and now she was back. It still wasn't anything long-term, and he was still going to get his heart smashed down the road, but he knew he needed to enjoy things while he could. "Coffee first. Any chance you want company in the shower?"

"Daisy likes showers?"

"You're not funny."

"I'm not joking." She waited, then grinned. "Now, Daisy and I would like bacon. Please serve us."

"You were in L.A. for a little too long, I think." But he was already moving, heading down the hall toward the kitchen, and when he got there he hauled out his cast iron skillet and the bacon. Ashley was back. She wanted bacon. He was going to give her whatever she wanted.

IT was a good thing Josh had been working so hard while Ashley was away, and a good thing, in a way, that he'd lost half his clients, because once she was back he didn't seem to want to leave the house. He made it clear that he didn't want her to have the barbecue and she reluctantly accepted his decision, but it seemed like even just the possibility of rubbing shoulders with a Hollywood star had brought a few more customers back into the fold, even without a payoff.

He sent Kevin on a few jobs, and spent one afternoon helping him when there was just no safe way for the guy to do the work alone, but otherwise Josh was on vacation. So was Ashley. They rode the horses all over the property and beyond. Josh showed her his favorite places, and she appreciated them just as much as he'd known she would. He cooked for her, a little, until she kissed him and told him to go sit down; she liked cooking, and he obviously didn't. And they spent a lot of time in bed.

But they did other things, too. Ashley was interested in the whole town, and she dragged him to one of her pottery lessons, off to Abi's café for lunch, and when she found out his aunt and uncle owned a garden center she insisted they buy flowers for the cabin. "We can get native plants," she said. "They'll look totally natural. Just a little bit flowery!"

Another day he took her over to go fishing with Mr. Ryerson, nice and early in the morning, and he watched as she charmed the old man with her enthusiasm. She peppered him with questions about bait and techniques and she actually pulled out a notebook and wrote things down when she got something she wasn't sure she'd remember. And then, when they reached the secret fishing hole that Mr. Ryerson had never even told Josh about, Ashley sat as quietly as a seasoned pro, casting and waiting and then casting again. She was a bit squeamish when she actually caught a nice bass and realized she'd have to touch it to get the hook out of its mouth. But when Mr. Ryerson moved to help her, Josh caught his shoulder. "No, she can do it," he said gently, and Ashley stared at him for a moment, and then nodded decisively.

"I can," she said. "I just . . . run my hand down like this?" She took a deep breath, and then she did it. "And I ease the hook around?" Her face was twisted but her hand was steady, and when she'd unhooked the fish and reluctantly set it back into the water, she'd turned to Josh with a triumphant glow. "I did it. Me! That was me who just did that!"

"I know. I knew you could."

"Yeah," she agreed. "You did." She shifted around in the boat, snuggled in a little closer, and Josh wasn't sure whether to ignore the knowing look from Mr. Ryerson or bask in it.

They went to Woody's one night with Kevin and Abi and a couple other people to hear Theo's band, and Josh just sat back at their table and watched Ashley have fun. He was proud of her and proud of being with her. Not because she was a movie star, but because she was Ashley.

"You got a long-term plan for this?" Abi asked when Ashley had dragged Kevin out onto the tiny dance floor. "Ideas of where you're going down the road?"

"Nope," he said, and he took a sip of his beer.

"You think maybe you should?"

"You think maybe you should be quiet?" She raised a challenging eyebrow at him and he sighed and extended his hand. "You want to dance?"

"You hate dancing."

"Not as much as I hate talking about this."

So she led him out onto the floor and it wasn't long until they switched partners and Josh realized he didn't hate dancing all that much, not when he got to do it with Ashley. It helped that Kevin was there, being goofy and distracting for everyone, and it was even kind of fun when Theo started making square-dancing calls from the stage, getting all dancers to swing their partners and do their own versions of whatever do-si-do-ing was.

Ashley laughed through it all, and Ashley made everything good.

So they had fun when they went out, but his favorite times were still at home with just the two of them. They rode, and they walked, and they went down to the creek and looked up at the stars. They also talked a lot, and spent most of one rainy afternoon inventing and playing a strange game of what-I'd-do-if-I-ran-the-world, a game so intense that they both started writing down strategies, doing calculations, and even making maps to show the way goods could be redistributed. Ashley's solutions tended to be more technology based, Josh's more agrarian, but they were both pretty confident that they'd get all their worlds' citizens fed and healthy.

"We may be the biggest nerds in the universe," Ashley said as she surveyed the bed. It was covered with stacks of paper, a laptop, and a demon dog wearing a paper crown. They'd both agreed that a figurehead monarch, especially a furry one, wouldn't hurt their political systems.

"Nerds might be a good choice to run the world," Josh said. He'd never thought of himself as a nerd before, but he was pretty sure it was the right word for the way he was acting. How else to explain his strange new fascination with climatic projections? Would he be able to stop desertification in time to keep the Sahel productive, or should he be allocating even more resources to dealing with refugees? Of course, he wouldn't have been so interested in any of it if the issues hadn't sprung out of a conversation with a beautiful movie star he happened to be in bed with, so possibly he wasn't a *classic* nerd.

That was when the phone rang. Josh answered, then handed it to Ashley. "Your manager," he said.

The lack of cell coverage at the cabin hadn't saved him from outside intrusions; they'd tracked her down. Now he couldn't do anything but watch it happen.

Ashley's face was flushed with excitement. "Really?" she demanded of the phone. "No, really? Adam, no. Are you sure? She really . . . oh my God, Adam, really?"

She was quiet for a while as Adam spoke, and Josh found himself going back to his old memorization tricks. He would remember the way she looked as she held the phone tight to her ear, pink and excited and so, so happy. He'd memorize the image, but maybe he'd pretend she looked that way because of something he'd done.

She hung up fairly quickly and just stared at him for a moment.

"You got the part. The Western thing."

She nodded as if testing how it felt to move in this new, brighter world. "I did. Adam said they were undecided. Then David McArthur called the director and told her I was trouble. Unstable and flaky. And the director told Adam that any enemy of David McArthur's was a friend of hers. They're going to give me a chance. The older sister. The part I wanted!"

"I'm happy for you," he said. It was true. For her, he was happy. For himself? Miserable. But that was too damn bad. "You want to celebrate?"

"I need to phone people," she said. "Oh. I need to phone Charlotte. He said they hadn't cast her part yet. Maybe I should wait? No, I'll call her. And my parents, and some friends—I need to call a lot of people!" She beamed at him, then leaned forward and kissed him, more enthusiasm than precision, and pulled away before he could find a way to hold on to her. "I got the part," she whispered, trying the sentence out at all different volumes. "This is going to change everything!"

He knew she was right. He gathered up the remains of their stupid game and she paced around the house, getting back in touch with all the people she'd left behind. She was laughing and yelling and almost crying with happiness, and he made sure he had a smile on his face every time she looked in his direction. Not that she did that very often.

*   *   *

ASHLEY couldn't believe how happy she was. A great guy and a great job, both at the same time? It was like a whole new world was opening itself to her. She'd been stuck, but she'd broken free. Josh and challenging, meaningful roles. Making a place for herself as an actor, not a pretty, likeable girl. She went out on the porch when she called her parents and she looked out at the beautiful forest wrapped around her, fresh and new after the rain, and she cried with happiness. Her dad was crying, too, even though he didn't really understand why Ashley was so overwhelmed. That was just the way her dad was. Her mom was, as usual, a bit confused by the emotional creatures in her life, but she was certainly happy and proud and excited.

"When does shooting start?" she asked. "Are they doing rehearsals? For a movie like this, they'll do rehearsals, right?"

"Two weeks of rehearsal and fittings and whatever," Ashley said. "Not a lot. Lauren doesn't like to take the freshness off the scenes." Then she cackled. "Did you hear that? 'Lauren doesn't like something' . . . like I have any more idea about Lauren Hall's directing style than anyone else does! But soon, I will! Soon I'll know how she does things, and she'll be working with me, and I only know a few of the others who are cast so far but they're all great and everyone else will be great and I'll be working with all of them, too, and every day is going to be like the best acting class I've ever been in! It's going to be exhausting, and intense, and *perfect*!"

She could practically hear her dad's tears starting up again, but her mother was the one who spoke. "And when does that start?" she repeated.

"Soon. They're working out a couple details. Probably the week after next, though."

"In Los Angeles?" her mother asked. "For several months?"

"Yeah! I get to live at home! It's about half soundstage stuff, and then they've found somewhere just outside town that'll work for a lot of the outdoor stuff. We might have to spend a week or so on location somewhere, but that'd be it."

Neither of them said anything right away. But then her father said, "And this boy . . . man . . . this fella you're so excited about. I thought you said he lived in Vermont?"

"He does," Ashley said slowly.

"So you'll have been seeing each other for a couple weeks by the time you leave? And—" Her father sounded like he might start crying again, but this time from a different emotion. "How's that going to work, honey? You're going to try to stay together over all that distance? Or would he be able to move down for a bit? But you'll be exhausted, working all the time, excited about your career, and he'll be . . . what will he be doing all day?"

She didn't answer right away. Instead, she tried to imagine Josh in Los Angeles. It wasn't like he was a total recluse. He'd said he used to hang out with the summer people; surely he could get his social skills back in gear. And, sure, he had a business to worry about, but how much could he be making from that? She could find some way to get money to him. Then she tried to imagine a situation where he'd accept her money, and she couldn't do it. Would she be able to trick him about it? Lie to him? But she didn't want to do that. Especially because she knew how hurt he'd be if he ever found out.

The audition had been such a long shot. She'd wanted to do it just for its own sake, for the fun and adventure and experience of it all. She hadn't ever really considered the possibility that she'd get the part. Not as something that actually might happen, in a non-dream context. Now that it had happened . . .

"Damn it," she muttered into the phone. "I'm not sure.

I . . . I hadn't really thought about that." She hadn't thought ahead at all, really. She'd been planning her career, sure, but she'd been living in the moment with Josh, and she'd never tried to put the two dreams together. It had been more fun to imagine a reality in which one or both of them ran the world than it would have been to think of a way to make Josh fit in with her career. "I'll talk to him," she said. "We'll figure something out." They had to. Ashley couldn't believe the universe would be so cruel as to make her choose between her two dreams. There had to be a way for her to have both of them.

She just needed to figure out what that way was.

The rest of the conversation with her parents was a bit more subdued. Ashley was just getting ready to say good-bye when Josh came out of the door. He had his work clothes on, right down to his steel-toed boots.

She stared at him. It was already late afternoon. And there was no way a call could have come in, because she'd been using his only phone line nonstop.

"I have to look after a few things," he said quietly. "I'll probably be a bit late. You can find dinner for yourself in the fridge, right?"

She frowned at him. Dinner wasn't the problem. "Hang on a second," she said into the phone. She put her hand over the mouthpiece and said, "Where are you going?"

"I started looking at my list of jobs, and there's one that I kind of missed. I need to get it taken care of."

She didn't like this. Not at all. It just felt wrong. But she couldn't tell him to not go do his job. "How late?" she asked.

"I'll work 'til dark, and then there'll be some cleanup. And I should check in with Kevin, see where he is with stuff. It'll be pretty late."

Their days and nights had blurred together lately; when you spent most of your time in bed it didn't really matter what time the clock said it was. "I'll wait up for you. Or if I'm asleep, wake me up."

"I'll probably be tired," he said. "Don't wait up. And if you're asleep, I'll leave you like that."

So, a "no" to both of her requests. She frowned at him. "We need to talk," she said.

"Yeah. Okay. But tonight probably won't be good."

She sighed. "Tomorrow, then."

He smiled in what she supposed was agreement, and then he was gone, striding across the lawn to the truck. She watched as it pulled out, then lifted the phone to her ear. "Sorry," she said. "Josh had to go to work."

"Josh," her mother said. "That's a good name."

"He's a good man," Ashley said. He was. And she wanted him. How the hell was she going to make that work when her career dragged her way across the continent?

JOSH worked until it was too dark to see the branches he was clearing. Then he turned the truck around and shone the headlights into the brush at the side of the driveway, giving himself enough light to keep going. The rain had stayed pretty steady as he'd worked, never hard enough to be a serious problem, but enough for him to add wet clothes to his list of miseries.

The job had been on his list for a while, but he was pretty sure the family who owned the cottage were in Europe until the end of August. There was no real urgency to get it done. But he'd needed to get out of the house, and now that he was out, he wanted to *stay* out for as long as possible.

Of course, he also wanted to go back immediately. What kind of idiot was he, staying away from that incredible woman because he was unhappy that he'd soon have to *stay* away from her? What? Had he learned nothing from her previous absence? But then again, what about his life before

Ashley? All the lessons he'd learned about summer people leaving?

The job was a good way for him to work out the frustrating contradictions, or at least to smash the crap out of some trees and wear himself out. Not a great plan, but it was the sort of thing he did when he had too much negative energy. As a boy, he'd found jobs splitting and stacking firewood for neighbors, sometimes doing it for free if no one would pay him. He'd spent his life taking out his frustrations on trees; no reason to go breaking habits.

"This is a hell of a mess," he heard from behind him. A familiar voice that made all the contradictory emotions he'd been trying to quell flare back up. He had no idea how Ashley had found him, and couldn't worry about it right then.

"I'll clean it up," he said without turning around.

"I wasn't talking about the path." She was closer now, and he knew he should turn to greet her, but he couldn't do it. "Kevin told me where to find you," she said, coming even closer.

He'd needed some time, and she wasn't giving it to him. He wasn't ready for this. He was still too raw, too uncontrolled, and if he said something now it would be truer than he wanted it to be. Because he wanted Ashley to be happy, and his truth would make her sad. "I need to finish up here. You should head back to the house. Or the lake, I guess." Or the city. Maybe she'd tracked him down so she could tell him she was leaving early.

"I'll help you. You're moving these branches over to the truck?"

He half turned, far enough to see her bending to grab a few of the branches he'd hacked off. "No," he said.

She looked up at him. "You're not moving them to the truck?"

"I am. But I don't need help." Which wasn't quite right. "It's rough work. Your hands will get all scratched up. If you grab them like that, your arms and your chest, too. I don't want you to get beat up from trying to help me."

"It'll be good for the part," she said brightly. "If I show up with a good set of calluses, that'd be excellent."

He turned away. He guessed she could carry branches if she wanted to; she wouldn't last long.

❧ *Twenty-two* ❧

"I'M TAKING THE part, you know." Ashley had the base of one of the branches in her hand but she hadn't started moving toward the truck; she wanted to get this all sorted out first. "I'm going back to L.A."

Josh turned and squinted at her. "I know," he said, clearly mystified.

"I thought about turning it down." She stared at him and tried to read his reactions. "To stay here with you. I realized that this thing with you and me is really new, and it would be hard to keep it going if I left right now. So I thought about staying." She took a deep breath as she shook her head. "But I can't. This part . . . it's my dream. You know? I mean, not this part specifically, I've only known about it for a few months. But taking my career in this direction. Being a real actor. Getting to live all those different lives, getting to be all those different people. That's my dream, and I can't give it up just for some guy. I can't do that."

"I never expected you to," he said, and she could tell he was being honest.

"Why not?" she demanded, and he just stared. "You never even thought about it? Because I'm still a summer person. Right? You've known all along that I'd be going home at the end of the summer, you've been thinking of this thing as something temporary, just a fling." She tried to throw the branch away from her to express her frustration, but it was heavy and awkward and the tip ended up jamming into the earth, bringing the base back around to painfully jam into her shin. "Ow!" she gasped.

And Josh finally moved. "Shit," he said, falling to his knees in front of her. He tugged at the leg of her jeans, rolling it up so he could see the damage.

"It's no big deal," she tried, but she was pretty sure he wasn't hearing her. "Just a scratch."

"It broke the skin. You're bleeding."

She grabbed the hair on the top of his head and angled his face up so he was looking her in the eye, not the shin. "People bleed. Then they get better. That's life, Josh."

He frowned at her. "Yeah, okay. I'm familiar with the concept."

"I'm not made of china. I won't shatter. I can get scratched sometimes. And you can tell me things I don't want to hear sometimes. You know?"

"I can tell you so you can ignore them," he said, calmly standing up. "Like tonight, when I said I was going to work and you should stay home. Like that?"

"You can tell me things about *you*. Not tell me what to do."

"I don't understand this conversation. Are we still talking about when you're leaving?"

"I'm talking about when you left, Josh! Tonight. You heard I got the part, and you were out of there. No time for us to talk about it, no trying to figure it all out. You just decided you knew exactly what was going to happen and that was it. You were back to old Josh, working hard and freezing me out."

"It's been about six hours," he said, clearly trying to hold his temper in check. "And you spent the first good chunk of that on the phone talking to everyone but me. I can't take six hours to get used to an idea without you saying I'm freezing you out?"

"Are you trying to say you weren't going to stay frozen? Are you trying to say I was wrong about what's going to happen?"

"You're going back to L.A., Ashley. That's a fact. I thought we had longer, and then I found out we didn't and I needed a bit of time to adjust to that before I could go back to being happy for you. It's not a fucking crime to need a bit of time."

"It's not a crime to tell me things, either." She was crying. Stupid, weak tears. Except she was still functioning, still having the conversation she needed to have, so "weak" wasn't the right word. "We're allowed to have feelings, you know. Negative ones, even. You can share those with me, just like you share being happy."

"How long 'til you go back, Ashley?" His voice was dead, almost as if he was wishing for her to depart sooner rather than later.

"A week and a bit, probably."

"And do you want to spend that time being unhappy and fighting? Or do you want to give me a little time to get my game face back so we can enjoy the time we have?"

"I want to spend it fighting," she said. "But with both of us on the same side!" She shook her head. "When I called Kevin, looking for you, he told me how things have been up here. He told me you lost a lot of business and took some crap from people. And he said you were just walking through it, head high. He said you were a tough son of a bitch." She pushed him so hard he took a step backward.

"So where the hell is all that toughness now, Josh? Why are you so . . . so *eager* to give up now? You think the only possible outcome is for us to break up. We couldn't possibly turn this into something more than a summer fling. That's what you think. Right?"

"Do you think something else?" His expression was almost scornful. Now that she'd got him talking she was wondering if she'd made a mistake. "You think . . . what? What Hollywood romance ending do you see for this? Do I suddenly realize that I've secretly wanted to be an actor for my whole life, and I go down with you and get a great part in your movie and we rule Hollywood together? Is that one of your plans? Because leave aside the part where it's a total fucking fantasy that could never actually happen. Even if it did happen, I *hate* people staring at me. Being an actor sounds like the worst job in the world. So there goes the Hollywood ending. Real-world version? I just go down to be your kept boy. But people would still stare at me, right? Wondering who the hell I was and what the hell I was doing with someone like you. I didn't enjoy the Hollywood gossip experience the first time around, so I don't think I'd want to sign up for a lifetime of it. Being in a city at all is something I can handle if I go down for a weekend or something, but by the end of it my skin's crawling and I feel filthy and stressed and I want to punch everyone I see. I hate the city." He shook his head and his voice was a bit softer when he said, "Not to mention that you wouldn't want me anymore, not in L.A. Not when you've got all those other guys to choose from. Smooth, rich guys in fancy cars with great houses. Guys who can take care of themselves, without mooching off you for everything they need. Guys who can help your career, and who look good next to you at whatever those glossy events are." He stepped backward and apparently the expression on her face was the one he'd expected. "Yeah. So that's not going to work."

"Maybe I could stay up here—" she started.

"You just said you were going down for the job. And you should. You don't want to get stuck up here. This is somewhere you vacationed, but you're ambitious. You don't want to be on vacation forever."

He was right. She *did* want to go back and work more. She wanted to prove herself and take exciting roles that would let her grow as an actor. She thought about suggesting that they try to maintain the relationship long-distance, but that made no sense, not if they'd never be able to live in the same place. Long distance was only reasonable for the short term. "So what do we do?" she asked quietly. "We just give up?"

"We stick with what it was originally supposed to be. A summer thing." He looked sad, but certain. "It's better to have a clean break so we can both look back at it as a good memory. Otherwise, if we try to drag it out? You end up hating me, or I end up hating you, or . . ." He smiled softly and reached out to run the back of his fingers down her cheek. "Maybe not hate. But we resent each other. It ends dirty instead of ending clean. I don't want that for us."

She hadn't known she was going to say it, but he was being honest with her and he deserved the same in return. "I love you, Josh. I know it's fast, but it's real. I've never felt like this before, and I'm scared that if I walk away from you I'll never feel this way again."

She was out of things to say, and it was just as well because Josh seemed to have kicked himself out of whatever wide-eyed shock he'd been in when she first said the words. Now he was moving, his mouth desperate as it covered hers, the kiss keeping her from speaking, thinking, or even breathing. All she could do was feel, and that was all she wanted to do. She loved him, and she was going to lose him. But he wasn't gone yet, and until he was, she needed to work on building the memories that would sustain her.

*　*　*

THERE was nothing but Ashley. No forest except for the tree she leaned against, no rain except for the water that fell on her upturned face. No darkness except for the shadows on her body, no light except for the way the headlights shone on her. No past, no future. Only Ashley, and only for the moment.

Josh abandoned all of his usual rules. He wasn't gentle, he wasn't carefully gauging her responses and calculating the ways he could bring her the most pleasure. It wasn't that he didn't care, it was just that he was operating on instinct now, touching her the way he just *knew* she wanted to be touched. And the way he wanted to touch. There wasn't really a divide between them, as far as he could tell.

When he pushed her back against the smooth trunk, she surged forward to meet him, her mouth hungrily claiming his lips, his neck—any exposed skin. And apparently there wasn't quite enough of that for her, because she tugged impatiently at his shirt, her warm fingers sliding under the hem and up over the bare skin of his chest, then whipping back out to attack the buttons. All the time her lips were on his, separating only for gasps of breath and for desperate, greedy whispers.

She got his work shirt off and he pushed her back with one hand, separating them long enough for him to pull his T-shirt off over his head. The rain and the cool night air hit his skin and gave him a quick burst of consciousness. The night was too cold, the location too public, the whole thing too hopeless. Then he looked at her and all the rest was just too damn bad. He'd have plenty of time to be disciplined and smart. After she left, and for the rest of his life. But not while she was still there.

"Your turn," he growled, and pulled her soaked cotton shirt up over her head. The rest of their clothes followed fairly quickly. There was some desperate tugging, a little bit of laughter, but soon they were naked, with a broad tree between them and the truck's headlights, and there in the forest, in the rain, in the darkness, they joined together as tightly as they both needed.

Josh was being rougher than he'd ever been with Ashley, driving into her body as if trying to mark her deep inside. And she responded by wrapping her legs around him and pulling him in tighter and harder. He wrapped his arms around her so she wouldn't bruise her back on the tree trunk and they strained together, wild and fierce and strangely triumphant, as if they were fighting against something, and as if they were, for the time being at least, winning.

They found their release together, and even then, as they both surrendered to the ecstasies of their own bodies, they still gasped and moaned in unison. They uncoupled slowly and gradually, but kept their bodies pressed together for warmth. When Ashley finally gave in and shivered, Josh kissed her forehead. "Your clothes are a mess, but there's a blanket in the truck."

"Will you drive me home?" she whispered. "You'll come with me?"

"Yeah." She could come back with him the next morning to pick up her car. And he could finish the work in the daylight.

But he needed to finish the work. And he needed to start another job when this one was done. Because Ashley was leaving. She'd be busy getting ready for the movie, and he'd better get busy trying to figure out how to live without her.

So they gathered up their clothes and scampered to the truck, Josh wearing only his underwear and boots, Ashley wearing nothing at all. He carried her over the gravel of the driveway and set her in the passenger seat, then got the truck started and pulled the rolled up blanket from the backseat.

"I'm glad you have cloth instead of leather," Ashley said

as he wrapped the fleece around her. "Leather would have given me a cold ass."

"But if I'd been rich enough to pay for leather, I probably would have sprung for seat warmers, too."

He shut the passenger door gently and circled around to his own side. She was watching him as he climbed in, but she didn't say anything until they were out on the highway. "You keep horses. Your house is pretty nice, and you own a lot of land. You have your own business, and Kevin said you do okay. You really . . . Money was tight enough that you couldn't afford leather?"

It was kind of a personal question, but maybe it was time to share a bit of that reality. "I could have afforded it," he said. "But it would have meant that I wouldn't have money for something else. I'm doing okay. I bought this truck new, and my old one wasn't totally dead. I could have nursed it along another couple years, if I'd wanted to put up with it being temperamental. I have a retirement account, and I have savings for a rainy day. I'm fine. But I'm not rich, Ashley. Nowhere near it."

"Does it bother you that I am?"

He thought about it. "No. Not really. I mean, the summer people thing, you know how I feel about that. But just you? For yourself? No. I'm glad you have money." He snorted a little. "I like the idea of you having the finer things and being taken care of, and I'm in no position to give you all that, so I'm glad you can take care of yourself."

She seemed reasonably satisfied with that answer. Then out of the blue she asked, "Does it bother you that I've done topless scenes? In movies? Some guys don't like that."

He took his eyes off the road long enough to give her a startled look. "Bother me? No, I don't think so."

"Have you seen them?"

"I don't think so."

"You haven't seen all my movies?" She frowned at him

and he made sure he kept staring straight ahead. "Wait a second. Have you seen *any* of my movies?"

"I'm not a big movie guy. But now that you've mentioned the topless scenes . . . if you could just write the titles of those ones down, that'd be great."

"What the hell, Josh!" She sounded like she wasn't sure whether to be amused or outraged. "Not even *one*?"

"Maybe I have," he said quickly. Then he grinned. "I just don't remember. It would have been before I met you. So, you know, I wouldn't have paid attention. But maybe I have. I don't like movies that much myself, but obviously I've watched them with other people."

She took a moment to think, then said, "You may have seen one of my movies while you were on a date with another woman?"

He nodded. "Yeah. You do mostly chick flicks, right? So it's not like I would have seen one of them on my own." This was kind of fun. "We can call some of my exes when we get home, if you want, and I can see if they remember. Hell, there was one girl I used to date who seemed to think the only reason movie theaters were invented was for fooling around. I had my own place by then, but she wouldn't want to come over. Said everyone would think she was a slut if they saw her coming out of my apartment. But the second the lights went down in a movie theater . . ."

"You may have fooled around with another woman while watching one of my movies."

"Well, to be fair, I probably wouldn't have been paying much attention to the movie."

She was staring at him and he glanced over and caught her eye. She was laughing, thankfully. "I've done some action movies," she said. "I was generally just the love interest and had to stand around and get rescued, but still, you could at least see *those*."

"Okay, you can write those titles down, too." As if he was

going to torture himself by watching her movies after she was gone. But it was easier to pretend that pain wasn't coming. "If you wanted to sort of cross-reference the two lists? Like, if there were any that were action movies *and* you were top-less? You should probably put a star beside those ones."

"Hey, Josh?" she said quietly.

He glanced over at her, and she raised her eyebrows, then dropped the blanket from her shoulders. "Right here, in person. Topless."

He made himself return his eyes to the road. "If I sped up and pretended someone was chasing us, it'd be the perfect movie."

It was so easy. That was what made it hurt so much to think about losing it. The warm affection, the easy jokes— the gorgeous, topless woman in his passenger seat. He had it all, and he was going to lose it all before he knew it.

"Daisy's going to miss you," he said quietly.

Ashley nodded. "I'm going to miss her, too. And Rocky. And your aunt Carol, and Kevin. And the lake, and the for-est, and the stream." She turned to him quickly. "That's what I want to do. On my last night here. I want to ride back to the stream with you, and I want to lie there with my feet on your chest, looking up at the stars. Floating. I want to do that. Maybe *every* night until I leave. Okay?"

"Okay," he said. It sounded a bit too much like she was dying, but he wasn't going to argue with her last requests, regardless. "Do you think you'll be back?"

Shit. He hadn't known he was going to ask that question. "No, don't answer," he said quickly. "It doesn't matter. And you don't know. . . . You can't know. Your life's changing and you need to be ready for anything. Next summer you could be working on a movie with . . . I don't know, I'm trying to come up with a big-name director and I'm drawing a blank. Steven Spielberg?"

She smiled. "I've already worked with him. But I'd love to do it again. And you're right, maybe this time it'd be on one of his more serious movies."

"You've already worked with Spielberg? Seriously?" Josh took a moment to collect his thoughts. "He made *E.T.*, right? That was him?"

"Well, yeah, but I wasn't in *E.T.*, Josh."

"Yeah, I know. But it's an excellent movie. You've worked with the guy who made *E.T.*?"

She laughed. "This is what's going to get you interested in my career?"

"Seriously, if you've been topless in an action movie directed by the guy who made *E.T.*, we should watch that movie right away. How do people watch movies these days? Would we have to download it?"

He wanted to keep joking and laughing about her movies. He wanted to keep driving, maybe forever, and he wanted to keep sneaking looks at the topless beauty in the seat next to his. He did not want to think about the end of *E.T.*, the part where the stupid alien went back to his happy spaceship and left the poor kid behind with a broken heart. It had been hard enough for that kid to watch his alien buddy leave, and he hadn't even been getting sex out of the deal.

Better not to think about it. "Absolutely," he said, and obviously it had been too long since anyone had said anything because Ashley gave him a look that made it clear she thought he was losing it. "The stream," he explained. "We'll do that. And maybe I can take a bit more time off and we can go kayaking at the lake. And Aunt Carol and Kevin will want to say good-bye—we could all go for a ride, if you wanted, one afternoon. I could borrow a four-horse trailer and we could go over to Merck Forest. They've got some good trails."

"Okay," she agreed. She settled into the seat and bundled

the blanket back up over her shoulders. He knew she wasn't hiding; she just wanted to be cozy.

He wondered what she'd say if he suggested they just keep driving, running away from it all and never coming back to their current lives. But he kept his mouth shut. He didn't want to hear her say no. And if she said yes, he'd have to deal with the guilt of messing up her dream. So he stayed quiet, and they drove back to the cabin. Back to the place that was, for a few more days at least, home.

❧ *Twenty-three* ❦

ASHLEY CRIED THE entire flight to L.A. Not deep, shattering sobs, just intermittent tears that snuck out before she noticed them coming. They'd gone to Woody's the night before and there had been so many people there who'd come just to say good-bye to her. Abi and Laurie and Kevin and his mom, and Josh's cousins she'd met at The Splash. Theo had hauled her up onstage and prodded her to make a speech, and for the first time in her life she'd been too overcome to give a performance. She'd just stood there and smiled and laughed and cried until finally Josh took pity on her and lifted her down and hugged her until she was strong again. They'd gone home and ridden to the creek and she'd looked up at the stars and tried to feel insignificant, because if she was nothing compared to the universe then surely her pain was even less than nothing, and she should be able to ignore it.

It hadn't worked, though, and they'd gone back to the cabin and made love and fallen asleep together, and then they'd woken up and Josh had driven her to the airport and she'd made herself walk away from him forever.

Adam had booked her two seats on the plane so there was no one beside her, and she was grateful to him, and then, suddenly, irritated. She was grateful? As if it were some personal gift from him to her, rather than an expensive luxury incurred on her behalf by his assistant, one that Ashley would end up paying for the next time Adam submitted his expense report. She had nothing to be *grateful* to Adam for.

Not until she landed and was escorted past security and made her way to the car waiting for her. But then she climbed inside the car and saw Charlotte, and heard Charlotte say, "Adam said you were a bit shaky. He thought you might want some company." Then Charlotte saw Ashley's face, blotchy and swollen, and said, "Oh, Ash," and Ashley was crying again.

"It's a great part," Ashley sobbed. "And you got your part, too! I get to work with you! I'm so excited," she tried, and then she sobbed. "I miss him so much."

"It's over, then?" Charlotte asked, gathering Ashley into her arms.

Ashley nodded. "He drove me to the airport and he kissed me good-bye and . . . it's *over*."

"I'm so sorry." Charlotte didn't say much more. She just held Ashley tight and let her cry.

"They wanted to cast Rocky," Ashley said eventually. She wasn't sure why it was important that she share this, but at least it was something to focus on. "Lauren saw the videos we took, of us riding around? And she said he was the perfect horse for the part. Someone called Josh and tried to set it up, and he wouldn't agree to it. He didn't even want his *horse* down in the big dirty city."

"Or maybe he was trying for a clean break," Charlotte said. "Isn't that what you guys were supposed to be doing?

It wouldn't be too clean if you had to come to work and see his horse every day."

Ashley cried a little more at that, wondering whether Josh had been looking out for her or for his horse. She finally regained some sort of composure and managed to sit up straight. "It really was that easy for you?" she asked. "Leaving Kevin? He seems fine, you seem fine . . . You're not just both putting on brave faces, are you? No. So, how did you do that?"

Charlotte shrugged. "We just never cared that much. We're friends. We've stayed in touch a little; he e-mailed me a few days ago and told me to brace myself for your arrival, because he was pretty sure you were going to be having a hard time."

"Kevin said that? Did he say . . . Did he seem to think Josh was going to have a hard time, too?"

"He said Josh would just go to ground. He said Josh never lets anyone help, but that you seemed a bit more sensible, so hopefully I could be useful down here."

"I don't like to think of him being all alone."

"Then stop thinking about him. Think about *you*. Rehearsals start tomorrow. We'll get you home, do your laundry, make sure you've got quick meals in the freezer just in case you ever manage to catch a bite at home. . . . What else do you usually do at the start of a project?"

"My assistant usually does all that."

"But you got rid of your assistant in the spring."

"Yeah."

"So should we be doing a quick-hire to get you a new one? Your contract doesn't specify that you get one?"

"No. Wait, does yours?"

"No," Charlotte said with a grin. "Relax. You're not being contract-snubbed. If you need an assistant, you should call Adam and get him on it; you'll have to meet the top candidates, and it'll be easier to do that during rehearsals than when we're actually shooting."

"No," Ashley said with a sigh. She leaned her head back against the hard window. "I don't want an assistant." She didn't want anything except for Josh. And he was the one thing she couldn't have.

"SHE'S going to stage some sort of weird guerilla mothering intervention pretty soon," Kevin said as he handed the wires down to Josh. "That's all I'm saying. It's been four days since Ashley left, and Mom's getting a bit intense. You can come over for dinner tonight and let her poke at you a little, or you can live your life in fear of her rappelling down the side of someone's cottage and shooting you with a stun gun before tying you up and force-feeding you chicken soup."

Josh ducked himself under the water and jammed the inflow pipe beneath the cement block with a little more force than was strictly necessary. The cottage he was working at had run out of water in the middle of a multi-guest weekend, and they needed their plumbing fixed, so Josh had called Kevin for help in order to get the job done more quickly. But he was regretting his decision. The summer people could have gone without water for a few more hours if it meant Josh wouldn't have had to listen to Kevin's nagging.

Josh stayed underwater for as long as he could, savoring the cool green peacefulness, but eventually had to put his feet down and poke his head out of the water. "Hit the pump," he ordered, and after a moment's hesitation, Kevin leaned over and flipped the switch. The hum was satisfying and Josh could feel the water at his knees being sucked slowly in through the end of the pipe. "Okay," he grunted as he heaved himself out of the chest-deep water and up onto the dock.

"*Okay*, you'll come for dinner?"

"*Okay*, let's see if the reservoir is filling up." Josh slipped on his sports sandals and stalked up the hill in his wet shorts, Kevin trailing behind him.

"Charlotte says Ashley's a mess," Kevin said quietly.

Josh turned to glare at him. "What the fuck are you doing? Is that supposed to help somehow, you telling me that?" Josh shook his head. "Seriously, Kevin, what's so hard about just leaving this alone? Do you think there's some magic solution? Do you think I could ever be happy down there? Do you think Ashley could ever be happy up here, for good?"

"It doesn't sound like she's too happy down there, either," Kevin said slowly. "And it doesn't seem like you're too happy up here. So you're both miserable. It just seems—"

"Seems what?" Josh prompted angrily. If Kevin could get this off his chest, maybe he'd shut up about it for a while.

"Seems like if one of you moved, then at least *one* of you would be happy. Instead of both of you being miserable."

Josh shook his head. "Nobody's miserable. We're adjusting. That's all."

"Adjusting," Kevin said slowly. "Oh. That's okay, then. Sorry about the misunderstanding. I guess 'adjusting' must look a lot like 'miserable' from the outside."

"Fuck off, Kevin." Josh swung down into the little concrete room beside the cottage's holding tank. He checked the pipes and then opened the hatch and heard water pouring into the reservoir. Okay. That was working, at least.

He climbed up and went to knock on the cottage door. Michael Montgomery answered, the glass in his hand combining with the angle of his posture to make it clear he'd found something to drink other than water. Cal's brother was one of the few locals who owned waterfront, and he could only afford it because his family also owned half the town, in addition to the furniture factory that was about the only year-round industry in the area.

"Water should be back up and running," Josh said. "Seems like your intake pipe got clogged. It'll take a half hour or so for your reservoir to fill back up; Kevin will stick around and make sure everything's working after that." He had more to say, a suggestion for monthly maintenance or at least a quick inspection, both of which could be done by anyone going swimming, but he'd save it for when the guy was sober.

"Great. Thank you," Michael said. Then there was a stir behind him and a thin blonde appeared at his side. Sheila Lambert was older, but well maintained, and considered herself the queen of the local social scene, at least through the winter. Josh was pretty sure Michael was actually dating someone else, but Sheila seemed to feel pretty at home at his place.

"You should come have a drink with us, Josh! We heard you had some fun up here this summer. Ashley Carlsen was here? How exciting!" She raised her eyebrows and smiled salaciously.

"I have to go," Josh said. He couldn't stick around to make excuses or be polite about it, and there was no way he was going to get dragged into their cocktail circle to discuss his "exciting" summer with Ashley Carlsen.

He turned and stalked toward the truck, and somewhere behind him he heard Kevin chatting away, covering for Josh's abrupt departure. Josh got behind the wheel and got the hell out of there. He had more jobs to do, more distractions to pursue.

More ways to pretend he wasn't totally miserable.

"I'M not seeing the power, Ashley." Lauren Hall leaned back in her rickety desk chair and took a sip of tea from her brown pottery mug. "In your auditions, there was an energy, an intensity that just burned up the screen. It made you *glow* with a fascinating, subdued fire." She waited for Ashley to speak, then said, "We've been rehearsing for a week, and I'm not seeing it. What's different?"

Ashley was supposed to be a professional. She was supposed to keep her personal shit at home, and if she was struggling with that she was supposed to deal with it, not go whining about it to her boss. But what other answer did she have? "I'm dealing with some stuff. Personally. I . . . I know it's not your problem, but I had to leave a guy behind to come down for this job. It's a choice I made. But I guess it's kind of . . . I guess I'm using all my energy to keep myself together, and it's not leaving enough to be intense in rehearsals."

Lauren looked at her for longer than Ashley liked. "Man trouble," she said with a nod. "Is this going to be something you can resolve by the time filming starts? Because I've got to be honest with you. As a woman, I sympathize. But I'm not at work as a woman, I'm here as a director. And as a director, I'm a little pissed off. I know you see this role as a chance. That's one of the reasons I wanted you for the part—I wanted to you to bring that desperation for change to the role you're playing. But this movie is a chance for me, too. Every movie is a chance. You want to be a serious actor; I want to keep directing the movies I want to direct. And that only happens if I'm successful. I need everyone on board to be giving me their best effort, and right now, I am getting something less than I expected from you."

Ashley nodded and fought not to cry. She couldn't argue. Lauren was right. This movie was important to a lot of people, and Ashley was letting all of them down. She needed to pull herself together or get the hell out of the way so someone else could come in and take over.

"We've got the weekend off," Lauren said, her voice gentler now. "I need you to take that time to pull yourself together and sort out whatever the hell is getting in the way of you being the banshee that you were in auditions. I want that fierce woman back, and I want this movie to be the vehicle that breaks her out of the supporting female roles she's been stuck in. I want this movie to be the first of many great performances for the adult version of Ashley Carlsen."

Lauren sat back in her chair and took another sip of her tea. "But that won't happen if you can't pull yourself together. And I won't let you drag this movie down. I *can't* let you."

Ashley still had nothing to say, so she just nodded.

Lauren nodded, too, ready to get back to business. "So I'd like a phone call on Sunday night. Not before that—I want to have this last weekend in peace before insanity descends. So on Sunday night you'll give me a call and you'll either tell me that you've got your shit together or you'll tell me that you won't be able to continue in the role. Better we lose a week of rehearsal than that we try to drag this out any longer. Clear?"

"Clear," Ashley said.

She made it out of Lauren's office and ducked into the bathroom before the tears came. She should call Adam and let him know; there were probably terms of the contract to be debated, requirements for how this sort of relationship could be severed, and the financial consequences of each choice. But Ashley didn't want Adam to call the lawyers. She just wanted it all to be over.

She was miserable. She wasn't doing her job. She'd given up true love to chase her dream, and now she was letting her dream slip through her fingers. "Fuck!" she roared, the obscenity echoing off the hard tiles of the room. There was the passion Lauren was looking for, but Ashley could only produce it in that one short burst, and only for her real life, not for the fictional trauma of the script.

She needed to do something. But she had no idea what that something might be.

"YOU need to keep the sling on for at least six weeks," Dr. Myles said with a frown and a firm shake of her head. "Six weeks, Josh. You can come back then and we'll take another set of X-rays to see if the bone's healed, but six weeks is the absolute minimum."

Josh didn't bother getting insulted about the doctor's clear suspicions. She'd known him since he was a kid, and they both knew he was going to take the sling off as soon as he could handle the pain. "Okay," he muttered, and he slid down off the exam table and looked around for his shirt.

The doctor handed it to him with a disapproving sniff and Josh wished he'd figured out some way to avoid coming to the hospital at all. The fuss, the attention—it made him want to crawl into a cave somewhere. He'd fallen off a roof. That was all. Kevin had acted like it was the end of the world, swearing up a blue streak as he drove Josh to the hospital, but Kevin was prone to dramatics.

"You need to be more careful, Josh," Dr. Myles was saying. "Those bruises on your torso haven't faded yet, and now you've fallen from a three-story roof? You could have died from that fall. You're lucky to be walking away with only a broken collarbone and few scratches."

"I landed on a shrub," Josh said. He'd already explained that, but maybe she hadn't been paying attention.

"But why did you fall off the roof in the first place? There are safety procedures in place to keep workers from falling—were you using those procedures?"

"Not in the strictest sense," he admitted. Then he headed for the door. "Okay, thanks for the sling and the drugs and everything. I feel much better now."

"You have someone to drive you home?" the doctor asked from too close behind him.

"I expect so," Josh said. "He's generally pretty hard to get rid of."

But when he got to the waiting room it wasn't just Kevin sitting in the hard plastic chairs. Aunt Carol was there, too, and she didn't look impressed.

"What the hell were you doing up on a roof, Joshua?" she demanded, storming across the room toward him. She stopped a couple feet away and added, "And what did you do to yourself? How badly hurt are you? Bad enough that I have to be nice to you? Because if you aren't, I have got quite a few strong words for your stupidity!"

"I'm fine," Josh said. "But I'm not really interested in hearing the strong words. Can we get out of here?"

"What the hell were you doing up on a roof?" Aunt Carol trailed after Josh as he headed for the exit.

"Well, he had to be on the roof," Kevin said from somewhere behind them all. "That's where loose shingles are." But before Josh could believe he'd found a champion, Kevin added, "The question to ask is why he fell off! Why weren't you tied off, Josh? Three stories? You should have had a rope and a harness. If I'd been up there, you would have yelled at me if I wasn't tied off."

"I was just checking something," Josh said sullenly. "I wasn't having a damn picnic. It was wet, I slipped, I fell. It's not a big deal." His whole body was sore and he had a broken collarbone and a bunch of scratches and he could have died, but . . .

"No," Aunt Carol said. They were in the parking lot now and Josh just wanted to go to the truck and go home, but Aunt Carol held onto his un-slinged hand. "It *is* a big deal, Joshy. You're working too hard. You're not paying attention. You're making stupid mistakes. And it's all because you're unhappy."

Josh scowled at her, then at Kevin. "It's a transition," he said. "It'll be okay. I just need to adjust, or something."

Aunt Carol's face softened and she peered up into his eyes. "Really, Joshy? If that's true, if you can look me in the eyes and tell me that, then I'll believe you, and I'll be happy. Can you do that, Josh? Can you look me in the eyes and tell me you're going to be getting better soon?"

He stared somewhere over her shoulder. Ashley was

gone. That was all there was to say. She was down in Holly-wood working on her dream job, and he was back in Vermont trying to pick up the pieces. Was he going to be getting better soon? Ever? "I'm doing the best I can, Aunt Carol."

"Well, it's not good enough, Joshy. So you need to let us help. You need to come over for dinner tonight and be with your family instead of moping around that house all by yourself."

"I was going to go over and finish the roof," he protested.

"No," Kevin said firmly. "You go home with Mom, and I'll take your truck to the site and finish up. You're not going up on that roof all drugged up." He looked at his mother and gave her a sweet smile. "And *I'll* use the appropriate safety equipment," he said smugly, and it earned him a pat of approval on his arm.

Josh was too tired to argue. He just wanted to crawl into his bed and dream of the days when he'd shared it with Ashley.

"No more of this," Aunt Carol said firmly as she guided him toward her car. "You need to get yourself together, Josh. Enough of this drifting around."

She was right. He knew it. He'd fallen off a damn roof and he could have died. He was miserable, and he really didn't see how the hell he was going to get past any of it. He needed a plan. A solution. He needed to find a way to make things okay again.

Twenty-four

ASHLEY FELT BETTER. Not good, exactly, but . . . better. She turned the rental car into the rough driveway and felt the tension draining out of her, absorbed by the embrace of the surrounding forest. This would be okay.

Still, she stopped the car just before it pulled out of the trees into the clearing around the house. Was she absolutely sure about this? Once she was there, once she was wrapped in Josh's strong arms, cradled against his broad chest, she wouldn't be leaving. She knew that. Was she really ready to give up her career in order to commit to a man she'd only known for a few weeks? One who had never even said he loved her?

The problem was, she didn't really have a choice. She was pretending she did, but she had no idea how to get herself back in shape the way Lauren needed her to. She'd spent all night Friday and all day Saturday thinking about this. Then she'd woken up Sunday morning, double-checked her priorities, and booked her flight. She'd call Lauren that night, as requested, and she'd step out of her dream role.

Better to quit than to be fired. For all Josh's worrying about how he was going to recover from their fling, it had turned out to be her who'd been stung. Losing Josh was unthinkable. Losing her career? It was terrible, frustrating, disappointing. But it wasn't unthinkable.

Better to lose the job and still have Josh than to lose the job *and* lose Josh. She didn't like what she was doing, but she didn't see an alternative, not really.

So she drove on to the house, but when she pulled in to park, it wasn't Josh's truck in the driveway. It was Kevin's. Josh usually spent Sunday afternoons at home, catching up on the chores of the house or hanging out with the horses. Maybe he and Kevin had just switched vehicles for some reason?

Ashley stepped out of the car and was almost knocked over by the grey and brown streak that barreled into her, yipping and whimpering with excitement. "Daisy," Ashley crooned, bending to greet the wriggling animal. "I missed you, too, baby! It's good to see you." She eventually stood, over Daisy's objections, and said, "Come on. Let's go see who's home."

She turned toward the house and caught her breath at the sight of the man on the porch, then exhaled in disappointment. Similar enough to fool someone from a distance, but that was Kevin, not Josh. And after giving up so much and travelling so far, she wanted the real thing, not the substitute.

He stepped down from the porch and walked toward her, his expression almost impossible to read. "This is unexpected," he said when he was close enough.

She nodded. She hadn't really had the words to share with Josh, and she certainly didn't have any to explain herself to Kevin. "I made a mistake," she finally said. "I thought I could forget about him. Thought I could move on. But I guess I was wrong."

Kevin's expression was changing, slowly. She'd swear he

was . . . The bastard looked amused. She'd given up so much, changed her whole life plan, and he was going to laugh at her? "So, if Josh is around, I'd like to see him. Do you know where he is?"

"Not exactly," Kevin said. He looked down at his watch, then back up at Ashley, and he wasn't even trying to hide his grin anymore. "I'm going to guess Nebraska, or maybe Colorado."

"What?"

"Well, you're right, it's just a guess. He left here first thing yesterday morning, I know that much. But I don't know what route he was taking, and he's a pain in the ass about roaming charges on his cell so I haven't called him. We won't know where he is unless he calls in from a motel or something. Which he isn't likely to do."

Ashley just stared at him. "What are you talking about?" she demanded. "Why the hell is Josh in Nebraska or wherever? Where's he going?"

Kevin clearly thought she should have figured this out by now. "He's going to Hollywood, Ash. Turns out he made a mistake. He met this girl, and then they broke up because they lived too far apart. He thought he could move on and forget about her, but then he figured he was wrong. So—"

"Wait." Ashley took a few more steps and sank down onto the wide porch steps. "He's going to L.A.? He's . . . he's *driving*?"

Kevin nodded again, his grin now so wide he was starting to look like a jack-o'-lantern. "He figured that would be easier for Rocky and Sunny. He didn't think they'd want to fly."

"Rocky and Sunny," Ashley said as calmly as she could. "He's going to L.A., and he's bringing horses."

"For the movie," Kevin said helpfully, lowering himself to the stairs beside her. "I guess some guy had called him and wanted to cast Rocky in the movie. Is that what it's called for horses? Getting cast? I think that word means something different for horses. But, whatever, Rocky had a job if he wanted it."

"Josh turned that down," Ashley said faintly.

"Yeah. And then he changed his mind. He called the guy up and said if they were still interested, Rocky could come, but Josh wanted a job, too. He could help look after the animals, or do carpentry, or whatever. If the guy could find a job for Josh, he could use the horse." Kevin shrugged. "I guess they really wanted that horse. The director herself called to agree to the deal. She talked to Josh for, like, five minutes. He said she wanted to know whether he was coming down to get back together with you. He figured she wanted to be sure he wouldn't be a pain in the ass if it didn't work out. I guess he convinced her. Or maybe she just really wanted that horse."

Ashley stood up. Josh was on his way to L.A. Lauren had made it happen. No. *Josh* had made it happen. He'd been the one to make the call, the one who'd decided he'd give up his whole life in order to travel somewhere he hated so he could be with Ashley. Lauren had helped, but Josh had been the one who'd started it all.

"What about the business?" She asked. She looked around her. "The farm? The other horses, and Daisy?"

"It was time for me to get the hell out of my mom's basement," Kevin said. "So I'm babysitting the place until he figures out what he's going to do with it. And Daisy'll miss him, but she'll be fine as long as she's got a home here. The business?" He made an unhappy face. "The business was a mess anyway, really. He finished up the Ryersons' job and the rest is all just little stuff. He can do some of the client contact over the phone, but mostly they want to see him face-to-face. I can do most of the physical work, but they don't really trust me the way they trust him. So, yeah, the business is going to hurt. Which is just as well, really, since there's only me to do all the work, and I'm not much good at hiring or supervising people."

"Josh is going to L.A.," Ashley said numbly. "To be with me." The rest of it was details. The part where Josh was going to be in L.A. was the part that mattered. "Josh is going to L.A., and I'm up here."

"Maybe you should cut your hair to buy him a watch chain, and he could sell his watch to buy you hair clips," Kevin said impishly.

"Was that a literary allusion, Kevin? Did you just reference an O. Henry story?"

"We had to read it in school," Kevin said defensively. "Josh probably did, too. When you see him, you can check if he remembers."

When she saw Josh. What a sweet, tantalizing thought. "Josh is on his way to L.A., and I'm here. This is not right. I need to . . . Oh, Kevin." The thought brought her up short. "Can Josh be happy down there? It's not fair, is it? If one of us has to change our lives, it should be me, not him. I love it here. I could be happy here. But Josh? In the city?"

"Well, if he's taking the horses he probably won't be right downtown or anything." Kevin shrugged. "You need to talk to him about it. In person. And I have no idea where the hell he is, so probably you want to get back down to L.A. and wait for him to show up. Right?"

Ashley stared at him. This wasn't what she'd prepared herself for. She'd thought she was resigned to giving up on the movie, but now that there was a chance of keeping it, she was stunned by the sense of relief she felt. "I could still do the part," she said slowly, trying the words out and looking for the trap. "I could have Josh *and* the part."

Kevin nodded. He wasn't laughing at her anymore. "Looks like," he agreed. "There was no point in both of you being miserable."

No. No point. So now Ashley could have it all. She frowned at Kevin and a bit of the elation drained out of her. She could have it all. But at what cost to Josh?

* * *

THE next time Josh drove a pair of horses across the country, he wanted to do it without a broken collarbone. Rocky and Sunny were both healthy, calm, generous horses, but that didn't mean he could expect them to just stand in a trailer for days on end like they were mechanical. So a few times a day he'd found a place to stop and let them walk around for a half hour or so, and each night had been spent at a layover barn where they'd gotten their own little paddock and a chance to stretch their legs some more. He'd done right by the animals.

But he'd pushed himself pretty hard. Long days of driving combined with restless nights, unable to find a sleeping position that didn't strain his collarbone. And now that he was almost there, pulling up to the farm where he'd been told to meet the film's head wrangler, he had a new worry. What if this was all a terrible idea? What if Ashley didn't want him there, or what if she did at the start and then realized that he was just an infatuation, just a guy who really should have stayed a golden memory? Even harder to imagine, what if she *did* want him there? Could he really commit to this? He was walking away from his family, his friends, his farm, his town, everything he'd known and loved for his whole life. Was he ready to give that up?

He pulled the truck into the parking area and sat there for a while. He thought of Ashley's slow smile, and the way he felt when he saw her snuggled up in his bed. The way she swam, as if she was a part of the lake, and her excitement at attaching a board to a dock or finding a half-assed waterfall. He thought of watching her drive away and how he'd felt while she was gone, and he knew he never, never wanted to feel that way again.

She'd been right when she'd said he was a coward. Well, she hadn't said that exactly, but she'd implied it. She'd said he wasn't fighting for this. For them. But now he was.

He swung down out of the cab and headed toward the barn. He'd get the horses settled, then go get cleaned up at the apartment the wrangler had said was available above the barn. Then he'd worry about Ashley.

He found his way to the door of the barn and took a deep breath. The familiar smell of horses and hay was calming. He was a long way from home, and his life no longer looked like anything he could recognize, but at least some things were still the same.

A teenage girl was sweeping the aisle and looked at him curiously. A brown horse's head bobbed over the stall door near her and she absentmindedly leaned toward the animal to exchange greetings as they both waited to see what the new arrival was looking for.

"I'm Josh Sullivan," he said. His whole life, that last name had meant something. Not always something good, but at least it had been *something*, a connection to a place and a history and a family. Way down in California, it was meaningless. "I brought a couple horses down. I'm supposed to be meeting Don Brady?"

The girl nodded and smiled as if he'd said the magic words. "Don's in the office," she said, and gestured to the far end of the barn. "It's the door on the far side of the tack room."

Josh headed down, looking around as he went. The barn wasn't as fancy as the ones he'd been picturing, the ones with the skylights and whatever, but it was well lit and well ventilated, and everything seemed to be in its place. The horses would be okay here. Safe. He hadn't just risked his animals in order to chase his own selfish desires. Another worry crossed off his list.

Of course, there was still the big one, but he put that out of his mind and knocked on the wooden door that he hoped was for the office.

The door opened to show a weathered face under a cowboy hat. The man was about Josh's height but whip-thin; his leathery skin made him look a little intimidating, but then he smiled. "Josh Sullivan?"

"Yeah. You're Don?"

"I am." He stuck out his arm and they shook hands. Then Don said, "We'll see to the horses in just a minute. But first, you need to talk to the boss."

"The boss? I thought you were the boss."

"Don't be fooled, son," Don said with a smile. Then he stepped aside and Josh looked past him into the room.

She was wearing jeans and a tank top. Her hair was in a ponytail, and if she was wearing makeup he couldn't see it. She looked . . . she looked just like she had at the lake. Perfect.

Josh just stared, and Ashley laughed, then charged forward. She threw her arms around him in something that was closer to a tackle than a hug, her lips finding his in a kiss that was more celebration than passion. Josh was vaguely aware that Don was easing his way out of the office and shutting the door behind him, but he didn't pay much attention to that. The only important person in the room, the barn, the whole damn *country* was standing in front of him, her arms around his neck and her body pressed tight to his.

"It's okay that I'm here?" he whispered when she'd pulled away far enough for him to find words.

Her face got a bit more serious. "For me? It's perfect that you're here. For you? We're going to need to talk about that." Then she stretched up and kissed him again, a little slower this time, her tongue tangling with his until she pulled away and said, "But we can have that conversation a little later."

"After I see to the horses," he managed to say. It wasn't what he wanted to do right then, but he had a responsibility to his animals.

"I can help," she said. "I was so excited when I heard you were bringing my boy down!"

"That's what you were excited about?" he prompted. "You're glad I'm here because I brought your horse?"

"Yeah," she said with an exaggerated eye roll. "What'd you think I was so happy about?" She followed up with a smile and a kiss, then pulled away a little and frowned. "You're only hugging me with one arm. Are you wearing a sling? Josh, what the hell happened to you?"

"I fell," he said. And because he was supposed to be fighting, supposed to be brave, he made himself add, "Fell for you, fell off a roof. They both knocked the wind out of me. Both left a mark. But I think the collarbone's going to heal a hell of a lot faster than the other."

She frowned. "I'm going to make sure the falling for me doesn't hurt you. Okay?"

He knew she was going to try, so he smiled at her and didn't call her a liar. "We should get the horses unloaded," he said, lacing the fingers of his good hand through hers. "They'll need some walking. You want to do that with me?"

"I do," she said, and they left the office together.

Don saw them coming and raised an eyebrow. "Heading out already?" he asked, and for the first time Josh noticed the keen light in the man's eyes, the way he was watching and thinking.

"Not out," Josh said carefully. He'd never really had a boss before and he had no idea how he was supposed to treat one; he decided to just do what he thought was right and let Don worry about what he was doing wrong. "I wanted to get the horses unloaded. Walk them a little, if that's okay? Doesn't look like you guys have a lot of grass, but there's that little patch around the side, if we could hand-graze them a little? Let them get used to the place?"

Don nodded slowly and Josh got the feeling he'd passed whatever test the older man had set for him. "Sounds good. Pull the truck into the side yard and unload there."

Josh did as he was told, Ashley tagging along and joyfully

greeting the animals. They all walked over to the little patch of grass and Josh saw the irrigation heads that kept this area green while the rest of the yard looked like a dustbowl. "Not quite like home," he said apologetically to the horses, but they were too busy sampling the exotic California produce to notice his words.

Ashley did, though. She looked around the farm and Josh followed her gaze. They were on the outskirts of the city, close enough that land was probably still pretty pricey. As far as Josh could see, there was the barn, a few fenced dirt yards, and not much else to the farm. No pasture, no hay fields, certainly no forest to ride in. But at least it wasn't wall-to-wall people.

"You hate this," Ashley said. He whirled toward her because she sounded like she was about to cry, but she just smiled sadly at him. "And you hate the city. Rich people, celebrities, everything that isn't real—you hate all that."

He shrugged. "Maybe I just need to get used to it."

She smiled again. "I don't think so. I think you'll still hate it."

No point in denying it. "Yeah. I think I probably still will." He took a deep breath. He'd come this far; he needed to go all the way. "I'll hate all this, but it's okay. Because I love you. That makes up for it."

And now she actually was crying, which was absolutely not what he'd intended when he pushed it all further. "Maybe not," he said quickly.

Her watery eyes flashed to his. "Maybe you don't love me?" she demanded.

"No. Maybe I won't hate it." He shrugged. "The loving you thing? That's . . . It's for sure. I wouldn't be here if it wasn't."

"Let's focus on that part for a little bit," she said, leaning up to kiss him. "But the rest of it? I'm going to make the rest of it okay, I promise."

"Kiss me again," he suggested. "When you're kissing me, there *is* no rest of it."

"Well, that is not a long-term solution," she scolded, but she kissed him anyway. He wrapped his arms around her, both of them barely holding onto the horses' lead ropes, and they stood there on their little patch of greenery with their horses munching happily away, and everything else faded away. At least for a while.

❧ *Twenty-five* ❧

ASHLEY REARRANGED THE flowers on the kitchen table and thought briefly of throwing them in the trash. At the store they'd seemed beautiful, simple and fresh. But she was pretty sure Josh would find them a bit fancy, and that really wasn't the impression she wanted to make. She wanted him to feel at home. Literally. She had no idea whether the apartment over the barn was livable, but she knew it was over an hour's drive from the studio, and even farther than that from her place. Once filming started she'd be working long, irregular hours, and everything would be easier if she could come home and see Josh, rather than having to drive out to the barn. She'd make the drive if she had to. If Josh couldn't be comfortable here, she'd drive. But if he *could* be comfortable . . .

She grabbed the bouquet out of the vase and whacked it on the side of the table. A couple stems broke, a few petals fell off, but it still looked pretty good. She whacked it again. And then once more. She stuffed it back in the vase just as the buzzer sounded to announce someone at the gate. She checked the camera and saw the familiar face in the familiar pickup truck. It was a bit strange to see Josh in the driveway of her Hollywood home, but it was strange in a good way. Strange the way it might be to find a unicorn roaming in a suburban backyard.

He looked like he was going through his own adjustment process as he parked the truck in front of the house and climbed the wide front steps. "Is it okay there?" he asked, gesturing almost nervously at the truck.

"If you leave your keys in it, I'll have the valet pull it around," she said, then grinned. "I'm joking, Josh. It's fine there. You drove down from Vermont for me; you can park it in the swimming pool if you want."

He nodded. "Okay. Yeah. But, you know, I drove down from Vermont for you; if you want me to drive ten feet farther and park the truck somewhere better, it's not a big deal."

"I want us to stop talking about the truck," she said, and when he smiled his agreement, she stepped forward and wrapped her arms around his neck. "Welcome to L.A., Josh," she whispered, and she kissed him. He kissed back, but not with quite the level of enthusiasm she'd been hoping for. That was okay; he was still adjusting. She eased away and wrapped her fingers around his. "I thought we could just order in for dinner, is that okay with you?"

"Yeah. That's fine." He followed her inside and she could feel him trying not to stare.

"It's a Greene and Greene house—they were the architects. But it's not as heavy as some Craftsman homes are, you know? Less stone, more wood, and all these gorgeous windows." She led the way into the kitchen and tried to make herself stop talking about architecture. It was strange how that was the main feature of the place she called home. The design, the materials. She still loved the house, but her appreciation felt a bit more distant than it used to, before she got used to the humbler and cozier life in Vermont. But she tried to recapture her enthusiasm. "I really like having breakfast in here, looking out over the city—"

"What happened to your flowers?" Josh asked, staring at the battered bouquet.

"Oh. Those. I dropped them."

"And then ran them over?"

"Well, if you must know, they parked in the wrong place so I had to beat them up to teach them a lesson."

Josh nodded slowly. "Bet they don't do that again."

"I'm really glad you're here, Josh." It was true. She just needed to fight through the awkwardness. "I like my house, but I love you. If you don't like it here, we can go somewhere else. To your apartment or to a hotel or something—whatever you want."

He stared at her. "This house is incredible, Ash. I mean, I'm glad I've got the apartment as a backup, like if you're busy or something, but overall, why the hell wouldn't we stay here?"

She froze, then smiled awkwardly. Possibly she'd been building this up a little more than she needed to. "I beat up the flowers so you wouldn't think I was trying to be fancy," she blurted out.

He nodded slowly, then grinned. "So, you're insane, is what you're telling me."

"Crazy in love," she amended. "Hey, want to see the master suite? There's a soaker tub . . ."

"Yeah," he said, and his gaze roamed over her body as he said, "I want to see everything."

JOSH lay back on the padded deck chair and looked out over the city as the sun set. He had a cold beer in his hand, the breeze was gentle and just a little salty as it blew in from the ocean, and Ashley was cradled between his legs, leaning back against his bare chest as he reclined. "Maybe I just haven't been doing cities right," he mused. "Maybe I like cities just fine, if I do them this way."

"That would make life a lot easier," Ashley replied, and she ran her hand down his thigh encouragingly.

"Probably at some point I'd need to leave the house, though." He needed to think about that. "I was wishing for a gun when I was driving over here tonight, that's for sure. I hate traffic."

"I could get you a driver," she said, rolling over and leaning her chin on his chest, carefully keeping her distance from his collarbone. "Or maybe a helicopter."

"It'd be a bit weird to pull up at the barn in a limo," he said. And now that he was on the topic, he supposed he should ask the question that had been bothering him. "Don said he was glad I didn't turn out to be useless."

"Well, yeah, I guess he would be glad. You were okay doing work with your arm in a sling?"

"I took it out when I had to." It had hurt like hell, but he'd survived. "But I don't think that was the part he was worried about. I'd told him about that on the phone before I came down."

"Oh," she said.

Just one syllable, but it was all he needed. "There's a lot of people who want a job like this, right? A chance to work in showbiz? And I don't really have any experience with the movie side of things. And he'd never even met me or seen me work with a horse before today. And I know Rocky has the right look for the movie or whatever, but it's not really that hard to find a scruffy brown horse with donkey ears." Yeah, that was all the evidence Josh had gathered through the day, combined with Don's close scrutiny as he'd worked. "It seemed like maybe Don wouldn't have hired me, if he'd had the choice."

Ashley sighed. "Okay. Look, I'll tell you everything I

know. I promise. But will you promise to remember the part where he's glad he hired you, now that he's seen you work? Because that part's important, Josh."

"What's the other part? Did you get me the job, Ashley?"

"No!" She made a face before adding, "Not directly. I was just . . . I had a bad week, last week. I was missing you, and wondering if I'd made the right decision, and I was kind of going through the motions at work. I didn't have the same intensity I'd had before." She sighed and kissed his chest, just over his heart. It was pretty hard to be mad at a beautiful woman who was kissing him like that. "I didn't know you were coming. I actually—you haven't talked to Kevin lately?"

He frowned. "No. I sent him an e-mail, told him we got in okay. But I haven't talked to him."

She sighed. "I went up there Sunday. Flew back to L.A. the same day, just about went crazy waiting for you to show up yesterday and most of today. I was going to quit and come live with you, and I was sad about the movie but it was going to be a hell of a lot better to be with you and without a job than without you, with a job. So that's what I was going to do. I didn't know you'd called down and asked about the job and I sure as hell didn't know you'd got it, or I never would have wasted a day flying up to Vermont and then turning around and flying back."

"You were going to—" he started, but she put a finger over his lips.

"Wait. I want to talk about that in a minute. I want to clear this up first."

"Yes, ma'am," he said, his lips moving around her fingers.

"I think Don called Lauren, the director, to see just how bad she wanted Rocky. And I think maybe she wanted to help me out. She definitely seemed pretty pleased with herself when I showed up at rehearsals Monday, and I know she was happier with my work. So, it wasn't me. But she knew I was missing you. I think she put in a good word."

He nodded, and didn't say anything. He wasn't quite sure how he felt about it.

But apparently Ashley interpreted his silence as something a bit more decided. "It's the way stuff is done down here, Josh! Probably up in Vermont, too, but definitely down here. You get chances based on who you know and who'll speak up for you, but once you've got the chance, that's when you have to earn your next chance. And if you don't like that, maybe you need to ask yourself if you'd be just as upset if a guy helped you get a job. Because it's just sexist if you'd take a favor from Kevin or somebody, and not from me!"

"Slow down," Josh said. "Take it easy. I don't think I'm too worried about it."

She froze and looked up at him suspiciously. "Really? Because I might have another couple arguments lined up if you want them."

"No. I don't think I want them. I'm okay with it."

"Really?" she asked again.

"You're making me paranoid. Should I not be okay with it?"

"No, you should be! It's a very good sign that you are! And I bet Don loves you. You're so good with horses, and you're strong, even with only one good arm, and—"

"Okay," he interrupted. "I get it. I'll be useful." He would be, he decided. He'd make Don love him and be grateful for Lauren's interference. He'd take this pity job and turn it into an opportunity. Ashley was right. This job was just his way to show that he deserved the *next* job. He wasn't quite where he wanted to be, but he was with the person he wanted to be with. He'd have to make the rest of it work, somehow.

ASHLEY watched the sun sinking and let herself think about keeping her mouth shut. Josh was willing to live in L.A., he had a job, and he wasn't miserable at the house. Maybe

Ashley didn't need to make the sacrifices she'd thought about.

But as she thought about it and realized she didn't have to change, she didn't feel relieved. She felt disappointed. She *wanted* to change, she realized.

"I'm going to tell Adam not to book me for anything after this project," she said.

She felt Josh's chest tense a little. "What does that mean?" he asked. "You won't be working?"

"Not right away."

"You don't have to do that. I mean, not for me. If that's why you'd do it, you don't have to."

"It's not for you. Well, it's related to you, but it's for me. I want—" She paused and tried to make sure she had the right words. "I want to finish this project, and I want to act my ass off. But after that? I don't want to go back to making whatever movie pays me the most and makes me look prettiest. You know what I realized? What I figured out I really like about acting?"

"The publicity and invasion of privacy?"

"Well, that's lovely, too, of course. But no. What I really love is the chance to be someone else. I was on *Mayfair Drive* from the time I was seven until I was eighteen, and that whole time? I got to have two lives. Maybe even three, if you count the public 'me' as separate from the real me. But I got to *be* a whole other person. Amanda Anderson was fictional, sure, but when I was playing her, I believed in her. That's what I love about acting; it lets me experience things I never would on my own."

Josh nodded his understanding. "Okay. So . . . you still love that, right? Why are you talking about giving it up?"

"Oh, I'm not giving up acting!" She grinned at him. "But I don't have to be in movies. I mean, if there's a great role, fantastic, I want to do it. But I could get just as lost in a part in a community theater or at a drama school. And maybe I don't always want to get lost anymore. Maybe I want to stay in this life a little more often, now that I'm getting it set up just the way I like it."

He was watching her closely, and she could see him trying to determine how sincere she was and how much she'd thought about what she was saying. She smiled at him. "I want to go back up to Vermont in the fall, and I want to see what it's like there without summer people. I want to see the snow, and the way everything greens up in the spring." As soon as she said it, she knew she was on the right track. "You remember when you said that English riding is all about forward movement, but a Western rider has to be prepared to go in any direction? I want to . . . I want my life to be Western. Not always charging forward, racing around and looking for the next jump. Sometimes I want to go sideways, or even backward. I want to spin around. You know?"

"You've spent a lot of time going forward," he said, and she knew he was trying to understand.

"I've been acting since I was tiny, doing it professionally since I was a kid. I loved it, but I've *had* a career. I still want to act, but I don't need to be obsessed about it. Meryl Streep lives in Connecticut—did you know that? She takes a couple jobs a year, if they're right for her, and the rest of the time she's at home. Being a mom, worrying about apples—whatever. She's just living. That's what I want to do. With you."

She twisted around and propped herself up on her elbow so she could get a better view of his reaction. He looked unsure. "I could still do movies," she said. "But only when it works. For us. If I could book jobs in the winter, that'd be great, right? So you could work up there when it's busy and maybe I could start a little theater company and we'd put on plays for the summer people. And you'd come down here with me in the winter, maybe. I could keep this house—"

"You should definitely keep this house," Josh agreed.

"And maybe we could build a place up north? For the

two of us? It'd be nice if it was on the lake, but it doesn't have to be. Maybe there's somewhere on your property we could build, near the stream. Daisy loves that property, right?"

"You can't plan your whole life around a demon dog," he said reluctantly.

"I'm not. I'm planning it around you. Around us." She watched him as he heard the words, and smiled. "I know. It's scary. It's scaring me, too. We haven't known each other that long. This is all new. But I want to do it. I want us to fight for it."

He looked out at the city lights for a while, then down to their entwined fingers. "Yeah," he said softly. "I want that, too."

So they sat there in the darkness, and they were together. When they looked up, they saw stars. Not as many as they could see in Vermont, and not as bright, but stars all the same. Ashley thought of ancient seafarers being guided safely home, and she remembered how she'd felt like she was floating in space when Josh had taken her to the stream. Floating, but with her feet firmly anchored to Josh. It had happened quickly, but that didn't mean it wasn't real. He was her constant now. Her earth. And she was his star.

KEEP READING FOR A PREVIEW OF THE NEXT
LAKE SULLIVAN ROMANCE BY CATE CAMERON . . .

Hometown Hero

COMING SOON FROM BERKLEY SENSATION!

"HE'S CALLED THREE times," Bonita said. "I'm your roommate, not your secretary. Call him back, even if it's just to tell him not to call anymore."

Zara buried her head further beneath the throw pillows on their comfortably ragged sofa. If she could just stay there in the soft darkness a little longer, maybe it would all go away.

But Bonita wasn't giving up. She lifted Zara's feet and slid onto the couch, then let Zara's feet fall into her lap and started massaging, her strong hands working through the calluses and tension.

"Or if he really *is* stalking you," Bonita said softly, once she had Zara nice and relaxed, "you should call Terry. The company has a security department for a reason."

Zara pulled her feet away peevishly. "I don't want to talk to Terry. And Calvin Montgomery's not a stalker," she grumbled into the cushions.

"Good, then," Bonita said. "So you can give him a call and deal with whatever it is."

"We've always e-mailed before." Zara pulled her head out from under the pillows and squinted through the late afternoon sunshine to see Bonita's face. "That's rude, right? If you set up a system of e-mailing, you shouldn't just switch over to the phone because you feel like it. Right?"

"Really rude. You should call him up and tell him so."

"I'm injured. When someone's injured, they don't have to talk on the phone."

"Actually, you're supposed to avoid looking at computer screens," Bonita corrected. "So the phone would be better than e-mail. Maybe your friend knows that."

"He's not my friend. And since when are you an expert on concussions?"

"Since my darling roommate keeps getting them. And if he's not your friend, what is he? He's got a pretty sexy voice. Nice and low . . . I bet I could get him to moan real nice . . ."

"Yuck. Stay away from him. He's an asshole."

"Really?"

Bonita sounded like she was asking for the truth, so Zara took a moment to try to provide it. "I don't know. Probably. I mean, he definitely *was* an asshole. But he's been good ever since then. You know, good to Zane."

Bonita already knew that story, so Zara didn't have to explain what she meant. Except for maybe an elaboration on just how very good Calvin Montgomery had been to Zara's brother. "He visits him more often than I do. He doesn't travel as much as me, and he lives closer, so it's easier for him. But still . . . he really stepped up. And Zane says he was good during the trial and everything, too."

"So, you're not returning his calls because . . . ?"

Because Calvin was part of Zara's old life in Lake Sullivan, and she needed to keep a bit of distance from that world. She'd moved on. She'd grown up, but it was still easier to deal with it through the remoteness of e-mail rather than the immediacy of a phone call. Besides, Zara had a pretty good idea of what Calvin wanted to talk about, and she didn't think she was ready for that conversation. Zane's impending release was exciting, of course, but also terrifying. What if he couldn't cope? What if Zara couldn't give him the help he needed?

But Bonita didn't need to hear all that angst. So Zara shrugged and said, "I'll call him. I just haven't yet."

And of course that was when Zara's phone rang. She made a face. She could just let it go to the message system, but then she'd have to either listen to the message or erase it without listening, and both options seemed a bit overwhelming right then. "One more time?" she said pleadingly.

Bonita sighed dramatically. "Absolute *last* time, you baby." She leaned over and pulled Zara's cell phone off the coffee table. "Zara Hale's phone." She listened for a moment, then said, "Oh, hi, Andre, it's Bonita. I think Zara's around somewhere. . . . Let me just try to find her, okay?"

She held the phone out to Zara, who reluctantly took it. Andre was her manager and, at least in theory, was in her corner. Not someone she should be blowing off. "Hey, Andre," she said, making sure she sounded chipper and bright. "You just caught me—I was on my way out for a run!" She ignored Bonita's raised eyebrow.

"Did the doctors clear that?" Andre sounded skeptical.

"Yeah, of course." They'd said she could start phasing in her normal routine again. She was pretty sure they'd meant, like, taking showers instead of baths, and getting dressed in real clothes instead of wearing sweats all day, but maybe they'd meant exercise. She couldn't be sure.

"Well, okay," Andre said reluctantly. "But you're looking after yourself, right? You're not pushing too hard?"

"Nope. I'm pushing just hard enough."

"Okay, good. You need to come back strong and ready. You're a major investment and you need to make sure you act that way."

Funny, she'd thought she might be something that *wasn't* purely financial. How naïve. "Yeah," she said. "Strong and ready. Got it."

"Okay. So, in the meantime . . ." Andre paused, and Zara could totally picture him leaning back in his chair, stroking his goatee, ready to drop the next line as if he was some sort of master of manipulation. "We have a new opportunity."

"Yeah? What? Not more modelling—that was a disaster."

"No. Not in entertainment, exactly . . ."

"Oh my God, Andre, do they want me to be an astronaut? That's so exciting! I mean, it's a surprise, sure, but I really think I can handle it!"

He gave her his best long-suffering sigh. It was more effective in person, and even there, it had long since lost its power against Zara. "No. Not an astronaut. But something almost as inspiring, really."

"Porn?" she guessed.

"No. You've made your feelings on that perfectly clear."

She shouldn't have *had* to make her feelings on doing porn clear to the manager of her mixed martial arts career, but at least he'd finally gotten the message. "So . . . what?"

"You like kids, right? You've been looking for a chance to work with them more closely?"

"No, not really. Kids are pretty annoying, aren't they? I mean, I don't know that many, personally. But they don't seem good." She thought back over her very limited experience with people younger than herself. Loud, undisciplined, out of control. "Yeah, I think kids suck."

"No," he said with exaggerated patience. "You like them. You've been looking for an opportunity to give back to the community. You had a tough start and you still have some rough edges, but people have been understanding about that and given you chances, and now you want to help some other disadvantaged kids get a chance. Right?"

"Okay, first off, nobody *gave* me a damn thing. I *earned* my chances."

"Fine. You earned them. And other kids should earn them, too. But they shouldn't have to fight quite as hard as you did. They should get a bit of help. A hand up, not a hand out. Right?"

"Maybe?"

"Work with me, Zara. You're at a crucial juncture of your career here. Two concussions is not good. Your opponents know to go for the headshot now. I know you're fast and you usually take them out before they can land a good hit, but obviously that's not always the case, or you wouldn't be injured right now. Right?"

"What's your point?"

"My point is, you need to take a break until your brain is solid in your head again. The company isn't going to let you fight anytime soon, even if we push for it. Their insurers and the PR department do *not* want their headlining female fighter pulling a *Million Dollar Baby*."

"She was paraplegic, not brain damaged."

"Whatever. The point is, you're valuable healthy, and you're a damn disaster if something goes permanently wrong. So they're not going to let you back in the ring until their doctors say it's safe. So unless you want to be looking at a layoff, we need to find ways to improve or at least maintain your value while you're recovering. It can't be physical. But it can be PR."

"With *kids*?"

"Not just any kids. This guy hasn't contacted you? This . . . Calvin Montgomery? He said he'd get in touch directly."

Zara's grip on the phone got a little tighter. "What the hell does Calvin Montgomery have to do with anything?"

"It's his idea. And he's got the company on his side, too.

I thought Terry was going to pass out, he was so excited about it all."

"All *what*?"

"He really didn't get in touch with you. Damn, he said he was going to." Andre sounded a little disillusioned with Calvin Montgomery, but charged on anyway. "He wants you to help him start up a community center, back in your home-town. What's it called? Lake Sullivan? Whatever. They've already got the place built and mostly staffed, but they're looking for a few more people. He says there's loads of disadvantaged kids there and they need some hope and someone to inspire them, and he wants you to be that person, and I swear, Terry just about came in his pants. Thinks it's a good way to improve the MMA image. He's throwing serious funding at the project. Some for you, some for the facility. It's excellent."

Andre paused for breath, and maybe Zara should have taken the opportunity to interrupt, but she was a bit too dazed by it all. "Montgomery wants your brother involved, which . . . I'm not so sure about. But, whatever, we can negotiate on that. But seriously, making you into some sort of Ripley character, like from *Aliens*? You're a fierce warrior woman with a soft spot for kids. It's brilliant. Just couldn't be any better. You work there for a while, you do whatever the hell people do when they start up community centers, none of it hurts your brain, you train enough to stay fit but don't bring yourself right up to the peak . . . I honestly can't think of a better way for you to be spending your time. Can you?"

The list of better things was so long Zara wasn't sure where to start. Should she organize the options alphabeti-cally or in order of preference? Best to keep it simple, prob-ably. "Anything but that." Anything but going back to rural Vermont and getting involved with the Montgomery family and dealing with a bunch of annoying children. "Maybe I could become a nun or something. They like kids, don't they? Some of them?"

"Nuns can't have sex, Zara. You still want to consider that option?"

"Maybe something else." Her sex life might be a bit slow, but she wanted to at least keep the option open. "I mean, there's plenty of messed-up kids in New York City! I can stay right here! And, you know, you can figure out photo ops or something, right? I don't have to spend a *lot* of time with them, do I?"

"People aren't as gullible as they used to be. It takes more than a few snapshots with some raggedy kids. We need testimonials from concerned locals, recorded tears from your protégés, poignant anecdotes about how much you've learned. We need more than a photo op, Zara."

"This is bullshit. We don't need any of that. I'm a fighter, not a humanitarian. I'm the MMA champion! I've got the damn belt—I'm looking at it right now. How is messing around with a bunch of kids going to make me fight better?"

"It's going to make you *look* better," Andre said, not entirely patiently. "You know how it goes. You get fights based on what the fans want to see, and right now . . . well, as long as you're defending the title, you're fine. But if you're out for too long and lose the title, or if you come back and aren't quite up to speed yet and lose it, you're going to need the fans on your side. And it'll do great things for your endorsements, too."

"I'm so tired of that crap. The men are allowed to just *fight*. They don't have to look pretty and flirt with reporters and work with damn kids!"

"Simple question, Zara. Because, I don't know, maybe I missed something. So let me just check. . . . . Are you a man?" Andre paused, just long enough to pretend he was waiting for an answer. "Oh, no, you're not? Okay, next question. Do you live in a fantasy world of total equality, or do you live in this world?" Another pause for effect. "Oh, you live in *this* world? Then stop wasting my time with your whining and help me manage your career as a female fighter in the current universe. Okay?"

Zara was pretty sure she was out of arguments, but that didn't mean she liked the idea. "By working at a community center? Seriously?" She paused. "Why the hell is Calvin Montgomery interested in making me work at a community center?" And the worst part. "In *Lake Sullivan*? They don't want me in Lake Sullivan, Cal. They practically kicked me out."

"They want you now. Being on the cover of both *Sports Illustrated* and *Maxim* will change a lot of minds."

"This whole thing is stupid."

"Give it some thought," Andre said soothingly. "It'd be good for your career, and like I said, Terry's willing to pay for it all."

"What does that mean, exactly? How much money?"

"We'll have to negotiate the details. But it'll be a hell of a lot more than you'd make lying around on your couch feeling sorry for yourself. And I'll talk to your sponsors, too, see if we can milk some extra out of them." He waited for her next objection. When it didn't come, he said, "Okay, then. Think about it. I'll talk to Terry and figure out some of the details. And look after your brain, okay?"

"Okay," Zara said grudgingly. She hung up, then looked at Bonita, who'd been listening to Zara's half of the conversation with obvious interest. "Fine, you're right. I need to phone Calvin Montgomery. Did you write his number down somewhere?"

"MR. Montgomery?" Allison's voice stopped Cal on his way out the door. "Zara Hale is on line three for you."

It was tempting to keep walking. He'd called the little

brat three times and she'd ignored him until he'd gone ahead and talked to her boss. Now she wanted to talk to him, but maybe *he* was too busy to talk this time.

Yeah, tempting, but not appropriate. He was the responsible one, after all. "I'll catch up," he told the people he'd been walking with. They were on their way to The Pier for lunch, so it wasn't like he was going to be missing a meeting or anything. "Order for me—whatever the special is."

That taken care of, he turned back toward his office. "Line three?"

Allison nodded from her desk outside his door. He hadn't liked the setup originally; Allison had been with the company since he'd been a toddler, and he was pretty sure she'd been assigned as his assistant largely to keep an eye on him. Having her stationed by his door made it feel even more like she was his sentry. His jailer. But he'd gotten used to her, just like he'd adjusted to the rest of it. And having her so intent on running his business life was actually a good excuse to delegate a lot of his work to her, so he'd started to think of her presence as a perk.

And there were other advantages to the job, he remembered as he sank back into his luxurious desk chair and swivelled around so he could look out the floor-to-ceiling windows toward the lake. Yeah, his work was boring and he had a babysitter assigned to him, but he made good money and worked in a pleasant environment. It could be worse.

He picked up the phone and said, "Zara? Thanks for calling back." He didn't bother to mention how long it had taken. No point in starting off with her on the defensive. "I guess you've probably been told about the plan by now?"

"Yeah, I've been told." It had been a long time since he'd heard her voice, but she still sounded about the same. Totally pugnacious and looking for trouble. "What the hell are you up to?"

"Zane's out in less than a month," Cal replied calmly. "He's going to need a job, and some stability."

"What? I mean, yeah, okay, but what's that got to do with me and a community center?"

"He can work there, too. He likes kids, and he told me he wants to find a way to start giving back."

"He's a convicted felon! You really think he's going to be allowed to work with kids?"

"His crimes had nothing to do with children, and there was only peripheral violence. I don't think there's any reason we can't trust him around young people. With adequate supervision, of course."

"Adequate . . . You don't expect *me* to supervise him, do you? He's my big brother! He's not going to listen to me. And it's not like I know anything about any of this!"

"No, not you. We've got a professional manager in mind. Good experience, relevant education, the whole package. She'll be in charge of supervising you and Zane."

"Okay, well . . ." He could practically hear her recalculating. "Okay, if this is what Zane wants and you can find a way to make it work, then, great, it sounds like a good plan. For him. But why am I getting dragged into it?"

"Because I *can't* find a way to make it work, not without some help."

"I really don't understand how I'd help anything."

"Two ways." Cal kicked his feet up onto the windowsill and leaned back in his chair. He was pretty pleased with himself on this one, but he tried not to let that come out in his voice. "One, you make the town more likely to accept Zane. You may not believe it, but you're a golden girl up here now. A celebrity. Local girl made good. Pick the cliché, and you fit it. So people who might object to *just* Zane working at the center will be okay with it if you're involved."

"You're right, I don't believe it."

"Well, if you ever came by, you'd know. As it is, you'll have to trust me."

There was no answer, not right away. Finally, Zara said, "That was one way. What's two?"

"Two . . ." This one was going to take a bit more finesse. "You being involved makes it easier for Zane to accept the job. He's a proud guy, Zara. You know that. He's never wanted to take favors from me, not if they involved money. So he won't want to take this job if he thinks it's me giving him a handout."

"You think he's going to be more willing to accept help from me? His baby sister? You're delusional."

"Well, no, I'm not. As a matter of fact, once I explained how you'd be involved, Zane agreed to go along with it."

"Bullshit."

Cal grinned. He wished this meeting could have been in person so he'd have been able to see the expression on her face, but at least a phone call was better than e-mail. "It's not bullshit at all. When I told him about his baby sister getting two concussions in one year and maybe facing permanent brain damage if she didn't stay out of the ring for a while? When I told him how you were pushing to get back too early because you had nothing constructive to do with your time? When I said I'd love to get you involved in this project, but didn't think I'd be able to persuade you if he wasn't involved?" Yeah, this had been a good plan. Cal was proud of himself. "He knew what he had to do. He's taking the job so that *you'll* take the job."

Damn, it would have been great if he'd been able to see her as she processed it all.

Finally she said, "Okay, you don't know shit about my career, or my health. So you're lying, really. And you're playing us off against each other, *for* each other? You've set it up so he'll take the job to help me, and I'll take the job to help him."

"Exactly."

"Why? Why is this any of your business?"

Interesting that she was the one asking that question, when her street-smart brother hadn't. But Cal had the answer already figured out, ready for when he'd been talking to Zane, so it was easy to use it now. "Because I want the community center to succeed. I want it to target kids who need it. Sure, everyone's welcome, but you know what I mean. The middle-class kids getting dropped off by their loving parents for an afternoon of basketball or crafts or something? They don't *need* it. But there are kids who do. A lot of them. And I think you and Zane will be good at reaching those kids."

"Why, because we're poor, downtrodden trash? We can speak to our people?"

"You're not trash. But, yeah, because you both grew up without money and without strong parenting. Because you struggled with finding your places in the world. I think Zane should be involved because he can be a good lesson on what goes wrong if you don't make the right decisions, and also a good lesson about it never being too late to change. And you? Obviously a success story. The kids need to see more of those. Probably the girls especially. You didn't get knocked up and start a family way too young because you didn't know what the hell else to do with your life. You broke free. The girls definitely need to see that."

He let her ponder for a moment, then said, "It doesn't have to be a long-term commitment. Just give it an honest try. See if it works for you. Okay?"

"I'll think about it. And I'll talk to Zane about it. This is my week to visit him."

"Are you safe to drive? With the concussion?" As soon as the words were out of his mouth, he knew they'd been a mistake.

"You don't know shit about my health," she growled. "Remember? And I can take care of myself."

"I know," he said quickly. "Sorry. I've been talking to Zane too much—you know how protective he is."

"How protective he wants to be, maybe. But he hasn't been able to do much for me for the last decade, and I've been just fine. I don't need either of you thinking you're in charge of my safety. No way."

"Absolutely," Cal agreed. And he did agree, at least in theory. A bit harder to convince his instincts about it, but his brain was certainly aware that Zara Hale could take care of herself, and then some.

"Okay," she said grumpily. "I'll talk to Zane about it."

"It's not that terrible, Zara. We've got a good facility, and the town has changed. Seriously, they love you here now. There are posters of you all over the place, and they sold tickets and did a huge event at the bar for your last pay-per-view fight. It sold out, fast."

"That fight lasted twenty-three seconds."

"And the cheering went on for hours. Every time they showed a replay, I thought the roof was going to lift off."

"You were there?"

"Of course. Everyone who's anyone was there. It was the social event of the season."

"Yeah, I'm sure your whole family showed up, furs and pearls and all."

Well, that was a good point. But he chose to ignore it. "You should come by," he said. "I think you'd be pleasantly surprised."

"I'll think about it. Maybe. After I talk to Zane. But if he's not really into this, there's no way I'm doing it."

"Fair enough."

They ended the call, and Cal sat and looked out his window. Zane and Zara Hale, back in Lake Sullivan. Back where they'd always belonged, before things had gone so wrong. Cal hadn't been able to save either of them then, but that didn't mean he couldn't help them out now. He'd been raised with every privilege, all the financial *and* the emotional support he could have ever wanted, and it had made him strong. It had also given him a pretty good dose of liberal guilt, and helping the Hales *and* disadvantaged kids was a great way to soothe his conscience.

Yeah. He was doing the right thing. He pushed out of his chair and strode out of the office with the energy that always made Allison frown suspiciously. Things were coming together. It was about damn time.

Discover Romance

berkleyjoveauthors.com

See what's coming up next from your favorite romance authors and explore all the latest Berkley, Jove, and Sensation selections.

See what's new
~
Find author appearances
~
Win fantastic prizes
~
Get reading recommendations
~
Chat with authors and other fans
~
Read interviews with authors you love

berkleyjoveauthors.com

M1G0610